YOURS TRULY

TWISTED SISTERS
BOOK 2

DAISY JANE

PROLOGUE

"I'm the part of the equation that doesn't work."

Trace

Two weeks ago

The sound of her heels clicking along the tile has me on my feet, grabbing at the back of my neck, trying to corral the irritation galloping rampantly inside me.

"Thank you for coming," I say as soon as she turns the corner and we lock eyes. "I know you didn't have to come, but thank you."

Tara, in blue jeans and black heels, a one-strap shirt clinging to her breasts, folds her arms over her chest. Her long dark hair is pulled back into a ponytail, and she looks great.

Gorgeous, really.

A burp hits me, and I smother it with my hand, willing the sickness to go away for the next five minutes.

"I don't have long. I'm leaving town today, so whatever this is, make it fast," she says.

"I'm leaving, too." I fall into the couch and quit pretending to be sober and feel great. Besides, Tara knows the truth. "The show released me from my contract." The truth is, I told them I wanted out two years ago. But until yesterday, they needed me as their cash cow. Now? I'm a liability to their image, and they don't want a cheater on the payroll.

Tara sighs, clicking her way to the couch, sitting down on the edge, next to me. "Did you ever love me?" she asks, fear trembling in those words.

I should tell her yes, because it will hurt her to hear the truth. But in the long run, it serves us both if I don't lie. "No," I say slowly, hating myself for letting the network talk me into an engagement I didn't even want. "I loved the idea of loving someone again."

She nods. "You know, I get that. Because... I don't know. When I saw you with her—" She stops, shaking her head. Tara believes, like the world, that I was caught with my assistant, cheating. "Doesn't matter, don't need to rehash. My point is, we would've been a bad marriage, me and you."

I nod. "You're going to be a great wife. I think I'm the part of the equation that doesn't work." That tracks. I've had two relationships and Tara is one of them.

She rests her hand on my thigh, the spot where her engagement ring once glittered now empty and untanned. "Good luck, Trace. A little therapy, less booze, you'll be okay."

I nod as she presses the ring onto the table. She must've been holding it, ready to give it back before she even entered the room.

"I won't tell the press anything," she says from the doorway. "Or, anything more, at least."

"Thank you," I reply, because I don't deserve the generosity she's offering me. Even though she doesn't know what she saw, I don't bother trying to set her straight again. She doesn't believe me, and that's okay.

I know what's true.

And right now, as Tara clicks her way back down the hall and out of my life, I know what's real for me. Not only am I done with fame and reality TV, but I'm done with the city and everyone here. I pick up my phone and call my only friend.

"How you doin', Trace?" Deuce greets as he answers.

"Remember how you told me Bluebell might serve me well?" I ask as last night's whiskey swims up my throat.

"Yeah, get your head fixed. You can't be fucked up out here with all these clear skies and open pastures."

That sounds awful. I pinch the bridge of my nose and sigh. "You still opening up the parlor?"

"Yeah. And I need someone to come bring it to life."

I flop down on the couch and ready myself for a 'don't puke' nap, then say, "I'll be out there in a few weeks."

ONE

I do not think about the pantiless cowgirl.

Ivy

I shouldn't have had that second handful of Kisses last night before bed. That's why my guts are twisted up in some sort of complicated sailor's knot.

It's *not* nerves.

I am a total badass artist with confidence and charisma. Baddies like me do not get nervous.

No way.

"Knock knock," my sister Juniper chirps through the door after softly knocking.

Traipsing toward the door, I pull it open, met with a steaming hot cup of coffee, mixed perfectly with my protein. Just the way I like it.

Juni transfers the mug to my hands. "Good morning," she

greets with a wide smile, her blonde hair braided around her crown, the rest down in waves.

"Sorry," I mumble, apologizing for my slight grouchiness. There are two people who do not deserve my mood, and one of them is standing at my door having just delivered me coffee. "Just... ate too much chocolate last night." I place a hand on my lower stomach, over my black leggings and long, acid-wash t-shirt. "My stomach is kinda queasy."

Sisters and spouses—the two S's that can decode your feelings, despite your best efforts. Juni smirks. "Okay, well, the coffee and some toast may help." She ushers me into the hall, the smell of breakfast meeting my nose. A rumble turns over in my belly as I follow her into the kitchen.

"I can't wait to hear how day one goes," she says as she slides me a plate of dry wheat toast and an open jar of my favorite jam—Juni's Jams, the flavor Ruby Rhubarb. Slathering the preserves onto the toast, I lift my shoulders in indifference.

"I have no idea what to expect. I mean, the only apprenticeships at tattoo shops I've seen have been on reality TV. And we all know how fake reality TV is."

My eyes lift to Juni's just in time to catch her arched brow. "Did you watch his show?"

I shake my head. "No," I say staunchly. "Never."

"How'd you know who he was back when you saw him at Hudson's house with Deuce?" Juni asks, recalling the first time Trace showed up at Dolly's husband's house ages ago.

"I subscribe to this tattoo and artistry website called Smeared Ink. A lot of his stuff was posted there and I became a huge fan. He was one of the only artists whose new pieces I really liked seeing. After staring at them for what seemed like hours, I'd sketch and sketch until my hand was numb trying to recreate them, just to try and figure out his process." I slow the admissions tumbling past my lips, realizing I said all of that in a single breath. "Anyway, when I read in the comments section one time that he was a reality star, all I did was say two words to myself."

Juni nods and in unison we say, "Ariana Grande."

A total Ariana Grande situation. We loved her music even though the three of us typically only shared a taste for jam. We stumbled across her stuff one day when cleaning the house, and fell for her hard.

We then made the rookie mistake of reading an article about her, sending us head first down a rabbit hole of interviews and snippets. Turns out, knowing Ariana makes a habit out of sleeping with other people's husbands and boyfriends makes her music far less enjoyable.

We should never have googled her. And I learned my lesson. When it came to Trace Calhoun, his pieces were so good and he had so much name recognition for not just tattoos but his drawings, I knew I could never, ever google him.

I *knew* he would be ruined for me if I looked him up.

Funny that I worked so hard to protect his image and within the first ten seconds of meeting him, I knew *exactly* who he was.

Arrogant. Egotistical. Selfish. Maybe even narcissistic.

The type of person who doesn't just think they're always right, but needs to get in the last word to remind you of their alleged rightness. The type of person no one would ever want to be around unless they had no choice.

Like me.

And even with one of his hands glued to a bottle and the other to some woman's ass, with his arrogant smile and infuriatingly sexy unkempt style, I will never deny that he is the most talented artist I know. Better than any magazine or TV special, his work is more detailed, creative and involved than any other tattoo artist I've seen.

I should be happy that the maestro of tattooing is my mentor. That I will be lucky enough to work with him for the next 12 weeks.

Yet as I nibble Ruby Rhubarb and listen to Juni whistle the theme song to *Friends*, I can't help the overwhelming feeling of dread that washes over me.

It's not *just* that he's a shithead.

He's a damn hot shithead.

And my toxic trait?

Being insanely interested in and jealous over hot shitheads.

"How long are you his apprentice again? Remind me?" Juni asks as she swipes a damp cloth over the counter. As the oldest of the three of us, she's always taken on the motherly role, even when our parents were alive. It's what fits her best and I can't wait for her to make my sister Dolly and I aunties. She'll be a really great mom.

"Twelve weeks," I tell her, an image of Trace in a torn, fitted white tee and black jeans with unlaced motorcycle boots fogging my mind. My neck grows hot, urging me to reach past the coffee to a canteen of water. Chugging it back, my senses cool and I get to my feet, itching to get out of this house for a lungful of fresh air. "Thanks for breakfast," I tell my sister, giving her a hug before snatching my lunch from the counter.

She stands at the doorway as I make my way to the car. "Bye," she waves me off. "Have a good first day!"

Despite the knot in my belly, I smile, telling myself it will be a good day. After all, I'm not nervous to spend twelve weeks with the hottest, most talented artist I've ever known.

I just ate too much chocolate, that's all.

〜

"And after you finish the total, you tap tender—"

With a curt smile, I nod, stopping Deuce from repeating himself yet again. "I know," I tell him.

He smiles at me before his eyes slide to the door, where we both fix our gazes for another hungry moment. Still, nothing and no one. A pigeon walks by, a piece of chocolate donut peeking from his beak. A shadow paints the sidewalk and for a second, my breath catches, thinking this is finally it.

He *finally* showed.

Except when the black boots come into view, they're not attached to a good-looking artist with greasy hair and a smarmy smile. They're attached to a man in all navy, a gold badge pinned to his chest and a holster of gear slung around his waist. Dash Foster, the police officer who has been pining after Juni for the last few weeks, appears, tipping his aviators up. He blinks into the reflective glass before he continues on, thumbs looped in his belt as he strides by.

"You can go grab something to eat over at Goode's," Deuce offers, likely feeling the weight of Trace's absence directly on his shoulders.

I hate when people do this. When they do something selfish, knowing how it's going to affect other people but not caring anyway. If this is how this apprenticeship is going to go, I'm going to need a lot of Ruby Rhubarb and Kisses to get through it. Because fuck Trace Calhoun and his lack of respect for anyone.

"No," I say sternly. "I'm here to be an apprentice. So.. even if he's not here, let me do apprentice things." I lift the broom by the handle, from where it's tucked between the desk and wall. "I'll sweep and mop, I'll wipe down chairs and clean the glass doors."

Deuce smiles, but it doesn't lift his usually happy eyes. "Thanks, Ivy. And... sorry he didn't show." He scratches the back of his head where his long hair is tangled in a man bun. "Probably got the days confused."

Our gazes linger for just one moment but we share the same unspoken sentiment.

He didn't get anything confused. He just doesn't give a shit about anyone.

But himself.

THE SLAM OF MY CAR DOOR ECHOES THROUGH THE QUIET little parking lot. Through the fog, I glare up at apartment number four, my eyes stinging from the cold. I usually like this time of year, when nighttime floods the sky around evening, making it feel much later than it actually is. It's the perfect vibe to cozy up in bed with my headphones on and my sketch pad out.

Tonight, though, the overwhelming darkness at just six in the evening feels foreboding. Ominous, even. I shake it off, literally giving my shoulders a quick shimmy, making the zippers on my worn leather jacket clink. Treading across the quiet lot, I make my way up the cement stairs, all the while wondering how many women have made this same walk with a whole other intention. The banister is so cold it stings my hand, making me quickly stash it into my jacket pocket. With my free hand, I make a fist.

Then knock.

No footsteps. No quiet chatter. No signs of life.

"No way," I murmur, roiling anger keeping me toasty in the cool breezeway. I knock again. This time, hard. So hard that my knuckles ache a little, and the door rattles noisily. Perfect.

Still... nothing.

Another hefty knock—the type of knock that would have

neighbors calling the police if there were any neighbors. Based on the fact there's a vacancy notice on the apartment across from his, and open windows showcasing an empty unit below, I think I'm safe.

Though if I'm being honest, I don't really care right now.

I lift my fist to hit the door again but before I can, it opens. Standing in the doorway is a leggy woman wearing nothing but a wrinkled, oversized t-shirt, her long red hair tangled around her face, her full cheeks ruddy and pink, her long lashes taking slow, heavy blinks.

It's six p.m. and I woke her up.

"Where's Trace?" I ask, bypassing any greetings or name exchanges. She blinks at me a few times before turning on her heel to walk away. And I watch her *completely naked lower half* head down the hall, back to whatever stinky rotten sex hole she came from.

"Trace," I hear her call as I step toward the open apartment door, peering in cautiously.

I jerk back, replacing my momentary curiosity with my simmering anger as Trace appears in the hallway.... Completely nude.

Suddenly my throat is tight, my pulse is tacky, despite the unfortunate pulsing between my legs.

He makes his way toward the open door with his head tipped down, long, stringy hair curtaining his expression. While he focuses on walking ten feet without falling over, I focus on his *third* leg.

Stay mad, Ivy.

Stay. Fucking. Mad.

You know those moments in movies where the sexy guy is walking through the crowded restaurant, and all the clatter of plates fades away, the heavily conversed room becomes hushed, and everything is fuzzy and out of focus, except him?

That moment always seemed so stupid to me.

But as Trace stumbles on a pair of bejeweled jeans with a pink cowboy boot still attached to them, I don't hear the litany of curse words stringing from his mouth. I don't hear that heavy thud of him steadying his feet.

I don't see anything but his massive, thick, long, veiny, mouthwateringly perfect cock.

I bring my black combat boots together, forcing myself to believe the rippling waves of heat coursing through my lower half is simply my body trying to stay warm.

Not the fact that in the last ten seconds I just envisioned myself naked, on all fours, that inked hand yanking my head back, that third leg filling me so full that I can't even speak as his body slaps against mine.

His eyes come to mine, and I watch his brain sort through the fog for a moment before familiarity hits. "Ivy."

I step toward him, still staying clear of the apartment threshold. "Our apprenticeship started today." I roll my lips together to keep the quiver in my chin at bay. "Be there tomorrow at 9 a.m. or don't come back."

The little pop of his head that he does when he smirks is beyond enraging. "You can't fire me."

Another step toward him for intensity purposes and I'm knocked back by a wave of Jack Daniel's and knock-off perfume. I wave my hand between us, pushing away his stink. "Read your contract. One more missed day and you're out." I glare at him, refusing to notice the way his eyes never leave mine, and the subtle twitch of his lips as he listens. "Deuce may be your friend, but Ink Time is his business." I take a few steps back, ready to turn and take the stairs before I add, "You're not God's gift and your shit *does* stink, so show up to your job or get fired, asshole."

And with that, I'm taking the stairs two by two, a little high flitting through my veins.

There's no contract but I'd be willing to bet that Trace Calhoun has not given a single iota of thought to this apprenticeship, so it's a gamble I'm ready to roll on.

As I drive home, I think about the sketches I'll be working on tomorrow—line work is where the apprenticeship begins, so I focus on the Wharncliffe blade in my boot, and how perfectly it lends itself to being the ideal subject.

I do not think about the pantiless cowgirl.

And I really do not think about that third leg.

Nope, not even once.

TWO

One drink.

Trace

"The first taste of love is—ohhh—bittersweet... and green on the vine. Like strawberry—"

SLAM.

The smell of improperly scrambled and definitely burned eggs causes my bottom lip to tingle with the oh-so familiar burn of nausea. Sinking onto the closed toilet, I focus on the steady hum of the shower as my head flops into my hands.

Did I dream it or... was Ivy just here?

"Knock knock," the waitress slash aspiring singer calls through the closed bathroom door (it's always waitress slash aspiring something—that much I've learned). Irritation wraps the back of my neck like an annoying hand, and my body goes tight and rigid. Do you need to say knock knock if you just fucking knock?

Letting out a sigh, I call, "What's up?"

"Breakfast is ready!"

"It's eight o'clock at night. And I'm getting in the shower," I mutter as I get to my feet, yanking open the door. Her eyes fall to my bare, somewhat hard cock. Without looking down I say, "It's not you, it's the booze wearing off."

Her face falls. "Eggs are ready."

"I hate eggs."

Her green eyes narrow, the freckles scattered along her cheeks deepening with her anger. "Then why are they in your fridge?"

I smirk. "The last girl who slept over liked them."

She rolls her eyes. "You're an asshole."

I close the door and through it, shout, "My wallet's on the nightstand if you need some cash to get home."

"I drove us here, asshole!" she shouts. But you know what? Her shouting asshole on her way out is a million times more tolerable than her singing 1990s country music while *staying*.

I never want them to stay.

Any of them.

Even the gorgeous redhead cowgirl whose name... escapes me at the moment.

I tug back the shower curtain, slowly stepping inside. My usual hangover dizziness hits. Lurching forward, I grip the wall and let the stream of hot water ease me into sobriety, washing the booze from my pores. After lathering enough times to leave my flesh red and raw, I wash my hair and step out, wrapping up in a towel.

Clean clothes sound daunting after such a hot shower, so I reroute from the bedroom to the kitchen, deciding coffee is more important than underwear at the moment. Caffeine is what I need to shake the booze and get focused.

The urgency to focus on my task tears through my body,

leaving me antsy and anxious, yet for the life of me, I'm not sure where I'm supposed to be putting my energy. I just know that it isn't on the redhead or the empty bottles on the counter.

My temples pound and my stomach curls as I enter my kitchen, a plate of browned and burned eggs on the counter. Acid climbs my throat. "Fuck no, not today," I groan, plucking the plate by its edge, dropping it into the garbage. I stare down at the steaming stench and swallow back the Jack crawling up my throat.

Yeah, I just tossed a glass dinner plate that my mother bought me ten years ago. But that's how fucking nasty those eggs were.

And how lousy I feel.

I reach for the carafe to discover *little Winona* made me coffee, too. I'd tell her thanks but the lack of purple g-string on my living room floor and inside-out jeans tell me that my dream came true: she's gone.

Perfect.

I fill a mug to the brim and drink it unreasonably fast, living for the sobering effects that hit just minutes later.

Glancing at the front door as I refill my World's Most Bitchin' mug, a memory flashes behind my sore eyes.

That dark-haired Firecracker, lost in a leather jacket, her gorgeous face all twisted up with anger. Yeah. Ivy did come by. Lowering my mug to the counter, I rub my temples, trying to sort out exactly why she was here.

From the counter, my phone lights up silently. I reach for it.

DEUCE

Will I be blessed with your presence tomorrow?

I reread his message several times before reality caves in

around me like a wall of crumbling bricks. "Fuuuck," I groan, exchanging the phone for the coffee mug. I finish the second cup as sweat beads on my forehead.

The apprenticeship started today. That's what she was going on and on about.

My work as a full-time tattoo artist at Ink Time started today.

Deuce has been a lifelong friend and one of the only people who has always been there for me. He's like the family I *thought* I had.

He's helping me finally "rebuild"—his Chicken Soup for the Soul prognosis, not mine. Yet here I am, halfway between a bottle of Jack and a pot of coffee, naked in my shitty apartment, trying not to vomit.

It's right then and there I make a commitment to show up at Ink Time. To show up for Deuce the way he shows up for me —the way a brother should.

And it's got nothing to do with that little Firecracker and her tight ass.

"WHERE YOU AT, MY MAN?" JOHN LAUGHS THROUGH THE receiver, the commotion of a full bar roaring in the background.

"Bluebell," I repeat, considering I told him this last week when he called. "Working for my buddy Deuce at his place here."

"Yeah?" John asks. "What for? You got the big exec connections, why are you in the sticks doing tramp stamps, dude?"

At that, I snort. Because it's an apt assessment of small town tattoo parlors. Though I haven't fully immersed myself in Bluebell, from what I've seen, Ivy Ellington and Deuce may be the only ones sporting real ink.

If I stay here to rebuild, I very well may be stuck doing tribal tramp stamps and baby feet on biceps for the rest of my career.

It's safe.

But boring as hell.

"I can't keep going at that pace, man," I tell him, in reference to the colorful life I was leading for the last seven years as the star of the reality show, *Needle Ninjas*. I traveled around the world, creating unique pieces for unique people, and let the network film me while doing it. My art is incredible—that, for once, isn't my ego talking, just the truth. But the show? It made me somewhat of a celebrity. I now have a line of pre-made designs I sell to tattoo shops around the world so that anyone can have Trace Calhoun's ink on their body.

But I was burning out.

Partying nonstop and somehow fucking even more. There were drugs, sleepless weeks, loud music, fast cars, nice jewelry, paparazzi and money. So. Much. Money.

So much that I got myself into trouble, lost the show and now I'm here. Trying to live the humble life as an artist in a small town.

I pull my sports car into a parking spot behind Ink Time, and stare through my windshield at the small parlor. It's closed now, since it's nearing nine at night, and all the lights are off. I don't know why I'd halfway expected Deuce to be here.

This place is exactly what I know I need.

Small space, eager minds, easy clients. And the shop itself? Clean, new, nice and safe. All the things I should want. Especially since I've had the rest—filthy, worn, naughty and dangerous. I've lived the most wild, off-the-beaten-path life that any tattoo artist could ever dream of. It's the natural progression to slow and settle down at this point in my career.

I shouldn't *want* to be pulled away from this, and it shouldn't be as easy as four words.

"Wanna get a drink?" John asks, the simple question rendering me motionless inside my sports car.

No. I don't want to drink. I want to go home and get to bed so I can show up in the morning– for Deuce, and for myself. I want to go into Ink Time with a coffee in my hand and teach that little Firecracker everything she doesn't know. I want to shine at Ink Time, and show the world that leaving the spotlight doesn't mean leaving the art.

But not as much as I want to feel warm and fuzzy, and forget all the reasons why I'm here in the first place.

And besides, it's just one drink.

I won't get drunk.

I'll get back early.

It's just one drink.

"All right," I muse, throwing my car into reverse. "One drink. Where are you?"

"Oakcreek," John replies. "I'm so glad you're coming out. I can't wait to fuckin' party, man."

Adrenaline spears through my arms and fingers, making me tingly and warm. The high has already started, and I haven't even touched a drop. "Just one drink," I tell him, lying to both of us but fooling neither.

THREE

He never showed up.

Ivy

Can you muzzle a bird? Are there little tiny leather muzzles out there that you can wrap around those tiny little beaks to shut those mini noisemakers up? Because that would be something I would invest in. Bird muzzles.

"Shut up!" I scream, kicking my feet in the sheets like a petulant child. I tossed and turned all night and my alarm is going to go off in less than ten minutes but still, that's ten whole minutes of rest.

Or it would be since bird muzzles have apparently not been invented yet.

There is a nest of scrub jay birds outside my room and right now, though I love all animals and all that shit, I want nothing more than a wild storm to hit and take them all out.

My diaphragm spasms as I let loose what feels like the tenth yawn in under a minute, but I push myself up in bed. Glaring through the curtains, I decide to get up and forgo those ten minutes. I guess the birds aren't to blame—I didn't sleep well. Trace didn't show up yesterday, so I wanted to get up early and get some sketching done before I have to sketch in front of him today.

Assuming he shows up.

Either way, there's no such thing as too much practicing. After turning off my alarm, I slip out of bed and grab my materials. I don't typically wake this early, and when I got this apprenticeship, I planned to start my day with sketching, coffee and some light yoga from 7 until 8. But because assjacket decided to no-show yesterday, that makes today the first day.

And sketching before I get there will leave me feeling prepared and less... irritated.

It is my personal pet peeve when talented people think being talented allows them to be shitheads. No matter how creative and gifted Trace is, he's got no right to leave Deuce high and dry. It's complete horseshit for him to flake on a fellow artist, too.

I don't know why it still leaves me ruffled. I should have expected it from him. It's not like he's got a reputation of an angel or a fucking saint. He's known for being a boozing, egotistical prick.

Still, as I rest my sketch pad on my knees and slip my headphones over my ears, I can't shake the frustration that rattles through me. Instead of getting rid of it, I channel it into the sketch I'm working on.

It's a detailed graphite-on-paper sketch of a knife. My favorite kind of blade. In fact, it's my favorite because I wear one in my boot every day.

Sure, Bluebell is a small town and we know everyone here.

Most murders are committed by someone you know, though. *Just saying.*

And you never know when having a knife on your person will come in handy. That isn't a scary thing – that's smart. Safe.

I get to work on the handle of the blade, focusing on the scratch marks near the base from the place I dropped it outside of Rhett's apartment last year. It hit the concrete at a weird angle, and the enamel wore clean off the bottom. I was using the butt of the knife to knock on the door, since apparently he couldn't hear my fist.

He heard the knife.

Drawing my knees nearer, I focus so hard on the tiny little imperfection on the bottom of the knife handle that I go through the last few songs on my playlist. I don't notice there's no music until my focus is broken by hushed, deep voices coming from outside my bedroom window.

Glaring at my clock, I see it's hardly even 7 in the morning. Across the way, Dolly and Hudson are definitely awake, but they wouldn't be outside our house whispering. I let my pad and pencil slide into the comforter as I crawl to the side of the bed, slip off and peer out the window.

With dust clouding their ankles and a tray of empty jam jars between them, Dash Foster and Sterling Ford stand outside. Dash yanks the tray toward him, sending the jars careening into his uniform-clad chest. Sterling's lips hardly move, but his Adam's apple bobs as he quietly speaks, the deep timbre felt but not heard. He tugs the tray, bringing the jars back to his own uniformed body.

I blink, watching Bluebell's police officer and garbage man argue over a tray of Juni's empty jam jars.

I've been single for a whole year yet I go into town nearly

daily. Meanwhile, Juni keeps to herself and spends the majority of her time cutting, mashing and boiling fruit, and here she is with two men fighting over her.

"Damn, Juni, what are you putting in that jam?" I muse aloud as I let the curtain fall shut. Whatever they're arguing about, it's not my business unless they make it my business. I head out into the kitchen and begin my morning coffee, smirking at my older sister as she appears at the island, her blonde hair braided, eyes heavy with sleep.

"I'm so sorry," she greets, closing the distance between us to pull me into a hug. "I wanted to know how your first day went but I crashed around 7."

On her canning days, Juni wakes up really early, which means by the time 7 or 8 rolls around, she's toast.

"Don't even," I drone. "I can just tell you now. It wouldn't have been worth waiting up. Trust me."

She arches a blonde brow as I froth my protein. "Not a good first day?" Her bottom lip juts out in disappointment.

I slide her a mug, knowing she's going to need a cup of hot tea to start her day. She wraps her lean fingers around the Bluebell Farmers Market mug, and waits for me to fill her in.

Pouring the coffee over the protein, I sigh. "He never showed up."

Juni makes a point to gently slam her mug into the counter, and while it could've broken, it didn't. And I like the sentiment. A smirk curls my lips. "Right? My thoughts exactly."

"What did Deuce say?" she asks, pulling the kettle from the stove. Steam wafts from her mug as she pours, curling the loose tendrils around her face that didn't stay in the braid. "That's bullshit, Ivy. I'm sorry. And you know that's him being a total douche and it has nothing to do with what he thinks of you."

Her words echo through my brain. *Nothing to do with what*

he thinks of you. I sip my coffee and lower it to the counter. With my hands now on my hips, I glare at her. "I hadn't even thought of it being related to me." An image of that huge cock swings through my mind. Err, *flashes* through my mind. "He's the problem," I say, "not me."

"Totally," she confirms, dunking her bag of Earl Grey. "It's not you, and that's all I meant. He's clearly going through something–"

I raise my hand to stop her from letting him off the hook. Hell, even if he's not here, he doesn't deserve it. "When I stopped by his place last night, he was "going through" a cowgirl with pink boots and a bottle of Jack," I deadpan. "And Deuce seemed..." I shrug, recalling his reactions from the day. "Sad, maybe? Disappointed?"

Juni nods thoughtfully. "They've been friends a long time. I know Deuce wants to help Trace get his stuff sorted out." She shakes her head ruefully. "I bet he's disappointed."

She sips her tea and I sip my coffee. The faucet drips. Outside, a bird sings. On the back patio, the wind chime sways slowly. "So you went to his place?" Juni edges after we enjoy a slice of Bluebell mornings.

"I went and told him he better show up today or else Deuce will fire him because of his contract."

Juni's eyes widen. "I didn't know Ink Time had official contracts."

I pluck a blackberry from the bowl of fruit on the counter. "I made it up."

My sister's smirk is contagious. "You've outsmarted him before day one."

"I always do." I shift on my feet, reaching for the coffee around my sister. As I refill my mug, ready to head back to my room and get some stretching done, I say, "Hey, by the way,

Dash Foster and Sterling Ford were outside this morning arguing over an empty tray of jam jars."

I watch my sister closely, but her eyes drop to her apparently very interesting mug of tea. "Oh, yeah, they're just returning jars. They're on the monthly delivery."

I narrow my eyes, trying to study the features on her face that she's hiding. We don't hide anything from each other, but in the recent months, Juni has been... different.

At first I thought it was because Dahlia moved out, got married and is on her second pregnancy. That all the change disrupted her the way it would a mother having a child go to college or something. I thought that's all it was. When I talked to Ev and Dolly about it, they agreed.

But now I wonder if it's something else.

"Do they... live together?" I ask, realizing as much as I see both Dash and Sterling, I don't know too much about them except Dash is Bluebell's favorite police officer and Sterling both owns and drives for Bluebell Waste.

Her eyes lift and finally come to mine. "They do. They're roommates."

I nod, trying to reclassify what I saw outside with this new information. "So... two middle-aged men live together and they eat 12 jars of jam a month?"

She shrugs. "Toast is their favorite meal."

I don't argue that toast isn't anyone's favorite meal. Instead, I don't push, because pushing Juni makes her shut down. It always has. "Anyway," she says, sweeping her fingers through my hair. "I hope today is a great first day with your mentor. Text me and let me know if he shows up."

"Oh, he'll show up," I snark, but deep in my bones, curiosity and nerves swarm. Will he show up? Will I have gone to his place and harassed him all for nothing? Does the apprenticeship only mean something to me? I smile at Juni as I move past her, out of the kitchen and down the hall.

"But I'll text you either way."

She calls after me. "Good! I'll leave your lunch on the counter. Heading out to the garden!"

My bedroom door closes, and I'm left with one glaring thought: what if he still doesn't show?

FOUR

Ivy doesn't give a crap about who I am.

Trace

"Here?" Corinne questions, pointing at the stop sign through the windshield. "Turn right here?"

Is it possible for someone's voice to make you nauseous? I mean, seriously. Something about the elevated pitch of her voice, and the way *here* sounds like "here-uh" has my stomach collapsing in on itself.

It ain't that single drink from last night, either.

I did have one drink—whiskey. I just so happened to finish the bottle.

"Yeah," I groan, catching my head in my hands as nausea bullies me, causing me to go fetal for a moment in the passenger seat of her Dodge Charger. She flicks her blinker on and the slow *tick, tick, tick* of the turn signal has me ready to tear my face off and jump out of this car, I swear. Everything is on my nerves this morning.

Mostly me.

"Okay, hun," she sings, popping her bubble gum. "We're here."

"How can you chew fucking Dubble Bubble at nine in the morning?" I crow, collecting my wet hair from my shoulders to tie it behind me in a messy bun.

"I don't drink coffee. It's my morning sugar," she says, reaching across me to pop open the door. "Call me?" she asks while also eyeing the sidewalk, hinting for me to get the fuck out.

I lift my shoulders. "I probably won't."

She rolls her eyes. "You're an asshole, you know that?"

The effort to get out of the car feels risky, as last night's booze churns in my gut. I attempt to shake my head, but the hangover renders me almost motionless. "Close the door so I can get to work," she says, tapping her long fingernail against the gold-plated name tag on her chest.

Corey. Fuck, did I call her Corinne or just think it? I bring my hands to my throat, where I close the last button on my long-sleeved black shirt. "Sorry," I mutter, pushing the door shut lightly so I don't turn the sidewalk into artwork with my brains splattered everywhere.

Hangovers aren't as easy as they were seven years ago.

Somehow it doesn't stop me.

Corey pulls away, and I turn, blinking up at Ink Time. The lights are on, Deuce's pickup is here, and the other artist I met a month or so ago is here, too. I see him crouched over his desk with a small lamp illuminating his private workspace. Slowly, I enter through the back and find myself in a small, dark hallway, face to face with my best friend.

He drops a hand to my shoulder softly, as if he knows I

can't stand a jarring movement. Something in my toes tingles, snaking a hot line up my calves and thighs, scorching my gut.

Fuck... I grab the back of my neck and pull at it as I look into Deuce's eyes. "I'm sorry," I admit, the words quiet as the feeling in my stomach registers.

Guilt.

I feel guilty.

Deuce's lips twitch. "It's fine." He looks over his shoulder to the place where the wall curves, and the hall opens into the studio. "Ivy's pissed, though."

Just hearing her name with the word "pissed" has a smirk curling my lips, and I don't know why. Something about that Firecracker always being angry—maybe I'm a masochist but it's some kind of fucked-up turn-on. I like it. Then it dawns on me. When Deuce drops his hand from my shoulder, I cup mine on his. "She came to my place last night, told me I'd get fired if I didn't show up."

"She cares, and she takes her craft seriously," Deuce replies just as the front shop door chimes with a new customer. "Make it up to her today by being a good mentor." I follow behind him to the front counter, where he hands me a stack of papers. "The tentative schedule for you and her. Follow it or don't, just make sure at the end of the twelve weeks, you've worked with her on all the main things here."

I don't get a chance to look at the book of shit he's placed in my hands because a woman is clearing her throat in an "*I need your attention*" type of way.

I get that a lot.

Only I'm startled to see it's—"Corey?" I look at her name tag for good measure, and she catches me, rolling her eyes.

"Did you really need to read my name tag, asshole?" She steps toward me, lowering her voice to a scathing hiss. "We had unprotected sex last night and now you need a name tag to know who I am?"

From behind me, Deuce clears his throat. "I'll give you a minute," he announces, but Corey likes an audience.

I'm not into voyeurism.

"This won't take long." She brings her gaze back to me, still chewing that awful pink gum. "I just realized I need the morning-after pill."

I blink at her. "So get it."

Deuce clears his throat, and Corey's return makes sense. I dig into my pocket and fish out my wallet where I pinch a twenty and pass it to her.

"Good thinking, Corey," I tell her, watching as she curls the bill and slips it between her breasts.

Out of nowhere, Ivy appears, her jet-black hair a vivid contrast to Corey and her blonde locks. She takes the twenty from between Corey's breasts, officially locking my attention on them. Ivy takes Corey's hand, and places a one-hundred-dollar bill in her palm.

"Get the morning-after pill, get a nice breakfast, and some heating pads."

Corey stares at Ivy blankly for a few seconds before popping her gum and saying, "Thanks. Are you like his sister or manager or whatever?"

Ivy shakes her head. "Nope."

Corey rolls the hundred, slipping it between her breasts again. She loops her arms around Ivy, her eyes squeezed shut as she embraces her. "Thank you, girl."

Then the door is dinging and Corey is gone.

I look between Deuce and Ivy. Despite the fact I'm showered and mostly sober, both of them look tired and unimpressed.

That sour feeling of guilt returns, and I realize I like the way it feels even less than being hungover. Deuce leads me to the lighted sketch table in the back, and Ivy follows.

"Line work. Second half of the day is booked with a client. Line work until then," he says, rocking on his boots.

"I thought you said I could decide the order as long as I did all the shit on the list," I argue, hating being told what to do by anyone. I knew working for Deuce meant he'd technically be my boss, but I never expected to actually be bossed.

Can't say I enjoy it. I'm the guy who's in charge. That's how I roll.

"You can. But line work is where every apprenticeship starts. Don't you remember?"

Our eyes hold. I don't know if he's asking me to go back to the start, to revisit who and where I was when I began my journey as a tattoo artist. If he is, he's asking me to jump back into the pain, either as a punishment or a reminder. I can't decide.

My voice is hoarser than I'd like when I reply, "Yeah, I remember."

I've been spending years trying to forget who taught me, and how much she meant.

I turn to face Ivy, whose black hair is knotted into two long braids, her eyes lined like a cat, large gauges filling her ears. I know it's wild to think considering my career but I've never traditionally been into goth chicks.

Something about the way she's glaring at me has me a little bricked up, though. I can't deny that her hate is attractive, and if that doesn't sum up my psyche, I don't know what does.

"You ready to do some line work?"

Her face and her tone bear no emotion when she says, "I was ready yesterday."

I cut my eyes to Deuce, then back to Ivy. I've apologized to my friend. He owns this place, he's the one who brought me here. I owed him an apology and I paid my debt. I don't owe her shit. Something tells me a smart-ass comment isn't my play with a girl like Ivy, but I just can't help myself.

Sliding into the leather chair on casters, I pick up my pencil and adjust the small light at the desk. "If today doesn't work for you," I say, splitting a smile between her and Deuce, "we can find another artist who wants the apprenticeship."

She's a firecracker for sure, but right now, she's icing over. I see it happen before my eyes. Her jaw swings before locking closed, blue orbs narrowing on me so sharply I almost feel her gaze poking my chest. Her shoulders are set back, chin high with both sexy defiance and snarling attitude. "Today is perfect."

I look down at my hand, already sketching from years of memory. I hide my smile as a few lines turn into a few more, and the outline of a pistol appears in my mind. As I sketch, a rush of coffee with raspberries and amber hit me.

The back of my neck pricks with heat and beneath the small table, my knee bounces. My cock thickens as I focus on my sketch, and not the insanely intoxicating scent that is Ivy Ellington.

"Yesterday would have been just as perfect," she breathes, just quiet enough for Deuce to miss.

The graphite swishes against the paper as my line curves, rounding over the same spot until the hammer looks right. I feel her eyes on me. I've been watched while sketching a hundred times. Maybe more. I've tattooed in front of massive crowds, viewed on reality television by the millions.

Something about *her* watching me, though. I find myself more focused than I've been in a long time. I find myself actually caring.

I take my time on the stock lines, switching pencils halfway through. "Ink Time is outfitted with pen machines," I tell her, keeping my voice low. "When I started tattooing, the shop I was at used rotary machines. I don't foresee technology moving past pen machines for quite some time, so take some solace in knowing you won't have to relearn your tool. Starting with the pen makes the most sense."

I switch pencils, opting for a sharper one with a thinner graphite tip. Finding the spot I left off, I continue on the gridded stocks on the pistol sketch.

"Obviously this ain't gonna be someone's ink but for the sake of teaching, I'll show you my process. Every artist establishes their own, but here's mine." Quickly, I add detail to the trigger and trigger guard, switching back to a thicker graphite to emphasize the angular opening of the barrel. "I sketch with pencil and paper first. Always. I know a lot of artists have moved to iPads, but my best work is done on paper."

"Same," she says, and that singular word has my hand pausing, my head turning, and my eyes meeting hers.

"You're young to be old-school," I comment, noticing a tiny cluster of gold near her left pupil, floating amongst the deep cerulean shade. Beautiful eyes this Firecracker has.

"I'm self-taught and was raised on a fixed income so iPads and tablets weren't really an option."

I nod, forcing myself to focus back on the last bit of the quick sketch. "Line work is the core of tattooing. See how this singular sketch embodies several different strokes to provide texture and depth?"

"Yes," she says softly, exercising a tone I didn't think she had. As shitty as it was for me to flake yesterday, she's letting it go because she wants to learn—even if I didn't apologize.

"I find it much easier to reach the level of complexity I want with paper and pencil. They swear to me it can be done digitally but like I said, I prefer this." I sign the bottom of the sketch from habit, and swivel in my chair to face the counter in the corner. "Now this is what I use, but other artists here at Ink Time have their own process, so it's up to you."

"Before you move on to the stencil," Ivy comments, giving me pause. I haven't even shown her the stencil printer, but she already knows. Then again, she was here all day yesterday. Without me.

I cock a brow, interested in her question, but I don't turn around. Not just yet. "What's up?"

"The pen you use, do you have a cartridge that holds different sizes or do you swap the pen each time you want to change line size?" She's intentional with her question, enunciating and speaking slowly. And when I swivel back to face her, I find her taking notes in an old spiral notebook.

I did that too when I first started. And I read through my own notes daily, staying up till all hours practicing each night.

"I use a pen with a cartridge, so when I need to change strokes, it's all in the pen. Same tool the whole time."

She nods, tipping her head toward her notebook to jot down my answer. When she's done, her gaze returns to the stencil printer on the table, and she waits.

"C'mere and watch," I say over my shoulder, hitting the button on the printer. Sensing her behind me, I feed the sketched paper through. "Some machines only print stencils from digital work, which means you need a separate scanner. This machine is designed for old-school guys like me. You put your sketch through and it prints it on thermal paper, giving you a nice little stencil."

I hear her graphite sliding along her notebook, and the sound lifts a thousand pounds of invisible weight from my chest, lightening me in ways I never expected.

Going back to the basics is all it is. Hearing her sketch reminds me of my start, before I was attached, before I was a big name, before anything. She reminds me of the pure love of the art that I felt when I started.

And that's the only reason my chest is light and my insides are fucking vibrating.

I ask her to sketch something quick and small, and stand behind her as she draws a small knife. I'm surprised by my urges to ask her what type of artist she wants to be, where she sees herself going creatively, and where she wants to corner herself in the tattoo world.

Truth is, I'm the one getting asked, I'm the one doing interviews, I'm the one with eyes focused on me while people wait to see what I'm up to. I'm not used to giving a shit about someone else. I don't want to care. It's too much of a liability.

But as her hand never leaves the paper, the dull roar of graphite on cardstock filling the space with beautiful, familiar music, I can't help myself. I've never wanted to know so much about a damn near stranger before.

She's captured my focus, and I don't like it.

"Could use some more depth and shadowing," I tell her, carefully placing bricks between us, one shitty comment at a time. Her sketch is beautiful and if I'm being honest, she's a whole hell of a lot better than I was at her age. "And if you're going to corner your sketches on—"

"Blackwork," she says, her pencil still moving as she focuses on the piece. "I'm a blackwork artist and I lean toward the macabre."

Same as me when I started.

No one would know that, though, because I made my name as Trace Calhoun, the Neo Traditional God of Ink. The Travel Channel sent me around the world as *Trace Tats*, which later turned into *Needle Ninjas* when my drinking got bad and they invited more artists. We traveled, covering people in the art they dreamed of, made into my style. Art Nouveau meets Art

Deco is where I thrive, but blackwork is where I started. The Travel Channel told me there wasn't enough showmanship and possibility in blackwork. And I wanted so badly to have something to move on to that I changed my entire style.

"Think you'll get a lot of customers here in Bluebell wanting dagger and skulls on 'em?" I question almost rhetorically, since we both know the answer. It doesn't matter who lives around the shop, she should absolutely follow her passion. What's the point of being a goddamn artist if you can't create the art in your dreams? But I don't wanna like Ivy, so I place another brick. "Okay, that's good enough," I slight her incredibly detailed knife sketch, despite the fact I'm hugely impressed that her line work is so clean, and that she was able to add so many layers so quickly.

There's a sparkle on the blade.

Engraving on the handle.

Blood pooling beneath it.

Wear on the serration.

It's fucking incredible. "It'll work for this. We're throwing out the stencil anyway," I add, the callousness of my words burning my throat. I don't watch for her response, though, because I'm feeding the paper through the machine, moving forward. "The button on the top is the power button–"

"Wow," she says quietly. "Let me write that down."

I turn to find her still sitting at the table, arms folded over her chest, eyes locked to mine. I'm being a prick, so she's being a brat. No one's ever challenged me in my career. When you're making a network millions, you live like a king. And women never argue with me, because they wanna suck my dick so bad.

But Ivy.

Ivy doesn't give a crap about who I am.

She stormed over to my apartment last night.

She's rolling her eyes at me.

"Show me already, you're not the only one with things to do," she snaps, yanking me from my thought which was masquerading as a deep glare.

I put my hand on my hip, the other one hovering over the start button. "You're my apprentice. What else do you have to do?"

She rises, and my heart pumps in the hollow of my throat. For some reason, my dick twitches a little, too.

"I work for Deuce, and so do you. When you're not training me, I have things to do around the shop." She closes the few feet between us with heavy steps in her combat boots. "Believe it or not, not everything is all about you, *Trace*."

With my eyes on hers, I press the start button. Her breath is warm against my chin as she blinks up at me, angry and defiant. The stencil machine works behind us, and only after a few seconds does she break her gaze and look back at it.

"It's fast," she comments, recentering us.

"Yeah," I say, still staring down at her. Freckles sweep her cheeks, curving the bridge of her nose, and her lashes are thick and long, making each blink of her eye intoxicating. That amber scent hits me again, and I step back, lifting the warm thermal paper from the tray. Handing it to her, I watch her eyes study the stencil of her work.

It's a sketch that took five minutes to show how the machine works.

It's nothing.

It will go in the garbage.

But I watch as her eyes rake over the paper, taking in each messy line and delicate curve. With one hand, she clutches the stencil like it's holy, using the other to lightly dust her fingers over the design. A knot forms in my throat as she blinks up at me, fighting moisture in her eyes.

"It's..." She clears her throat. "It's cool seeing my sketch as a stencil."

Heat flares in my chest, sending a shot of desire down my sternum, into my groin. Witnessing someone's amazement– that first hit of excitement in a new business– that's all my response is. It's not her. It's the symbolism. It reminds me of the best time of my life.

That's all.

And I get it.

And I feel that amazement for her, through her. My hands burn, itching to reach out and hold her against my chest and tell her *yes, it is cool, you're great, this is where you belong.*

Instead, I swipe the stencil from her hands, causing her gaze to jerk up to mine, an angry pinch between her brows.

"There will be hundreds more. It's nothing to cry about." I let the stencil sail into the garbage can directly under my hand as I release it, then say, "Now you know how the stencil machine works."

She swallows thickly, folding her arms over her chest, hiding that acid-washed and torn-up Metallica t-shirt from my sight. "Got it."

The door whooshes open, the little bell tied to the arm jingling only when it sails closed. From the front, Deuce hollers, "Trace, your mid-day appointment is here."

"You gonna watch me draw it up and ink him or you gonna sweep floors because, you know, you're the shop apprentice and not just mine?"

I give her credit—she's quick to release the tight set of her jaw and the anger in her brow. "I'm glad to hear you acknowledge that you know I'm not yours. But yes, I'll be watching you work today since you're actually here."

And then she's pushing past me, stomping down the hall with her ripped tights and her salty attitude.

And I'm left to adjust my dick behind her.

FIVE

Is my thing being a masochist?

Ivy

"Seems like a dumb reason to celebrate," I say, stuffing my socked feet into my boots. Dolly nudges me with her elbow from her spot next to me. We're sitting on my bed, catching up before dinner.

"One month is a milestone!" she says, watching me feed the laces around the hooks before tugging them tight and tying them in a bowed knot. "You know... it's *my* house you're coming to. You didn't need to put your boots back on."

Now that Dolly is married to Hudson, the *neighbor's* house is now my sister's house. The age gap and quick onset relationship would make some families nervous. Not me. I had years to process that the older man next door would definitely be related to me by marriage one day. I knew it from the first time she snuck into his house to taste his leftover coffee.

When my sisters or myself set our sights on something, we *achieve*. Even if that achievement is making someone ours.

"It's not that I'm not comfortable," I explain, pulling my hair out of the braids I'd worn them in today. "It's just... I don't know. I don't feel like going out at all. And if I have my boots on, I'll come home quicker so I can take them off again."

Dolly wraps her arm around me, the smell of Hudson's cologne so overwhelming I think my pores are clogged. "You smell like you just took a bath in Hudson's cologne."

A wicked grin sweeps her pink lips. "We just made love."

I push against her shoulder, sending her careering into the mattress as she giggles. "I don't want to know about it." Now that Hudson is our brother-in-law, the specifics have slowed and I'm grateful. Something about watching your sister's husband and baby daddy cut the Christmas turkey when you know *where* his other hand has been is... surreal.

She sits up, smoothing her hands through her hair, her blonde waves tangling on that massive ring on her finger.

"Okay, food's gonna be ready in forty-five minutes. I'm gonna waddle down to the creek and let the guys know. See you in a few?" She rises and moves to the doorway, where she spins on her bare feet to face me, waiting for my confirmation.

Sighing, I smile. "See you in a few."

As soon as I hear the front door open and close, I flop back on my bed and let loose a wild sigh. One I've been holding in since yesterday when that jerk let me know just how unimportant this job is when he no-showed. It's only the second time since the first day, but still.

Obviously as Dolly's stalking enabler for the last few years, I knew as soon as Hudson was officially hers, they'd be worse than bunnies in spring. They're already on their second pregnancy together. But having to hear about all the good, hot, wicked sex she's having with the man of her dreams? While I had to hunt down Trace to get him to come to work? I'm a little grouchy. And I will be happy to celebrate Dolly taking back-shots from Hudson all day long.

I'm just not there yet.

I wish I was. It's not about being grossed out—I realize Dolly is a woman with needs. Just because she's my flesh and blood doesn't mean that urges aren't there. I've been next door to her rubbing one out plenty of times.

It's their *happiness* that made me put my boots back on.

I love it for Dolly so much, and I'm stoked that she got what she wants for her life. I am. Truly. I am not an asshole that can't be happy for someone else, or who feels threatened by other people's wins. I'm not.

But right now, maybe it's starting this gig, I don't know, but whatever it is, I'm not strong enough to pretend it doesn't affect me.

I long for a partner to leave his scent on my clothes, for his touch to linger on my skin all day, to slip my hand into my pocket only to find a random love note, to find my car with a full tank and a playlist just for me. I'm at the point where I want more than Juni to come home to, I want to plan vacations with more than just my feet in the sand— I want someone to take them with.

Someone to rub against me and ask me how sore I am after he fucked me ruthlessly the night before.

Trace comes into my mind, and I slap my palm over my forehead to knock him free. Only, he of course defies me even in a fantasy; standing casually at the reception desk at Ink Time, one elbow bearing his weight as he leans over, right leg stacked against the other. His hair is down and wavy, the vivid ink on his throat nearly glowing as he tosses his head back in raucous laughter.

Why does he have to be the one to pop in my head directly

following the "fucked me ruthlessly" thought? Dolly's thing is stalking. Is my thing being a masochist? Do I really want to embark on having the hots for a total turd of a human being?

I roll over onto my stomach, pulling my phone from my pocket. Google is open and my fingers are ready.

Do I *want* to do this?

I looked up Rhett after we met a few times. Learned everything there was to know. Every last detail. And what happened? He cheated on me, but before that, he never expended energy getting to know me. There was no chance in hell that Rhett was ever holed up in his room, googling me because he was so interested.

I'm not doing that anymore.

I'm energy matching.

In the capacity in which I know Trace Calhoun, he is a total butthole, skeevy, gaslighting, self-indulgent jackhole—wait, I already used *hole*—jackass.

I don't need to search Google for some semblance of redemption so I can write off his shitty qualities, obsess over the one good one, fall in love with him, then get my heart broken when he undoubtedly doesn't share my same feelings.

No. No fucking way.

I shove my phone away before I google, and move through the house toward the door, only dragging my Doc Martens a little on the way.

I know they just want to celebrate me and the hard work I've been doing at Ink Time for the last month. I love them because of it.

I have learned a lot, and it was day one of the official apprenticeship when I realized that I don't just like art—I actually do love tattooing too. But all of that "I'm chasing the right dream" high has been smothered by the aggravating, intense, annoying, and irritatingly sexy Trace.

If he isn't playing devil's advocate with everything I say, he's ignoring me or glaring at me from across the studio.

I've given the mental middle finger more times in the last month than I have given the *actual* finger in my entire life.

And that's saying something.

Fresh air stings my eyes as I lock the front door behind me, turning to head just twenty feet away. But I stop in my tracks when my eyes catch Deuce slipping from his truck, heading toward Hudson and Dolly's place.

As if he senses me frozen, he twists his head to meet my gaze and nods. "He's not coming," he says, adding, "don't worry. I didn't invite him."

"Good," I breathe, dropping my head, watching clouds of dust coat the tips of my boots as I close the space between us. We walk to the front door together but he stops me before he opens it, his large hand covering the knob in entirety.

"Good," he repeats, studying my eyes intensely.

"Yeah," I say as a bead of nervous sweat slips down my spine beneath my oversized t-shirt. "Good."

Deuce's eyes remain lost in mine, searching for something as they volley back and forth. Without another word, he pushes the door open and the weirdness dissipates as Dolly wraps her arms around me.

"You came!"

I snort. "You were at the house, like, five minutes ago watching me get ready. Of course I came." I tuck my waves behind my ear, making my way to the barstools in the kitchen. It's where Dolly and I always sit when we talk.

"They're at the creek skipping stones until dinner," Dolly says to Deuce, without him needing to ask. She checks on Honey in the playpen, kissing her cheeks a million times before returning to me.

"And my–" Deuce's sentences dies on the vine as Everly

comes out from the hall, a sleepy toddler tucked into her chest and nape. "There's my whole world," he croons softly, his soft tone throwing bumps along my bare arms and the side of my neck.

I don't have a thing for Deuce.

But there's baby fever in the air, between Ev and Deuce and Dolly and Hudson, and I think it's very contagious. Because my insides tighten at the pink-cheeked baby folded into his mom, and the tender way Deuce greets them both, his strong hand sweeping gracefully down his son's back as he presses his lips to Ev's.

I want that. It's shitty timing to want a relationship and a family so badly because I'm starting my career and all, but still, I can't deny that the clock inside me isn't ticking—it's ringing loudly, begging to be noticed.

I've wanted to be married and have a family since I was too young—just eighteen. But I promised myself I'd wait- finish school, start my career, all those things.

I wanted Rhett to be the one.

But he turned out to be a total lizard instead.

"Heading out to see Hud and Bear at the creek," Deuce repeats to Ev, who nods knowingly, her wide eyes fresh and sparkling.

"Okay," she whispers, "we're just waking up from a nap so it'll take him a minute to adjust anyway."

Deuce and Ev share another private goodbye consisting of soft kisses and hushed words, and then it's just us girls and the babies. Ev sets her son down next to Honey in the playpen permanently laid out in the living room- I say permanent because my sister is so fucking obsessed with her husband, I can't see a time when she won't always be pregnant.

Seriously.

Breeding kink on steroids over here.

"I relate," I say, nodding to my tired niece as I bite into a fresh strawberry. Dolly has a full spread of fruits, chips, cheeses, breads and nuts laid out, and suddenly I feel bad for having dragged my toes to come tonight.

"What do you mean?" Ev asks, smoothing her fingers through her hair as she takes a seat next to me.

"Ace needing a few minutes to calibrate," I repeat, adding, "I need that when I get to work every day. A few minutes before I can fully process Trace Calhoun."

She snorts as she reaches for a bowl of barbeque chips, taking a few at once. "How's it going, by the way? I kept meaning to come take you to lunch and find out how you're enjoying it but," she motions to the playpen with an orange chip, "he's kept me so busy lately."

"It's going good," I reply, unsure of what's socially acceptable to bitch about. Her husband owns the place and is my boss, after all.

"I don't see her car at home until 11 sometimes," Dolly says, dipping her own chip into guac.

"Barbecue and guac?" I question, my nose wrinkling at the abhorrent combination.

"Some combos are so obvious. Like hot dogs and ketchup. It's the less obvious combos that really win for me." She dunks another chip into guac. I'm not sure if she and Hudson are part of this metaphor, or if it's me and Trace. But... Why would she put me "with" Trace? She wouldn't. Because there's no... "us." Not like that. "This is one of them. And also, it could be a gross pregnancy craving," she finishes.

"I'll have to just trust you." I dunk my tortilla chip into guac. "And the reason I'm home so late some days is because Trace drags his scraggly ass in hours late. And I force him to stay so that I can get the full eight hours."

Ev arches her brow. "Force him?" Her lips quiver with a smirk.

Smiling, I tell her another reason why I really like her husband as a boss, and as a human. "I keep reminding him of the contract he signed with Ink Time when he took the job—" We pause and think back to the story of Deuce signing Trace.

He was drunk, it was a catastrophe and ended up with Deuce making many promises of good faith to the Bluebell Police Department.

"Well, we all know he can't remember and the fact that he can't is really his own fault," I say, grinning, completely ignoring the tiniest bit of guilt in my stomach. I'm sort of tricking him, even though it's true that he's a moron and a half for not knowing basic information about his employment.

I guess when you're loaded stuff like that doesn't matter.

"Oh my," Ev says, going for Dolly's barbecue and guac combo. Her face scrunches as she says, around a mouthful, "Not for me." She wipes her mouth with the white paper napkin, her brows pulling together as she eyes me. "What does Deuce say?"

My smile widens. "He... goes along with it." I laugh as I recall Deuce this morning. Trace was late–only eight minutes but still, I've established myself as the thorn in his side and I like it there. I'm cozy.

I reminded him of his contract and Deuce said, and I quote, "You better listen to her."

"Your husband is so cool," I sigh, my heart rattling as Trace flashes through my mind.

He has beautiful hands.

A wedding band would look sexy as hell on his finger.

Wait, *what the fuck?* Metaphorically I shake my head, refocusing on what I should. His hands touching me, not what they'd look like with a ring on.

His hands... *okay, his hands.*

Fuck his hands are hot.

His fingers would feel so good inching up my thighs, swiping my panties aside.

"Hello?" Dolly makes me jump.

"Huh?"

"You just zoned out." Dolly presses her finger into my chest, and I notice Ev is no longer across from me. "You better not have a crush on Deuce," she warns.

"What?" I jump up, looking around for Ev.

"She's checking on Ace." She licks her lips. "You were fantasizing. I saw it in your beady pupils."

My hands fly to my hips. "My *beady* pupils?" I scoff.

She nods. "Yeah, so tell me who if it isn't Deuce."

I roll my eyes. My beady eyes, apparently. "Trace, you idiot. Of course I wouldn't fall for a married man." I step toward her, lowering my voice. "That's grounds for murder."

She nods. "Absolutely."

"Anyway," I veer back to the topic at hand. "Don't... I don't know. Just... don't say anything or talk about it or think about it or... fuck, don't even remember I told you, okay? Just, like, forget it." Sweat beads on my upper lip and my heart is suddenly racing. I feel like I'm hooked up to a polygraph and she's the tester.

I feel so exposed.

I've admitted out loud, and that makes it real.

I *do* like Trace. It's almost all physical, with a tiny, itty, teensy bit more. Still...

He's a complete fucking asshole to me and I want him bad... what does that say about me? I swipe my hand along my forehead and take a deep breath. "Please just don't say anything."

She pulls her fingers through my long, wavy tangles. "I would never."

Ev returns, settling back in her spot, taking her glass of white wine by the stem. "I love that he doesn't even know and you're using that. And I love my husband for going along with it." She takes a sip, and her eyes wrinkle as she grows thoughtful.

"I think discipline is what a guy like Trace needs," Ev finally says, slow and intentional, like she's thought about it before.

I can't help but ask, "You... Think about what Trace needs?" I hope it doesn't come across as jealousy.

But I am.

I am seething with ridiculous levels of jealousy that Everly knows Trace so well that she even has the ability to form an opinion about his life and what he may or may not need.

She gets access to an intimate side of him that I don't, and I hate her for it.

Even though I love Everly through and through.

Right now, my fingers curl into my thighs as I breathe through the intense wave of jealousy that washes agonizingly slow over me.

Ev nods. "I do because he means so much to Deuce." She sips her wine, then seems to urgently correct herself as her gaze bounces between me and Dolly. "I mean, of course I care about Trace," she amends. "But Deuce has this bond to Trace that I'll never understand."

Is there a side to Trace that is even deeper than what she gets?

A new level of jealousy for me to reach?

As I think of Deuce, I'm suddenly angry to know they share some secret, intimate connection. My body burns to be the one intimately connected to his talented brain, his skillful hands and his jagged heart.

He has to have a broken heart. He has to.

It's the only way to explain how he behaves. Sleeping around endlessly, always drunk. The signs are there that something is off.

But then again, it's been years. He's been doing this for years.

"Discipline is what he needs," Dolly agrees finally, shaking us from our silence. "He needs something to control him a little, even if he doesn't realize it."

Control him.

That's something I'd love to do. God, I'd love to be the one finally playing devil's advocate to him, while he's somehow at my mercy. I'll never be the one to mentor him in tattooing, but if in some reality I can be at the helm of his well-being and sanity, so help me I'll do it.

To torture him the way he tortures me, constantly critiquing me.

"Yeah," Ev says after another sip of Pinot grigio. "He needs a woman to take control of things and shape him the hell up. The only woman who broke his heart did lasting damage but he's beyond a simple repair now. He needs tough love."

"I thought I saw he was engaged not too long ago," I say, recalling what Ev told me before Trace moved here, and something I briefly saw online. I usually don't pay attention to tabloids, and this time was no different.

Ev dismissively waves it off. "Yeah, that... wasn't what it looked like. Trust me, Trace was the victim there as much as Tara."

I stuff my face with chips to hide my smile. He didn't cheat and he needs tough love. I like both of those things, especially the tough love.

I want to be the one who does that.

I will be the one who does that.

Ivy Ellington is absolutely fucking good enough for reality star Trace Calhoun.

THE URGE TO LOOK HIM UP IS STRONGER THAN EVER.

All of these thoughts I'm having about Trace have been so hard to suppress—tonight it feels like I no longer can.

It feels like I have to make him understand he's a total asshole, but also make him understand I want him to be *my* total asshole.

That I like him despite the hole-ery.

He was hungover at work today. Every time he leaned over my shoulder, I smelled last night's whiskey. And a trace of perfume.

I'm vibrating with jealousy on a daily basis.

But from his perspective, I'm just full of attitude.

Lying in bed, stomach sated from Dolly's delicious dinner, I cave and snatch my phone from the nightstand. Typing his name into Google, I wait for the top result to be his Wikipedia page and for the next one to be the network page for his now off-air show.

I've never read his Wikipedia, but I know he has one.

And I know he was on a reality show.

But the way I know Trace is his uploaded art. I watched his feed. I didn't get involved in any media version of him—I fell for his work.

And when I met him? I was sad to find out... he is my exact type.

Brooding and grouchy, sullen but not without purpose.

Inked and immersed in art, a passion for consuming other art forms—my dream guy.

I'd deny ever saying that, though.

Results flood the page and my eyes burn from the sheer volume glaring back at me, bold blue colored links littering each listing.

TRACE CALHOUN'S BODY COUNT.

Sickness creeps up the back of my throat, burning my nose. My eyes mist over. I hate myself for having such a visceral reaction to this. Obviously he's a womanizer.

And obviously I have no claim to him.

Still. The knife I keep in my boot? It feels like it's burrowed in my stomach right now, and I hate what that means.

I *really* like Trace.

I drop my phone onto my stomach and drape my arm over my eyes. I sigh, because I haven't really liked anyone like this... ever.

He will be a challenge, but he will be mine.

He has to be. I don't waste my feelings.

SIX

I'll talk to my best friend Jack. He always listens.

Trace

Last night was the last night.

The stench of coffee burns my nose hairs as I suck down yet another paper cup. The shit here at Ink Time is just that—shit—and I'm gonna let Deuce know.

Just as soon as I get my bearings.

I'm a little... *off* this morning.

Tired and a tiny bit hungover.

Just a tiny bit.

But my sour stomach and throbbing head are not what I'm focused on.

For an incredibly annoying reason that I wish not to name, I'm worried Ivy will recognize the signs, see I'm hungover again, and hate me more.

She does hate me. I feel it in the pinch of her gaze, the shortness in her words, the subtext in her body language.

She loves my work, there's no questioning that. And I do take pride in the fact that someone as incredibly talented as Ivy looks up to me. But otherwise, she can't stand me.

She's in good company feeling that way.

I crumple the third paper cup and toss it into the wastebasket. "Good morning," she says, passing me on her way in.

I got here early today. Not just for copious amounts of coffee but to specifically make sure I wasn't late. Again.

I lift my eyes and welcome the expected drop of my stomach when she doesn't bother looking down as she walks past.

Of course she doesn't look at you, fucking dum-dum. You're a prick to her all the time. "Look who's late now," I chide as she slides her little black-and-purple lunch bag under her desk. It's got an ice pack in it, and whenever she takes it out of her bag, I wonder if she's ever used it on any of her boyfriends after giving them a black eye.

"I'm not late, I'm on time," she says, adding, "nice try, *Trace.*"

Shit. Ivy saying my name makes me shiver. The way it slithers off her tongue, full of venom but deeply intriguing. My dick perks up.

Not wanting my hard-on to intensify, I finish my fourth cup, crumple it and toss it into the wastebasket. "I have a morning session today," I tell her, but as I do, she nods, flipping open her little black spiral planner.

"I'm aware. I booked it."

Did she? I stare at her day planner as a moment from last week crashes through my memory. Me hungover after I'd been in Oakcreek the night before. I went to find a cool place to sketch and connect with nature, but I found a bar with $3 shots instead. The next morning I barely held it together. Ivy forced me to finish the project I was working on, didn't let up when she wanted her lesson on depth of needles in the skin, and she never once asked me how I was feeling.

That same day, she *did* ask if I could do a morning session this week.

I remember now.

"What's the note on the session?" I ask as I find myself following her to the reception desk. Deuce runs reception for now since we haven't hired anyone, and though Ivy is my apprentice, she does a lot for the shop itself. Including running reception when she can.

She opens the computer and starts swiping and typing. It's office work, nothing grand, but something about the way she owns and destroys all the spaces she's in—she reminds me of a young, eager me. Only... smarter and, honestly? More talented.

The tattoo she gave herself on her inner ankle the other night is incredibly good, and not just for a newbie. I mean, it's just plain good.

A serrated knife piercing a chopped-off tree trunk, with wild vines growing around the handle. I don't know what it means to her, if anything, but I haven't been able to stop stealing little glances at it. It's the kind of artwork that makes you want to think, and it's unusual to find young artists creating pieces like that.

"This," she finally says, making my gaze jump from her inner ankle up to her glaring eyes. She definitely caught me looking, but we both ignore it in favor of the design on-screen. "He emailed it over. You have two hours to sketch it and stencil it."

I look at the screen for a second, then my eyes veer back to her, where her lips twitch. "You're not on TV anymore, Trace. These are the things the people of Bluebell want."

I narrow my eyes at her, both hating and loving how satisfied she is by this.

I was creating large-scale, custom Alphonse Mucha style pieces – ethereal and beautiful, bold colors and sweeping shapes to highlight the chiseled features of a woman, usually some sort of warrior or champion. Wild flowers or animals would accompany each piece, and when I was done, people would stare in awe, cupping their hand to their mouth, sending photos to their friends, writing on message boards, recording the episode on their DVRs to show their own tattoo artists.

And now I am tattooing a large belt buckle replica that says "HOWDY" with a rope and spurs beneath the words.

"Great," I say finally after I take in the large brass belt buckle image for a minute. It may not be what I'm used to—typically people come to see me and they want what I have to give them—but I realize in a small town, people don't care much about my art. They just want a capable tattoo artist.

That's me.

"A lot will let you create whatever you want. But they have to trust you first, or know of you. Just... hang in there," she says softly, as if reading my mind. I hate that she knew what I was thinking.

"Did you get dimensions?" I ask Ivy as she gathers herself a cup of coffee from the snack station behind reception.

She sips her steaming brew. "Dimensions are in the file, which you can access from the iPad at your workstation."

I blink at her, twirling my favorite sketching pencil in one hand.

"You can't use an iPad?" she asks, and it's just now I'm noticing her long, dark hair is wavy today. But, like, curled wavy. And her lashes are darker. My eyes drop to her pouty lips, and I notice their usual pale color is now dark and bold, brave like permanent dark ink.

I was so into her just being here earlier that I didn't even notice her looks.

Awareness jolts through me, and I reactively sink into my seat at the sketch table and give her my back. I move my pencil from memory, knowing I need to see the damn buckle again but right now, I can't look at her. I can't talk to her. I can't do anything with or related to Ivy Ellington.

Because I didn't notice her black lips and curled hair.

I was thinking of her. Will she notice me? Will she acknowledge I'm not late? Will she approve of me?

Those are questions that only come when I give a shit.

"I *can* use an iPad, Ivy, I'm not four," I gripe, the shape of the buckle already easily visible on my paper. "Print me the image and leave it here," I tell her, still keeping my back to her.

I don't want to look at how fucking beautiful she looks today. So I reach under my desk and grab the little flask I have taped to the underside. I feel a bit like a junkie hiding booze but moments like this, I'm relieved. I take a quick swig and return it.

I have no business doing anything but getting comfortable at Ink Time in Bluebell. I need to find comfort and stability and happiness in this type of tattooing. I need to stop drinking. I need to focus my efforts now on being a local legend, not the guy who once was.

And falling for someone just like her... who reminds me so much of the woman who destroyed me... that's not part of the plan.

A moment later, a printed image of the belt buckle is pushed onto the desk next to me.

"Thanks," I grumble, and am surprised when a gruff tone replies.

"Welcome," Deuce says.

Swiveling, I look up at my friend. I've known him before

his hair went salty and lines filled in around his eyes. I knew him when he didn't know Everly, when Ink Time was just something we talked about in the back of our buddy's van while we passed a joint and stewed on dreams.

Now he's wise and mature. He's a father and a successful business owner. The thing I'm most proud and jealous of is his role as a husband.

We always thought it'd be me first.

It was going to be me first.

"You ready for a full morning session?" he asks, his eyes darting around my station. Thankfully the flask isn't out.

"I'm not drunk, or even hungover," I say, leaving off the 'anymore' weighing guiltily on my subconscious.

"Not what I meant per se," he says, thumbing through a stack of sketches on my desk. It's the stack of stuff I've told Ivy I need to get through. The stuff she wants me to look at. The truth is? I've looked at every single piece of art in that pile at least ten times.

I can't bring myself to tell her how good they are, how good she is—so instead I pretend I'm too busy to even look at them.

It's fucked up, I know.

"Those are hers," I comment on the sketches as Deuce plucks one from the stack, holding it up to the lamplight on my desk.

"I know," he says, his eyes full of wonder as he takes in the sketch. A woman—one who reminds me of Ivy herself—lots of ink, long wavy hair, a scowl on her face, plump lips and a stubborn little nose—holds tight to a circular piece of wood, knives sticking out of the board. Beneath the sketch of the salty woman having withstood a barrage of knives, two words written in beautiful cursive. *Magician's Assistant.*

That one's my favorite. Deuce turns the piece so I can see it, nodding as he says, "She's good."

I shrug, focusing on the rope I'm currently sketching. "She's not bad," I say, hating that I can't just agree with him. She's not even around. It would be okay to admit to Deuce that Ivy is incredible. Hell, it would actually be the best time to do it. Get it off my chest, make her look good to her boss, which she absolutely deserves, and purge it from my soul so I don't accidentally slip and tell her she's good or something.

I lower my pencil to the paper and get to my feet, facing my friend. Looking over the stations, I don't see Ivy but still, I keep my voice low.

"You picked the right person for the program. She's a gifted artist."

There.

Easy.

The right thing to do is now done.

In my mind, I'm swiping my hands together to be rid of the guilt, and patting myself on the back for giving her the credit she deserves.

Maybe I'm not such an asshole after all.

Deuce claps a hand on my shoulder. "I already knew that, asshole. Why don't you tell her instead of me?" He glances down at the sketch I'm working on then back at me, adding, "Good luck on your morning session today. I was only asking if you're ready because it's been a while since you did a few hours."

I nod. "I'm good."

He moves out of my space, toward the front. "Good. Because I'm heading out. I'll be back around lunch. Ivy, too."

I arch a brow. "She's not going to watch my session?" I scratch at the back of my head, trying to ignore the free fall of disappointment in my stomach that she won't be here this morning. "Isn't that, like, the point of the apprenticeship?"

"The point is to learn the business and art of tattooing, which she's doing."

"So where's she goin'?" I ask, ignoring the urge to look around the studio. She was just here, so where the fuck is she now and why isn't she staying?

"Connor is taking her to look at needles at the supply store twenty minutes North."

"Oakcreek?" I ask, my throat suddenly dry and uncomfortable.

Deuce nods. "Yeah. She'll probably be our buyer once she's ready and secure—and Connor is dying to pass off the responsibility. He did it at the last shop we were at and he said he'd do it in Bluebell to get us on our feet but he doesn't want to be our buyer. And Ivy would be great at it."

"You're offering her a job when she hasn't even graduated from the apprenticeship?" Why I am arguing against Ivy when I know firsthand she's capable of doing anything, I don't know.

"She's talented and sharp, and she works hard. And last time I checked, I don't need your permission to run my business. That opportunity came and went years ago, didn't it?" Deuce says before pushing open the front door with a ding, disappearing onto the sunny sidewalk.

At one point, Ink Time was our dream.

But I met Cat and everything else happened so fast.

By the time I signed onto *Trace Tats*, Deuce had already put down money for a lease on the first two shops.

The shop falls silent without Deuce. I guess Ivy must've slipped out the back when she went to meet with Connor.

Connor. Psh. I know she didn't choose him over me, she just chose to learn a new task today instead of sit and observe. I can't fault her for that. Truth be told, I think it's sexy as shit that she's so hungry to learn the business.

I'm not mad because she's not here.

I'm disappointed.

And that's *way* fucking worse.

THREE HOURS LATER AND I'M PACING THE SMALL STRIP OF space between my station and the reception area. Ivy and Deuce still aren't back yet, and neither is Connor.

This has never happened to me. Never.

I thought I'd get whiskey dick and not be able to get it up with a woman before this ever happened.

Honestly.

I run my fingers through the sides of my hair for the millionth time, the sound of my boots shuffling on the tile driving me mad. I look down at my phone sitting atop the reception desk. Where the fuck are they?

"Find it yet?" Angus asks from the tattoo chair where he's patiently waiting for me to find the antibiotic ointment. I look down into my hand where the brand-new tube waits.

"Not yet," I call, sweat making my t-shirt cling to my back.

As if the heavens open and a ray of beauty and truth shines down on me, the shop door opens and Deuce trudges inside, smelling like french fries.

"Hey," he greets, sipping from his cup, the top of the straw chewed up. "How'd it go?"

He sets his cup down at the reception desk as he shrugs out of his leather jacket, eyeing the tube in my hand. "He's still here?" Deuce drops his jacket on the hooks behind the desk, eyeing my client still at my station. "Took more time than you thought, huh? Well, how's your wrist?"

Deuce knows my wrist gets sore if I go a few weeks without working. Tattoo artist's undiagnosed carpal tunnel. I shake my head and grab him by the arm, dragging his big ass into the hall.

I lick my lips, staring at my friend who's brows are pulled together. "What?" he questions, confused but smart enough to keep his voice private.

"I... fucked up."

Deuce's eyes fall to my hands, where he watches them for a second. I know what he's looking for. I snap.

"I'm not drunk," I say defensively, though in truth if I were, at least that would make sense for what's coming. I lick my lips and swallow the shame lodged in my throat. "I fucked up his ink."

Deuce blinks, glancing over where Angus is lying down, then back to me. "The belt buckle?"

I nod.

"How'd you fuck that up? It was simple. I've never known you to fuck up a single design." He leans in, sniffing around my mouth.

"I said I'm not drunk," I growl defensively, hating that I don't truly have the right to be super angry at the thought or accusation because for a long time, I've been drunk more than not.

His brows raise as he rocks back on his feet, shoving his hands into his jean pockets. "Okay. So you messed up the buckle. How bad can it be?"

My nostrils flare. The front door sails open as Ivy strolls in, pink heart frames resting on her face, her inky hair full of body from being outside. My chest tightens as she pushes the frames to the top of her head, drops her bag and another white bag on the ground before settling into the reception desk.

She never even looks my way.

I move so my body acts as a shield from her as I whisper, "Go fucking look."

Deuce snatches a pair of black gloves from the station and snaps them on, settling into the rolling stool near the bed. He moves the lamp and takes the ointment from my hand, smoothing it over the edge of the buckle as he makes small talk with Angus, the client.

"How's your daddy's ranch out there faring since the last storm, Angus?" he asks. This entire town knows each other. Everybody goes to a farmers market together out at Ivy's neighbor's place every weekend. It's wild how close small towns are. How safe they are.

I loved the chaos and fury in cities when I was on the road. Everyone knew me no matter where I went but I didn't owe them anything but a good time and an experience, since my presence was always fleeting. Here in Bluebell, though, everyone knows everyone. And there's permanency and comfort in that.

Angus and Deuce make small talk as Deuce smooths the ointment over the ink, still not meeting my eyes. After a few minutes, he tells Angus he came by to say hello, and that I'll be back to wrap up the design.

He pinches me by the elbow, my stomach in knots, and drags me back into the hall. I should be focused on how to fix this, but instead, all I can think is... *Ivy won't be able to hear this, will she?*

"That is..." But he can't finish his sentence, because Ivy appears, a grin on her lips.

"HODWY?" she mimes, spelling in the air, "H, O, D, W, Y. What is hodwy, Trace?"

Deuce levels his gaze on Ivy, providing a barrier between her amusement and my shame. "A great learning opportunity," Deuce says. "You want to take your first stab at a correction?"

Her amusement at my mistake immediately falls away. "Seriously?"

Deuce nods. "Seriously. He'll walk you through it. I'll go

talk to Angus while you get ready." Deuce looks my way. "Let me worry about Ang, you devise a plan and help her."

I nod. "Thanks."

Ivy disappears, going to put her hair up and wash her hands, leaving just me and Deuce in the hall. "How'd it happen?"

My gaze follows Ivy down the hall, watching her plump ass test the fabric of her leather leggings. "I don't know."

Only I *do* know. I was so busy thinking about how I feel about Ivy, I fucked up.

Deuce squeezes my shoulder. "Draw something up, get with Ivy, and meet me in a few. Don't worry about Ang. Trust me."

She fucking did it. She turned my epic disaster into a beautiful scroll, error-free. Where cowboy lettering once read HODWY, now amazing cursive spells HOWDY over an old parchment scroll, detailed with tear and wear.

It looks better than the original design, if I'm being honest, and I'm sort of peeved I hadn't thought of the alteration myself.

Right before we sat down, I heard her questioning me leading her through the fix. She'd said to Deuce, "Shouldn't you walk me through the fix?" Deuce told her that everyone makes mistakes, and that my mistake changes nothing. I'm still an incredible artist and she's still here to learn.

She didn't give me a single word of grief while she did the fix. We sat thigh to thigh, the harsh light of the lamp creating a glow for us to live in for an hour. Silent but side by side, she worked and I watched, every single second comfortable and easy. When she was done, I asked her to take off her gloves and I shook her hand.

"You did good work," I said.

She just nodded.

Now, Deuce is walking Angus out as I sink into the reception desk, reaching for a cold can of Coke instead of the flask in my boot. Ivy appears, pulling the clip from her hair, dark waves falling all around her face and shoulders.

"Thanks for letting me work on a person today," she says quietly, her jaw tight. I think she's using every ounce of willpower not to taunt me, and right now, with how shitty I feel, I appreciate it. I don't deserve it, but I appreciate it.

"Thanks," I say, sipping the overly carbonated drink.

The door closes and Deuce treads back toward us, sighing. "Well, the first few are usually rocky."

I snort. "No, it's not. You don't gotta say shit to make me feel good. I fucked up, and it's on the house."

Deuce grips the edge of the desk. "What?"

This is the part I'm not used to—not making the rules as I go. Deuce has rules. And now? I have to follow them. "Sorry— I'm not used to house rules. I told him the piece was free, because of the mistake."

"We fixed the mistake," Deuce says, "and I never told him it was going to be free."

"The final piece was better than what he brought in," Ivy inserts, giving me a reason to finally look her way. God she looks beautiful, traces of ink smeared up her forearms, accomplishment and pride lifting her shoulders. Her dark hair is messy from being down then up then down, and her black lipstick is faded in the center from where she sipped her drink.

The drink that matches Deuce's. Meaning, Ivy, Deuce and Connor all caught lunch together while they were out.

"That was a 1700-dollar piece and your entire morning," she chides, her hands going to her hips. Feeling defensive and angry and not at all jealous that they all went and enjoyed lunch without me, I snap back.

"If you were so worried about the fucking money, where were you? Hmm? Off playing footsies with Connor was more important to you this morning, so don't stand here all mighty and righteous now." I pull my wallet from my back pocket and grab out a few hundred-dollar bills. I slam them down on the reception desk. "There. That's what you care about."

I turn on my heel and stomp back to my station, where I begin sanitizing the area. We spend the rest of the day in complete silence but for the times Ivy needs to ask me questions about where the ink caps are at and how many I need for tomorrow's setup.

She gives me the personal silent treatment and I think Deuce does, too.

It's fine. I don't need to talk to them.

Once I'm out of here tonight, I'll talk to my best friend Jack. He always listens.

SEVEN

Does it do something with a banana?

Ivy

"Oh, come on," Dolly whines, stomping her bare foot on the kitchen floor. "Please?"

I dunk the knife into the open jar of mayonnaise one more time. "Only one more swipe, right?" I look over at Bear who is perched atop a barstool, his little legs swinging. He nods.

I slather the bread again, pressing the slices together to spread the condiments around. Peeling the wax paper off a slice of precut cheese, I add it to the bread to begin the ingredient layering. "I let you host a one-month celebration dinner already. That was... enough."

"Enough?" Dolly harrumphs as Juni appears at the top of the basement stairs, using one of her bare feet to knock the door closed behind her. Arms full of empty canning jars, she waddles toward the island and sets them down with a sigh. "What was enough?"

"Aunt Ev wants to have girls' night for Ivy but Ivy doesn't wanna," Bear says, dipping an animal cracker into the little dish of fresh jam Juni put out for him.

"It's not that I don't wanna... I mean, I love hanging out with you guys," I amend, immediately feeling guilty and selfish.

It's just... wine and comfort is the literal recipe for secret spilling.

Dolly knows I want Trace. For that matter, I'm sure Juni does too considering she brought me my coffee every day for the last week and I made no effort to hide my sketch—which was of Trace's hand holding the tattoo machine.

She didn't ask whose hand it was but she's met Trace and it's highly unlikely that I'd be sketching a *different man* with an octopus wielding eight knives. Yep. That's what Trace has on the top of his hand. Three legs coiled beneath its body, the other five fingers bearing a leg with tentacles, a different bladed knife held by each.

From what I've seen, that's the only maritime ink he's got. And I have seen him naked.

That monstrous veiny thing of his flashes through my mind. I chew the inside of my mouth to keep the groan from flying out of me.

"C'mon," Juni joins, "Ev said she's using her fondue maker. She hasn't used it since she's been married." She uses the end of her sundress to wipe sweat from her face, then pulls her hair into a messy bun. "Pop the fondue cherry with us."

"Girls' night," Dolly begs.

If I don't go, I'll stay home and work on my sketch of Trace's hands, then masturbate while I think of his hands (and other long, thick, swinging things) and then force myself to fall asleep while frustrated, horny and excited.

"Fine, I'm in," I agree as I finish layering ingredients onto the slices of bread. I cut the sandwich and pass it to Bear. "You gonna be at girls' night or what?" I ask him.

He wrinkles his nose. "Heck no!"

Juni gasps for dramatic effect. Dolly winks at him while she balances Honey on her hip. "Tell your aunts what you're doing instead," she says, standing at his side as she smooths her long fingers through his hair. I watched their relationship start, from the first time she watched him as a baby in footie pajamas, all the way to pulling him from the creek and giving him mouth-to-mouth. Dolly is the embodiment of a mother, loving that child hard, as if he came from her. Watching Dolly have a child with Hudson has only intensified and validated her natural role as a mother. Bear, Honey and now their new little one growing in her belly are so lucky.

"Gettin' tattooed," Bear grins, a smear of mayo at the corner of his mouth.

I smack my hand on the counter. "And you're not having me give you your very first tattoo?"

He sets his sandwich down, using his little white napkin to clean his hands. Serious expression on his face, he says, "It's not going to be a real tattoo Ivy. I'm only six."

I fight the laughter threatening to spill out. I take his hand and hold it. "Thank goodness," I breathe. "Promise you save your first for me, okay?"

He returns to his sandwich, saying, "Okay, I promise. Tonight, Trace is gonna give me a cool temporary tattoo while Daddy and Uncle Deuce install something."

"Something?" I mimic, turning to look at Dolly. "What are they installing?"

She shrugs. "I dunno." A smirk curls the end of her mouth. "I mean, Huddy told me but as he was telling me he was also undressing for the shower so... you know me. I can't hear a damn thing when that man is N U D E," she smiles, spelling her inappropriate behavior so that Bear doesn't catch on.

I roll my eyes. "Your obsession is admirable." It doesn't surprise me that her passion hasn't waned even a little bit.

Ellington women set their sights on things and very rarely break stride.

It's why I'm terrified to want Trace. To have set my sights on him.

And it's not for any "he's out of my league" type of self-loathing bullshit either.

I'm a badass. I know it. If my dad and Juni taught us anything, it's that nothing attracts people more than confidence.

But Trace is complicated. Something is weighing on him. He has a break in him somewhere that he hasn't addressed, and I see that manifest in boozing, sleeping around, snarky remarks and now, tattoo mistakes.

I want him. It just might take some... work.

I'm not afraid of a little hard work.

Never have been.

I'm afraid of bad tattoos, soft rock and products labeled both "new" and "improved." But hard work? *Psh.* Bring it on.

Especially when the prize is Trace.

God I'd die before I let him hear me say that.

While Bear finishes his sandwich, I change into yoga pants and a crop top, pull my hair into a ponytail, grab my tumbler of water, and head across the way to Dolly's place.

I promise myself to stick to water instead of the wine, so my secret stays with just my sisters.

I'm not sure I'm ready for Ev to know. She'll tell Deuce and I think I may die of embarrassment if Deuce knows I like Trace.

It's so... expected.

In his eyes, I'm probably like every other woman who meets

Trace. Immediately falls for him, and doesn't care that he's an asshole. Though that's where Deuce would be wrong—if he found out and if he thought that, I mean. Because I didn't just fall for Trace.

I fell for him when I saw his tattoo of Edgar Allen Poe on a woman's sideboob years ago. I've followed his work online ever since.

"Hey, Ivy," Ev greets, pulling open the door to her brother's house. She's wearing jeans and a white tank top, her feet are bare and her hair is up, but there's no baby on her hip.

"Where's Ace?" I ask as I move past her into the house, kicking off my sandals.

Ev closes the door and twists the deadbolt, eyeing my bare feet. "In the playpen napping." She looks me over. "No boots. You actually wanna be here tonight, hmm?" Her smirk is contagious.

"So you know my trick," I say, a tiny tinge of guilt swimming down my spine. "You know, it's not you, it's not Hudson's place, it's not anything but me. Sometimes I'm just not in the mood to be... anywhere but my bedroom."

She touches my arm gently as she smiles. "I completely get it. I'm just giving you a hard time. I've been hanging out with Deuce and Trace too much. I'm turning into a shit talker."

We make our way to the kitchen. "If that's your shit talk, you've got a long way to go."

Ev plunks down on a barstool and lifts her glass of white wine. "I'm glad. And I'm glad it's a no-boot night."

"Me too," Juni says, appearing from around the corner, a tray of roasted asparagus in her hands.

Bear, Juni and Dolly walked over while I was changing clothes because the guys arrived and goodbyes needed to be said. Even though this is just a couple of hours, Dolly couldn't go without tonguing Hudson's face off before they left.

I wonder if Bear even got to say goodbye?

Ev takes a pull of her wine. "Deuce says you're incredible. And since all I've seen today are shapes and colors, please tell me you brought your book with you."

Blinking, shocked, I cave and pour myself a small glass of wine. Not the size of glass that spills secrets or brings tears, more so, the size that makes your cheeks warm and your tension fade. I take a sip.

"Excuse me," I draw out. "Did you say Deuce said I'm incredible?" A flush eats up my cheeks, but it's such a proud moment that I don't care that Ev sees it. And I certainly don't hide my emotions from my sisters.

I don't hide anything from them, and them from me.

"Yep," she nods, finishing off her wine as she empties the rest of the first bottle into her glass. "So show me. If he loves your work, I'll probably be obsessed."

Dolly mimics her fingers walking as she pops a piece of asparagus into her mouth. "Trot back and get your sketches. I'm dying to see your current WIP anyway." She winks and I cast her *the eyes*. You know the kind. The eyes that say *shut up or I'll kill you* in just a singular flare.

Dolly laughs, then buries her smile in sparkling cider.

"Fine," I groan playfully, as if getting my sketches to get complimented and doted on isn't the literal best thing in the world. It is. Don't get me wrong, as an artist, getting lost in the process of creating is beautiful.

But getting atta girls for my hard work? I'm here for it, since all I get from Trace are comments like "if your clients like slop" and "if the goal is an ironic tattoo then that's great."

Yeah, kudos from the girls might turn this girls' night from great to epic.

～

"Then you just... strain it," Juni calls from her spot on the couch, her third glass of wine in hand, bare feet stacked on the coffee table.

At some point during bottle number three (which is worse than it sounds since Dolly has her own bottle of sparkling cider) we decided we'd make our own butter to go with the bread for dinner. Juni, already tipsy, decided she'd teach us from the couch.

"We don't have cheesecloth," Dolly hiccups from the bubbles of her sparkling cider, staring into the appliance drawer. She gently closes it so as to not wake a sleeping Honey. "I'll go get one from your place, can you keep your ears perked if Honey wakes?" she says to me, and though I only know her as Hudson's girl, it still sounds weird every so often for her to refer to our home as my home, or Juni's home.

I nod and she rushes out, tearing through the distance between our houses.

A few minutes later she returns with a grocery sack full of stuff. Pulling one item out, she asks, "Can we use this?"

Juni, one eye squeezed shut, peers at us across the home. "That's an organic coffee filter, not cheesecloth."

Confusion knits my brows. "They both just strain though, right?"

"Sieve size," she says. "It won't work."

Dolly digs around in her bag like Santa looking for the perfect gift. "How about this?" she laughs, pulling a metal cage from the bag, balancing it in the center of her palm for us to see.

Juni sits up, lowering her glass to the table next to a *Field & Stream* copy. "What the hell is that?"

Ev takes it from Dolly, turning the device over in her hand time after time. I press my palm to my lips to smother the smirk growing.

I literally cannot wait to tell them what that is.

"Does it do something with a banana? Or like…" I watch as Ev presses her fingers into the wide metal slit at the tip. "Does it, like, strain the egg white from the yolk or something?" She hiccups.

Clearing my throat, I take in Ev's, Juni's and Dolly's interested faces. Ev moves the item around between two hands now, her glass of wine taking a back seat to her curiosity. "It could be–"

"It's a male chastity cage," I deadpan.

Juni actually physically startles back.

Ev brings the cage closer to her eyes, inspecting it further.

Dolly moves around the counter, standing next to her sister-in-law, and smooths one fingertip down the metal. "Wow," she says, as if she's staring at the Grand Canyon.

Ev's nose wrinkles. "I love you, Dahlia, but please take one step back if you're thinking of my brother while touching this."

We pause, and a moment later, Dolly steps back, causing all of us to erupt into laughter.

"Where'd you get it?" Juni asks, coming to study the metal device with the others.

"*Why'd* you get it is the better question," Ev says, wiping beneath her eye as she sets the chastity cage between the soft cheeses and roasted asparagus. A strange charcuterie.

"You know how my first official solo session is coming up, right?" I ask rhetorically because of course everyone in this room knows. This room is full of my people.

It's why I wanted to apprentice and work in Bluebell. Because my people are here. My sisters—and now Dolly's extended family—are everything to me. Family is everything.

When Deuce said he was opening an Ink Time here, it felt like kismet. Like the gods of fate coming down from the sky to gift me with all the tools I need for a perfect, peaceful life. Now I just have to work to make it happen.

I can't wait for my first solo session. It's going to set the tone for my entire career.

"Well, the piece I'm doing is on a female domme. And it's of her submissive's chastity cages." I wrinkle my nose. "Well, a replica of one."

"So she's a dominatrix?" Ev asks, sipping her wine, staring at me like I'm about to reveal the world's biggest secret.

I shake my head. "No, not really. She's just the dominant in their sexual relationship, as well as their emotional one. I don't think it's about heels and corsets as much as it's about an equal exchange of power, with a reward system, too."

"Interesting," Ev says, drawing circles around the top of her wine glass.

"Her partner has his thingy in a cage all the time?" Juni whispers, making Ev and Dolly laugh.

"Yes, Juniper, his penis is in a cage and she takes him out to reward him," I say, refusing to use the term *thingy* about male genitalia. "And she wants his cage inked onto her to always remember the dynamic and their experience. For when it ends."

They sip their drinks in unison, and I sip mine too, all four of us turning our heads and narrowing our eyes to imagine the cage in action.

Trace's third leg comes to mind, and I get a vision of his lean, toned body covered in art from head to toe. He's naked, his hair is wet, his feet are bare, and his hands are working to close the cage. It hangs heavily between his thighs as he outstretches his arm, a silver key hanging from a delicate chain. "Take my control," he rasps as the key rests in my palm.

"To each their own, I guess," Ev finally says with a sigh as Juni and Dolly move into the kitchen to work on the food.

My lower half surges with heat and desire at the fantasy of

Trace naked, in the cage, at my mercy. Ev did say she thinks Trace needs discipline…

"I've been using it to sketch. Working on the design." I take my sketch pad from nearby and slide it along the white marble counter for Ev to flip through.

She's silent—even at the chastity cage sketches—and takes her time moving through each page as Juniper and Dolly talk about chicken glaze and roasted potatoes.

Finally she turns to me, the wine making her cheeks rosy and her voice soft when she says, "You're so talented. You remind me so much of the girl who taught Trace."

My eyes drop to the sketch pad where Trace's hand is on full display. We both stare at the detailed octopus leg swimming down his pointer finger, curled around a tattoo machine.

I keep the rattle from my voice, despite the way my chest echoes with unanswered questions and frayed nerves. "Who taught Trace?"

"Before his show, he was trying to just work his way up the chain like everyone else," Ev says as Juniper slides her a plate of food—roasted chicken and potatoes, steamed vegetables and a slab of garlic bread that makes my mouth water. My plate is next. I can't eat until I know. I can't do anything but push a potato around with the tines of my fork and scream SPIT IT OUT in my head.

"Anyway," she says after blowing on a bite of food. "He connected with this artist. She was his age but had already been working for a few years." She finishes her wine. "They bonded over art and fell in love."

I knew he had heartbreak in the past, but now I need to know what happened.

"And?" My pulse is echoing in my brain as I stare at stray pepper flakes on my dinner plate.

"She… got him connected to the agent where he got the TV

deal." Ev takes another bite and I swear to Henry Cavill I'm about to take the fork out of her hand, throw it across the room and scream SPIT IT THE FUCK OUT, EVERLY.

But I stay calm because flies with honey, flies with vinegar and all that.

"But she also cheated on him in one of the most horrific ways. She broke his heart and left him right before he was leaving to start the show." Another bite, only now that I know what happened, I almost need a second to process. Except now she keeps talking as my heart races and my stomach coils with pain.

He was betrayed by the person he loved most, by a person deeply entwined in his art and dreams.

That had to feel awful. Beyond awful.

"Is he in Bluebell to get better?" I question, not even sure what I mean by 'get better'? Sober? Healthy? Heal his heart? I don't know. But Ev understands the subtext of the question.

"Deuce wants him to stay. Now that Trace is out of contract with the network, he wants Trace to lay down roots here in Bluebell and live the life he dreamed of before his TV deal."

"What kind of life is that?" I ask, afraid to know the answer. Selfishly afraid it won't fit into my dream.

"Small town, family he loves, wife he adores, doing the work he was born to do."

"Simple," Dolly comments on the dream.

"Perfect," Juni replies.

Silence falls between us and I don't know what they're thinking about, but I'm definitely thinking about Trace. He doesn't feel grounded, he doesn't give off the energy that he wants to stay. Hell, he's racing off to Oakcreek to drink almost nightly.

But I want him to stay.

For myself but for him, too. Bluebell could heal him.

I could heal him.

"I don't think he was ever the same. He'd only loved her and he hasn't been in love again.... He definitely loves Jack Daniel's... and fucking random women."

"Everly!" Dolly giggles. "You said fucking!"

"I say it all the fucking time when I'm drunk!" Ev laughs. "And stop full-naming me." She grins wickedly. "I'm only Everly when I'm on my knees in the bedroom."

"Hey!" Dolly laughs, slicing her hand through the air. "If I can't talk about Hudson, you can't talk about Deuce."

"Deuce isn't your brother!" Ev laughs, and their laughter has me and Juni laughing, too.

We eat and we talk, the conversation moving back to the chastity cage, then dominance, and then somehow we're deciding who would win a naked wrestling match between Dwayne Johnson and Liam Hemsworth.

But the entire time, even with the flurry of booze in my veins and the high of being complimented on my work by Ev, all I can think about is Trace.

And his broken heart.

EIGHT

It's time to get better.

Trace

"Sal, don't forget the cooler by the door!"

"Ay, I won't, I told you a thousand times I won't forget it!"

"But you forgot it last week so don't tell me you know, just grab the bag already!"

Shuffling and rustling, followed by four minutes of my upstairs neighbors arguing in a language I'm too hungover to decipher, and then they're finally gone.

A sigh escapes me, and I roll onto my back, swiping my hands beneath the pillows to find the pockets of cool, undiscovered sheets. Thankfully there are no stupid birds building nests and chirping around here like at my last apartment in Hollywood, so when my eyes close again, I start drifting.

I'm on the cusp of sleep when a loud noise sounds at my front door.

"What is this fuckery? Is the world conspiring against me right now?" I roll out of bed and grab my gold watch, bringing it close to my eyes. It's not even *eight* in the morning, and I'm pretty sure it's fucking Saturday. "*Whaaat?*" I shout angrily while trudging through the apartment hallway, my foot catching a stray pair of panties from the floor. I kick the pink thong off, and it ends up on a lampshade. That makes me smile.

Without looking through the peephole because I'm not a wimp that needs to peek out front to make sure I'm safe, I yank open the door and find Deuce on the other side.

"It ain't a work day," I launch with no preamble. I've known Deuce for the better part of twenty years. We've said *hello, hi, how's it going* enough for the rest of our lives. "It's early and it's Saturday. *What?*"

"Hello to you too, sweetheart." He smiles, pushing past me in his leather jacket and blue jeans. God, so cliché. Then again, I guess I am too.

Fuck.

Leaving his boots on, Deuce sinks back into the couch, jerking forward to pull a woman's bra out from under his ass. "I came to talk and since you're part naked and definitely not strong enough to throw me out, you're gonna listen."

"I could throw you out." I grab an old t-shirt off the countertop—one I took off in the throes of passion. By the way it smells, those throes were a few days ago. Maybe even a week. Boxers intact already, I sit down across from him on the edge of my coffee table. I'm not sure a cup of coffee has ever been on this table.

My bare ass while a beautiful woman rides me? Yes.

A naked woman covered in cocaine? Yep.

But a cup of coffee and, like... I don't know, a newspaper? Fuck no. That's for grandpas.

"Want some coffee, peepaw?" I ask as Deuce eyes my place,

judgment heavy in his brow. Okay, maybe I don't know that he's judging from just his face but... I also do. He's been judging me for years. Even when I was on the road and we'd FaceTime once a week, when the topic veered from art and ink into my personal life, his brows would pull together. He'd get really kinda bitchy.

I sense that coming now.

He snorts. "You even *have* coffee to make me? And by the way, we're the same age."

I shrug. "You seem much older."

"Listen, I'm too tired from Ace being up all night cutting teeth. I have no silk to wrap this up in, so I'm just gonna empty my apron, got it?"

I scrub a hand down my face. When's the last time I shaved? "I'm not followin' that metaphor but say what you came to say so I can get back to sleep."

He steeples his hands beneath his chin, gaze surprisingly calm as he takes me in. After a sigh, he says, "I got a proposition for you. It's the next leg of the Get Trace Back tour."

"Get Trace Back tour," I repeat on a snort, shaking my head. Though the booze lingers, leaving my neck and brain sore as shit. Instead, I run a hand through my hair and rest my elbows on my knees. "I'm here in Bluebell. I'm at Ink Time. I've done what I said."

Deuce's head tilts sadly just like in a country music song, and an equally empathetic expression curves his lips. "Sober up and live your life. Get back to caring about tattoos because showing up at Ink Time and giving 30% of what you're capable of isn't *being back.*"

We don't use words like addicted and sober, because it brings a level of reality I'm sure we both realize I can't handle. But today, he's telling me to get sober, and as much as the words bring a knot of emotion to my throat, I fight them.

I fight back when someone cares, when someone wants to show me love. I push them away and I pick them apart and destroy them all, because it's easier to be a hated, drunk asshole than to be devastated.

Lost.

Heartbroken.

"I ain't gonna talk around it anymore. I'm not pretending that we don't see it, me and Ev." He scoots to the edge of the couch, hands still steepled as he speaks low and calm. "Come live in the house next to me and Ev. It's ours. We bought it to fix it up and flip it but now with Ace, and, well, you..." He grins, making a joke to break the mounting tension, but I don't smile.

"Live in the house you bought and fix it up?" I question. What a legendary plan.

He nods. "You live there for free—"

"I got money," I say, knowing we both know that much. I'm just so used to using money to keep my problems away. We sit in silence a moment before Deuce continues.

"I don't need your money for rent. You live there and instead of coming home from Ink Time and drinking, come back and use your hands. Fix that place up for us."

"Free labor, eh? I can see why this plan works for you." I get up, knocking over a half-drunk beer with my ass. It glugs onto the table, and neither of us move to clean it up. Instead, I go into the small kitchen, ducking beneath the cabinet to see him as I fill a glass with water. My head is throbbing.

"Call it repayment for all those free tattoos you're giving out at *my* business," he says. A dig at the fact it could've been ours had I not chosen reality TV? I don't know. But he isn't wrong. I fucked up the other day.

"One tattoo. There was only one free tattoo." For some reason, it seems important to punctuate that truth. I only fucked up once... and it was because I couldn't get my mind off of Ivy. And then I couldn't stop thinking about how she's the first woman I've thought about like that since... her. Since Cat. "I was just... in my head."

"Get out of your head. Use your hands to get it out, whatever it is," Deuce says, his hands now resting open-palmed on his spread knees as he speaks. "You gotta get better. And if you don't think you deserve it, do it for Ev."

That same lump of heat and tension coils in my throat. My eyes burn. Everly has become like a sister to me. Taking care of me in my darkest times. When I'd crawl back to Deuce, my only goddamn friend in the whole world, the only person who didn't want a thing from me but my friendship, she'd be there without questions, without judgment, free of lectures.

She'd have water. Food. Tylenol. A pillow. A ride. Words of wisdom. Sometimes just a hug. But she's always been there. I'm pretty sure she can't stand me, but she's been there.

Deuce has too, but the thought of hurting or disappointing both of them gnaws at the soft spot deep inside me.

"Come. Come live by us. It's time to get better."

"Better, huh?" I know what he means. I know I'm not living a path of longevity. And without the show, without the fans, without the continual hype, my partying and drinking will only become more and more out of place. More and more of a problem. As if it's not already.

"Don't get angry. Don't fight me. Don't fight this."

"I'm good, man," I say, my ego choking the rational parts of me, not allowing me to admit that he's right. Not only do I need to get better, but this is the place to do it. And with the people I love? The only people I love? It's time. But I fight. Because admitting that I'm broken—admitting that I let her break me—it's a jagged pill I refuse to swallow.

There's a knock at the apartment door, jarring our focus. I

slam the glass of water and come around the counter to the door.

Opening it, there's a woman on my porch. Black makeup is pooled beneath her eyes and her hair looks like it would benefit from a brush. At eight in the morning, she's wearing a pink miniskirt and black cowboy boots and nothing for a top except... a bikini.

She looks past me to Deuce, who lifts a hand to silently say hello. Smiling awkwardly at him, she returns her focus to me. Despite the whisper she's using, I know Deuce can hear her. For Christ's sake, he's less than one foot behind me.

"Hey, Trace, umm, I think the condom is stuck inside me. You know, after last night."

I twist in the doorframe, facing my friend. The sign that he's right is asking me to pull last night's condom out of her. And I haven't even had my coffee. "Fine. Whatever. I'll... I'll move into the place next door. I'll start fixing it up. I'll... Fine," I say as Deuce gets to his feet with a grunt.

The girl eases her way inside. "Help me get it out?"

"That's my cue," Deuce says, shimmying past her. From outside the apartment, he outstretches his hand and we shake on it. "Come by my house after... this," he says, nodding to the girl. "I'll give you the key and show you the place."

He leaves and ten minutes later, she's gone, too.

Deuce was tired because his son was teething and as I stand beneath the spray of the hot shower, washing away this morning's condom retrieval, I think about how I want to be tired for good reasons, too.

Deuce really is right, damn him.

It's time to get better.

NINE

You have dick on the brain.

Ivy

"Shading."

My mouth is so dry, confidence is challenging but I manage. "Shading," I repeat slowly. Trace nods and I do my best not to stare at his bustling biceps and all the gorgeous ink covering them as he tightens his bun.

I especially do not glance at the tempting strip of skin between his jeans and t-shirt, and the thatch of dark hair above his waistband. I do not look at those little muscular dips of his waist, and I definitely do not pay extra attention to the heart wrapped in barbed wire inked on his belly.

Nope.

"Yeah, I mean, your first solo session ain't too far from now, so I figure you work on the shading on today's piece." He rolls his neck, and the cracks make me jump.

"That doesn't hurt?" I ask, nodding.

"If it hurt, would I do it?" he snaps back, his nostrils flaring.

"*No* would've worked just fine." I roll my eyes while internally flipping him the bird. Pushing past him, I move to the backlit table in the back of the shop.

He doesn't apologize for his snarky comment and I don't expect him to. He never does. Maybe no one taught him that simply acting like it never happened isn't an apology. Or that gifting or giving someone something after you treated them like crap doesn't mean it's okay.

Settling in at the table, Trace comes and sits next to me, his large leg bumping mine beneath the top. I wonder how many tables have seen future lovers bump knees, hands sliding onto thighs. Heat swims through my leg and into my center, making my stomach clench and my pulse spike.

The scent of his pine aftershave hits my nose, and my nipples grow hard and plucky beneath my oversized DARE t-shirt. Trace reaches up, flicking on the lamp, before he pulls his portfolio out, laying a sketch across the table for us both to see.

It's a lighthouse. So far just black and white from the graphite, but highly detailed. Sun pours over the solar valve on top, leaving a cascade of perfectly angled shadows along the tower. Small but full of detail, I pinch my gaze on the tiny window on the tower, where there are living quarters inside. A man stands with one palm pressed to the glass. He's so small that his expression is unreadable, but the fact that the detail of a person alone in the lighthouse has been added is ethereal and eerie.

I love it.

"Not all lighthouses are red and white striped," he adds as I continue to silently peruse the beautiful sketch. "I explained that to the client and they'd prefer black and white anyway."

I press my finger to the base of the tower where wild grass shades the bottom of the piece. "Will I be doing this?"

A hint of whiskey hits me as Trace leans over, wrapping his hand around mine before moving it to the tower. Letting go, he leans back and says, "This is what you'll be shading."

I swallow thickly around excitement and surprise, both emotions I do not want him to know I feel. "That's the main part of the piece."

He doesn't say anything until I turn my head to face him. He's studying me already, his dark eyes pinched on my features, his body language relaxed. A gorgeous paradox. "I know."

My heart thuds loudly in my ribs and I drop my palms to my thighs, wiping away the sudden slickness. "You think I'm ready?"

Trace tips his head to the side, a tiny little smile lifting only the corner of his lips. "You're ready to do the whole thing. But they paid for Trace Calhoun to do it. So I'll outline it and you'll do the shading."

I'm... shocked. Speechless. Surprised.

Flattered.

And because I'm more like Trace than I'd like to admit, I don't say all the things I'm feeling. Instead I say, "I guess you losing your touch is advantageous to me, huh?"

As soon as the words leave my mouth, I'm swarmed with regret. Loads of it.

I hate his salt and snark, and yet when I'm around him, I can't help but give it back as good as he gives.

Even though I want to say thank you, I want to say that I feel honored that he trusts me, I want to hug him even.

Instead, I watch his calm expression slip away, and right before my eyes, the wall comes up. "Yeah, well," he says, getting up from his chair, leaving my side. I miss the heat of his body and his scent immediately, even though missing anything Trace Calhoun feels wrong. "Don't get too cocky, Firecracker. Everyone makes mistakes."

Firecracker.

He hasn't called me that in a while, and I've missed it. Between my legs, everything grows warm and fuzzy. I swallow, reaching for an apology. One that he deserves because my comment was jerky and no matter how much of an assjacket clown he is to me, I have to do better.

I have to teach him to move past those salty quips, too. If we're ever going to progress our relationship, we have to get past this bickering and arguing we're always doing. He snatches the sketch away from me, and turns on the stencil printer adjacent to us.

Instead of saying I'm sorry, I say, "I'm sure I'll fuck something up sooner than later." After snapping on a pair of black gloves, I load the cartridge into the pen. "You're right, everyone makes mistakes."

The light on the machine flickers and I watch his large, dexterous hands feed it through, the pulsing in my panties still present and powerful. I practically choke on my tongue, trying not to imagine those beautiful, skilled hands working that monstrous dick of his.

Stay focused, Ivy.

"Yeah, and you'll make a lot of them. I have no doubt," he snaps back, yanking the thermal paper from the machine the moment it's done. He smacks the stencil down on the table. "While we're waiting for the client, why don't you draw up a replica of the stencil, to practice your shading?"

I feel like Beetlejuice in the graveyard when Barbara and Adam call him there. I know my head isn't *actually* spinning three hundred and sixty degrees, but it feels like it.

I was nice after I was mean. And what did he do? Was he nice back? No. No, he fucking wasn't.

I smooth my hands down my thighs and turn to tell him he's an asshole, but he's already gone, standing up at reception with Deuce and the new girl he hired.

She started today. We went to high school together so I'm well aware of Sandi and what she's about.

She's about getting dicked down by anyone who tells her she has pretty eyes, that's what.

Trace smooths one of his hands over his hair, the veins and ink making my mouth go dry. He's so fucking handsome. And sexy. And God, it destroys me how talented he is. He drew up this lighthouse in an hour and it's one of the most breathtaking maritime sketches I've ever laid eyes on.

And it was effortless for him.

Sandi can't appreciate what an incredible artist he is. But something tells me all he wants Sandi to appreciate is his cock.

Jealousy spikes through me in cruel, unrelenting surges, leaving my hands and feet tingling and my mind spinning. Sandi reaches out, dusting her fingers along his forearm as she giggles about something that I'm ninety-nine percent sure isn't funny at all. In the last few months I've gotten to know Trace decently well.

There's nothing he can say at this hour of the morning when he's still sweating off the Jack that is dab-at-your-eyes funny. *Sandi, quit kissing his ass.*

Deuce catches me watching, and I turn back to the sketch at hand, getting to work on the layers of wild grass beneath where the lighthouse will be.

Trace is letting me shade today.

I need to focus on that.

After forty-five minutes, the sketch is complete. Deuce and Connor appear at my back, surveying it.

"Looks..." Deuce trails off.

I turn to look up at them, sliding my pencil through my ponytail. As I work out a cramp in my palm, digging my thumb into the center, I ask, "Good?"

Connor chews his bottom lip, shares a look with Deuce, then turns back to me. "Ivy, the linework and shading are great. The work itself is done really, really well."

"Why do I sense a but coming?"

At that moment, Sandi and Trace, who took a walk for coffee (gag me), come in through the back, ending up right behind Deuce and Connor.

Trace slides his sunglasses to the top of his head, his gold watch glittering as he points to my sketch. "Cockhouse."

"What?" I ask, immediately spinning to face my sketch. From behind me, Sandi giggles.

"Looks like a peen."

A hand comes down on my shoulder, squeezing. I glance at the fingers and spot a tentacle clutching a shearing knife. "Got cock on the brain, do ya?"

"What?" I blink at my sketch. My attempt at weathering the tower, in this light, does kind of look like *foreskin*. And when I narrow my gaze and make the whole thing the tiniest bit fuzzy, the solar cap and cupola without question look like the head of a penis, the crown surging forward excitedly out of the foreskin. I slam a hand over my mouth. "Oh god."

There's some subtle movement behind me, and a moment later, I'm left with just Trace and Connor.

Connor brushes his finger along one of the cracks in the tower. "I know this is wear on the tower, but if you get rid of it, that may help. And the cupola could be resized to look less—"

"Like a big cockhead," Trace offers, a pleased smirk curling his lips. I know violence is bad and stuff, but God if there was ever a time I wanted to slap someone, it would be now.

"I once sketched a memorial design for a woman who lost her husband and the flower looked like an aroused vagina," Connor offers with a soft smile. Trace grumbles something inaudible under his breath, but I keep my focus on Connor.

"What did you do?"

"I redid it. Thankfully I caught it before it went to skin, but it happens. Art is special but when it becomes your job, sometimes, no matter how passionate you are about your art, your mind wanders." He shrugs. "It's natural."

"I wasn't—my mind didn't wander to..." I start, but find myself unable to say I wasn't thinking about cock.

The truth is? I was. I was and have been since Trace showed up at Hudson's house a few months back.

I tried not to go full Dolly. I mean, that's not my style anyhow. But no matter how hard I tried to stay focused on art and working, helping my sister get her man, helping my other sister grow her jam business, it didn't matter.

Knowing that the man whose work I've followed for years is living in my little small town, working with a family friend? I began dreaming. Seeing far-fetched things like us being a couple together, despite the fact I'd never even met him. Then after I *did* meet him and observed him as a human, my interest should have waned.

It should have circled the drain and slipped away instantly.

He's arrogant. He's pompous. He's drunk most of the time. He sleeps around.

But God smite me down, I can't help it.

I've only begun to want him more.

And what's worse? Now that I know him, wanting him is different than it was all those years before. Because now being rejected is actually on the table whereas before, everything was just a fantasy between my fingers and the sheets.

"Focus on the shading today," Trace says, his eyes pinned to the back of Connor's head before they slide over to me. "Try not to make the grass look like a bunch of cocks."

My nostrils flare. And while I want to punch his lights out, my skin heats. My lower half pulses. And I want more than anything to be pushed onto this light table and fucked ruthlessly right now.

I smile. "Hodwy."

~

TRACE AND I DID A WONDERFUL JOB OF AVOIDING ONE another for most of the morning. When his client came in, they watched me sterilize the space—something we do in front of clients at Ink Time so they feel comfortable with our setup.

After sterilizing the tray, I set it down wearing a new pair of gloves. Trace and the client speak quietly to one another about the way tattooing works—he explains that he isn't an hourly artist but rather, by the piece. While they chat, they watch me. I catch Trace's gaze here and there a few times as I affix the barrier on top of the tray. I tear off a ton of sheets of paper towel for easy access, get his favorite sterile fluid ready (I know from an interview he did with *Tattoo Times* that his choice witch hazel, which he uses to remove excess ink), check the design notes in the iPad to know which pigments he's using, set out and fill the ink caps, load his cartridge into his pen, and proceed to wipe down both chairs before setting out a few bottles of water and a new box of gloves.

Trace rises, moving from the casual spot he sat to the chair where he'll work. It's not the first time I've seen him work since we started the apprenticeship but this time feels different.

Despite the bickering, we're cohesive in our processes today and it fills me up in ways I hadn't expected. The nerves from my upcoming shading opportunity fall away as he nods, thanking me for an excellent setup.

Excellent set up were his exact words.

I sit at his side, watching, taking in the moments he explains his strategies—less pressure, changing cartridge sizes depending on degrees of depth and darkness in design, giving the client a moment to acclimate to the longer portions of the session—and listen. I listen to his conversation with his client, which ebbs from casual to emotional every so often. He isn't afraid to ask why when the client shares that the lighthouse holds meaning to him personally, and he isn't afraid to stop the machine, rest his hand on the man's arm and tell him he's sorry when he shares his story.

Being close to him while he works is truly a magical experience.

When it's time for me to take over, he sits behind me, peppering quiet words of wisdom in my ear, reassuring me when he senses my insecurity. And he does sense my insecurity —how? I don't know. But when I pull back and survey what I've already done, and I find myself rolling my lips together in silent panic that I'm not good enough and that I've ruined someone's beautiful, meaningful piece of work, his hand curves my neck and he squeezes gently.

"Imposter syndrome is all it is." I turn to face him, finding his dark eyes soulful and focused... on me. "The work you've done is incredible so far."

Speechless with my stomach aflutter and heat unfurling in my belly, I smile and nod. "Thank you."

He doesn't return the smile but rolls back, giving me space I don't want. "You got it from here, Firecracker."

And though it's just grass in the sun below a lone lighthouse, when it's all said and done, I think it's the best work I've done yet.

~

As I'm repacking my lunch bag and slipping into my HUGS NOT DRUGS hoodie, Trace appears, hands shoved into his pockets.

I'm beginning to think his hands are so sexy that seeing them in pockets is like seeing a nice big cock in sweats. Tempting and arousing. And I feel like a complete creep for thinking it, and for privately sexualizing him in a way I wouldn't appreciate if it were coming my way.

But I can't help it.

He's so frustrating but each day that passes, I want him more and more.

"Thought I'd see if you wanted to head across the street to Goode's to celebrate your session today," he says, nearly stopping my fucking heart.

Trace Calhoun just asked me to dinner.

Okay, maybe he didn't use the word *dinner* and it is literally fourteen paces away from where we currently are, and we aren't changing into nicer clothes and he isn't picking me up but... the Kelly Kapoor in me is squealing "It's a date!"

I shrug. "I could eat."

Trace smirks, tapping his back pocket. "Got my wallet." He eyes me up and down, and I stand proudly before him in my torn leather leggings and my HUGS NOT DRUGS hoodie. Landing on my slipper-covered feet, he points that gorgeous finger at me and asks, "Where'd your boots go, Firecracker?"

God, I swear, that nickname coming off his arrogant but perfectly shaped lips sends my ovaries into a tailspin. I swallow, purposely clenching my jaw to hold back the smile. I may love when he calls me that, but I don't want him to know it.

"My feet were cold and I thought I was just going home

so... I put my slippers on." I look down at the oversized gladiator feet slippers Dolly got me last year.

He blinks a few times before meeting my eyes. The shop is empty but for us, and the lack of noise and movement has our eye contact feeling... intense. "Those are funny."

I drape my palm over my chest in faux shock, ignoring how fast my heart is hammering. "Was that another compliment?"

"Another?" He cocks his brow, his nose ring catching the light as he flares his nostrils. God I love that he's pierced, too.

I want piercings.

"You told me I was good in there," I nod toward the spot where we had our session.

He moves toward the door, and the jingle of the bell as it opens into the private night causes bumps to rise up on my arms beneath my hoodie.

Grabbing my bag, I sling it over my shoulder and head out, taking a discreet breath as I walk past him in the doorway. His scent hits me between the legs, and after he locks up Ink Time for Deuce, he comes by my side. We walk across the street together in silence, and Trace opens the door for me at Goode's, too.

I don't think I can take sucking in his pine-laced-with-sweat scent again, so I hold my breath as I walk past him into the diner. Lucy, the waitress who's been at Goode's since my earliest memory, waves at me from the kitchen in the back. "Ivy! Seat yourselves."

I smile and nod, then survey the place for the best seat.

A few old couples are here having decaf with a slice of pie but for the most part, Goode's is quiet. I choose a table and slip into the booth, eager to sit and ease the aching between my legs.

Trace slips into the booth across from me, a rush of his scent enveloping me. It's almost annoying how good he smells after a full day of work and it's more annoying that he can't at the very least wear a cologne I hate.

I love pine. I love the outdoors. And I love a man who smells like the things I love. Pine trees and hard work are essentially the formula for sex with me.

Lucy appears, sliding us two laminated menus and two glasses of ice-cold water. I've been here a thousand times and don't need a menu, but I don't know about Trace, so I tell her we need a few minutes. She agrees to come back and as she walks away, Trace stops her.

"Lucy, could I bother you for a cup of coffee?"

"Decaf or the good stuff?"

Trace chuckles. I don't know if I've heard him chuckle. Snort? Yes. Snark? For sure. But an actual little chuckle? It's deep and rich and so sexy that the pine takes a back seat as his timbre washes over me, leaving me achy and wet.

"What's good here?" he says, his eyes moving up and down the three tiers of food broken down by breakfast, lunch and dinner.

I roll my lips together. "Well, I like the Cobb salad and the chicken tortilla soup, but really, everything's pretty good."

His focus is on me when I glance from Lucy across the room back to him.

"Cobb salad, huh?" he says, tearing the white paper from a straw on the table. He drops it into the glass of water Lucy brought over and takes a sip. "That actually... sounds good."

Heat cruises up my neck. "Wow. So agreeable today."

He clasps his hands together on top of the menu and stares at the surface of his water. "You did good shading work today."

Inside, I'm absolutely howling. Squealing and screaming, even. "Thank you."

He sips his water again. "I even liked the cockhouse."

Lucy reappears. "What'll it be?"

"Two Cobb salads," Trace says, ordering for me, which no one has ever done. Even as a girl, my father told me I should grow up to be a strong woman, unafraid to use my voice. I was ordering Shirley Temples and tuna sandwiches on my own by age five. I don't need to be rescued, but someone knowing my order and placing it for me? Kind of nice.

Surprisingly sexy.

Once she's asked us about our drink orders—Trace surprisingly sticks with water and decaf coffee—she leaves us and I'm able to respond to his comment about my stupid lighthouse sketch.

"I'm embarrassed it looked so... *phallic*." I choose my words carefully because I'm already swollen and aching for him. Damn pine cologne. And gorgeous hands. And cool ink. And—okay, it's the whole package.

He shrugs. "Maybe you have dick on the brain."

He has no clue how right he is.

Or does he?

I push hair behind my ear, tucking it there to buy me a second. After a sip of water, I agree. "I probably do." With my eyes locked on his I say, "It's been way too long since I've fucked."

He blinks a few times, startled by my choice of words. "I guess you don't know about that," I add, spreading the paper napkin over my lap.

He makes no comment back, surprisingly, and instead says, "I'm moving out of my apartment."

My heart stops.

"You're leaving Bluebell?"

The back of my neck grows hot. The diner around me grows blurry. This is the man I've been idolizing for years. He's here. And he's leaving?

No. No fucking w—"Naa," he says, shaking his head, his

response sluicing through my chaos. "I'm moving into Deuce and Ev's investment house." Lucy appears with two plates, and slides one in front of each of us. Trace thanks her and takes his fork. Piercing lettuce and hard boiled egg with the tines, he says, "Gonna work on it at night instead of... being bad."

"I bet Ev's happy about that—she's been wanting to get that place fixed up and on the market for a while," I say, scared that if I comment on him being bad, he'll shut down. Besides, I know what he means. It's not a secret, and if it is, he does a horrible job of keeping it private.

He drinks too much and he parties too hard.

After a few bites, he finally says, "I don't know. I just came to this conclusion with Deuce the other day. I haven't talked to Ev." He takes another bite and around the mouthful of food, he says, "You're the only person I've told."

"No family to tell that you're settling down out here?" I question, because I've yet to hear Trace mention a mom or dad.

He shakes his head. "Folks are dead."

"No siblings?" I ask, feeling preemptively a bit sad if he says no, because my sisters mean so much to me.

His eyes lift to mine then back to his salad. "None," he finally answers.

From there, we eat our salads in silence, but it's comfortable, and that should be weird but it isn't. In sync, we pass and share the pepper, he sips decaf while I eat a piece of peach pie, and at the end, he drops a hundred-dollar bill on the table to pay.

"Thank you," I say quietly, feeling suddenly nervous.

He walks to my car, taking a few steps back into the street as he waits for me to get inside and buckle up. With my headlights on and the door open, I say, "See you tomorrow."

He doesn't smile but he shoves his hands in his pockets. "See ya tomorrow, Firecracker."

I look in the rearview and spot him watching me drive off. Today was a very good day.

TEN

I'm jealous.

Trace

I peel the label from the bottle, looking at the tiny bits of adhesive and damp paper stuck to my fingers.

"Why are we here?" Deuce asks, peering around the counter at the bowling alley. "We're the youngest here."

It's senior night at the bowling alley, where I asked Deuce to come meet me for a drink.

A non-alcoholic drink at that.

Sweat slides down my spine. Ivy. That's why we're here. She's fucking me all up. No woman has ever pushed back, questioned me, argued with me, glared at me, made me sweat. I've never fantasized about waking up with a woman. Going to bed, sure, but waking up, never. I've always had access to women of all walks and not since my first love have I wanted to wake up the next morning with a woman... over and over. In fact, I've never really fantasized about a woman, period. Much less... the nonsexual aspects.

And that's why we're here.

"It's safe, that's why," I say, plucking the last bit of label from the root beer. Deuce clinks his orange cream soda against my bottle.

"I support that, and these," he says, making note of the bottle before lifting it to his lips for a long swig. "Damn, this is pretty good."

I sip my root beer. "Yeah, it's all right."

He twists his head, one eye shut as he peers my way. His dark hair is down and messy, and he's wearing a hoodie and gray sweats. I pulled this man from his comfortable life with his wife and son to listen to my bullshit. I tell myself I'd do the same for him, even though I'm not so sure. I also tell myself I'll make it up to him by one day being the friend to him that he has been to me.

"Spit it out, Calhoun."

I clear my throat and meet his gaze. "I was thinking of losing the Calhoun, actually." I finish the warm root beer. How come I can slam a beer in ten seconds but getting through a root beer has taken me ten minutes? I'm stalling. "Since I'm here in Bluebell now, working at Ink Time, I thought I'd go back to Wade."

A faint smile curls Deuce's lips. He takes another sip of soda and strokes his inked hand down his beard. "In my heart, you've always been Trace Wade."

I roll my eyes as he enjoys his mocking, his chest vibrating with quiet chuckles.

"I mean, Trace Calhoun is the guy on *Trace Tats* and *Needle Ninjas*." I shrug, plucking invisible lint from my long-sleeved flannel. "I ain't him anymore."

Deuce makes an aggravating show of looking around us.

"Last I checked, the only Trace is right here, and all versions of him are here, too." He shakes his head, peering at the mirror backing of the bowling alley bar. Old, partially empty bottles of bright-colored alcohol rest beneath a layer of dust, and below them a rack of old beer glasses sit upside down. An older woman in a pin-striped apron works the length of the bar, where a total of nine old men are scattered about.

I hate when he goes thoughtful. Deuce is smart, and he always finds a way of hitting me with a dose of truth when I'm at my weakest. I always need it, but it brings a wave of emotion that I could live without.

Finally he faces me again after finishing his soda, catching a burp with the back of his hand. "*Needle Ninjas* Trace and Ink Time Trace are the same guy. When you separate yourself into versions, you're setting yourself up for disappointment. Working here in Bluebell as a tattoo artist ain't ever gonna be the same as what you did before. But the part you aren't seeing is that... it ain't supposed to be a replacement. It's the next step. And you can look at it as going downstairs, and if you do, then that's what it'll be. And you'll stay buried in bottles and pussy forever, because you've made yourself a victim of your situation."

"It ain't about losing the show," I grumble, eager to defend myself. Habits are hard to break. Trace Calhoun isn't wrong. He never is. That's what the viewers liked, and that's what my ego needed at the time. To win. Over and over and over. To prove to myself I'm not second best.

"No, it's not. But you're gonna use that as your reason, so you don't gotta tackle what happened *before* the show," he says, making note of the months I'd begun to spiral before I was signed to *Needle Ninjas*.

I don't say anything.

He knocks his elbow against mine. "Don't clam up. I'm in a

bowling alley full of senior citizens with you. My wife is at home in bed, and my son is asleep. Don't you dare clam up."

Opening my mouth, I snap it closed a moment later, embarrassed.

"Spit it out," Deuce says, voice brimming with impatience. We may be middle-aged men, but I have no doubt he'll drag me outside and square off with me if I don't comply. He's got every right to be over my shit.

"It's fucking embarrassing, man."

From my periphery, I see his arm lift. A moment later, the old waitress appears. "Hey ya, Deuce, how ya doin', honey? Another?"

He smiles. "Hi, Sally, yeah, I'll take another and so will my friend."

My eyes lift to the woman with the paper pad in her hands. She smiles at me, crow's feet pinching the corners of her eyes. She looks like someone I kind of remember, but since I've never been to the bowling alley in Bluebell, and she doesn't strike me as someone with a tattoo, it's unlikely I know her.

"Another root beer, baby?"

"Thanks." I dip my head.

She scribbles on the pad and scampers off.

"Sally is Lucy's mom," Deuce says, reading my mind. "Lucy is the waitress at Goode's."

I nod. "Makes sense. She looked familiar."

"Yep, and I'm telling you because Bluebell is small, and you gotta start learning 'bout people here." Sally returns with our drinks. After twisting off the tops, Deuce clinks the neck of his bottle to mine and continues. "Tell me what you're embarrassed about. If you make me guess, you're gonna leave here feeling a lot worse." He smirks.

"Is that right?"

He nods. "You embarrassed by your ugly face?" he prods, sipping his drink to hide his smirk.

I roll my eyes. "Fine."

He gives me a minute and I need it. It's been years but this is not something I talk about with anyone. Ever. I spin the bottle in my hand by the neck a few times, take another sip and keep my gaze focused on the bartop. "I'm embarrassed that it's still the root of everything. That I let it control me ever, much less... for this long."

Deuce nods, though I don't feel brave enough to look him in the eye. "Cat?"

I haven't said the name aloud in what feels like forever. And I haven't heard anyone else say it, either. My heart leaps for one single beat before steadying again. I nod. "Cat."

Deuce lets loose years worth of angst in one sight. "Where are you at with this, because I can't help if I don't know what level you're on?"

I arch a brow. "Level?"

He motions with his hand. "You know, are you still madly in love or, like, you want to exact revenge or, like... you just want to move on but you can't?"

I narrow my eyes. "Exact revenge?"

He shrugs. "I don't know, man. You were gone for so long. I don't know where your head is at now."

"I'm here," I tell him. "My head is here. I don't want revenge. Besides, don't you think I'm about ten years late on that?"

"Like I said, I don't know where your head is at. You've been going hard for years." He sips his drink and drops his voice. "Did you going hog wild all start with Cat and—"

I lift a palm, not wanting him to finish that sentence. "Yes, it started because of Cat."

"Right," he continues, dragging out the word cautiously.

"That was a long time to still be hung up on it." The exact reason I told him I'm embarrassed.

"Gee, thanks," I mutter, sipping my stupid root beer.

"C'mon. You aren't in the bowling alley with my old ass because you're doing fucking great."

I smirk at him. "I like that you just kinda burned yourself, too."

He sighs. "Talk to me. You want to. It's why you asked me here. Unless you just want some quality time with me, in which case, great. I'd like to talk and the first thing I want to gossip about is you and what's up."

I sift my fingers through my hair, unsure of why I feel nervous and embarrassed. Deuce knows the truth, and he knew what happened all those years ago. Still, talking about it still feels... surreal. I clear my throat, finally brushing off the hesitancy.

"All these years I kept thinking that if I was rich enough, famous enough, talented enough... one day she'd..."

"Come back?" he offers quietly. Something about my best friend using his soothing tone, the one he uses for his toddler son, makes me want to cry.

Goddamn it.

I cough through the lump in my throat, using the *"I've got allergies, I'm not emotional"* cough used by people who hate emotion. "I guess so, yeah."

"Do you want her back?"

I shake my head. "No. Fuck no. Of course I don't." I reflect on the last ten years. "I don't think I ever did. But I did want her to recognize that I'm the good guy. That she chose wrong. That she was wrong."

Deuce rests his hand on my forearm, making the backs of my eyes burn with unshed emotion. "She was wrong. You are the good guy. And you shouldn't need her to tell you that to know it."

I nod. "I'm realizing that."

"Oh yeah?" Deuce asks, digging a few bills from his wallet. I smack his hand away, appreciative that the emotional moment has somewhat passed.

"I'm paying." I scratch at the side of my stubbled jaw, then run a fingertip along the hoop in my nose, thinking. "And yeah. The thing is, I never cared about addressing shit until I came to Bluebell. When I was on the road with *Needle Ninjas*, I kept thinking, Cat's gonna see this. She's gonna realize she fucked up. It's gonna be so fucking sweet when she reaches out and tells me how much she regrets what happened. What she did."

"And you don't want that anymore?" he asks.

I shake my head. "I don't know if I ever wanted that, I just thought I did."

"What do you want?" he prods softly.

"I want to be happy." I face him, exposing myself in a way I never have. "I want a girl. A family. I want a routine. Weekends with the people I love, evenings around a barbecue with those same people. I want a beer to taste good because it's hot and I've worked hard in my yard and earned it. I want to have sex and have it mean something. I want to create art that enriches me, fulfills me. And when I'm in the studio, I want to enrich other people with great art. Fulfill their vision. And I want that all here, in Bluebell."

"That's a big epiphany."

"Nah," I say, leaning back. "In my heart, since Cat and the bullshit with Tara," I start. Best I can do to avoid the cringe that comes with an admission so raw is to not make eye contact, so I keep my eyes on my boots. "I've known what I wanted for a while. I just... didn't think I could have it. I thought they broke me or I think I owed karma for what I did to Tara."

"What changed your mind?" he asks, his bottle almost to his lips as I turn to face him.

"Ivy."

"You're really going to let me shade the entire design for your afternoon session?" Ivy asks, her eyes, today lined with bright purple, go wide. "Seriously?"

I shrug, full of nonchalance. "Why wouldn't I?" With my sunglasses still on, my eyes drop to her breasts, which are more on display than they've ever been.

They're fantastic tits, as I knew they would be, but still, it angers me that I can tell they're fantastic.

Because if I can, so can other men.

She's wearing some black bodysuit thing that disappears into her skirt. Her very fucking short skirt, I might add. Her legs, while covered in tights, peek through the tears in the fabric, revealing velvety unmarked flesh on one and loads of ink on the other.

Fuck, she's hot.

With combat boots on her feet and her jet-black hair down around her face, she's a wet dream in the flesh, I swear.

"You know," I start, irritated and jealous at how gorgeous she looks today, at how I want her to be gorgeous for me, and me only. Except, I treat her like shit and am almost never open with her about anything, so would she ever want me back? "Acting surprised that I'm involving you in so much work tells me you're insecure about your skills."

I flip my sunglasses up; though I haven't got my fill of her, I'm also not the kind of asshole who wears shades indoors all day, either. Fuck that guy.

"If you don't want to shade the American flag—"

"I want to," she snaps, the excitement and happiness she held just a moment ago now in pieces on the floor. "I'm not insecure, Trace," she hisses, the long slither of the C in my name making my cock stir. "You're just an asshole and I was surprised you were being nice."

"I wasn't bein' nice," I say, reaching for the arm on the coffee pot behind the desk. I've been here on time for two weeks straight, I might add. Haven't touched a drop of booze for that long, either. "You're an apprentice," I point at her, and her anger grows. "I'm," I hook a thumb to my chest, and she goes fire engine red, "here to teach you. Part of teaching is hands-on."

I'd like to get my fucking grubby hands all over that young, delicious little body. I'd tear those tights off, shove that skirt up her hips and rut my way inside of her all while she tore her vocal cords screaming my goddamn name.

"Did I hear you're shading Trace's afternoon session?" Connor questions, walking up with his shining white smile. He bugs me. He bugs me because he's all... fucking... manners and bleached teeth and... drinks water all day and talks about running and watching the news. Fuck this guy and his ideal everything.

Connor looks my way, extending his hand to me. "Morning, Trace. How are ya?"

I'd be better if your teeth were on the floor and my boot was in your ass. Now quit flirting with Ivy. "Solid, man, thanks," I reply, shaking his hand for the least amount of time that is socially acceptable. "And yeah, she's shading." I narrow my eyes at Ivy. "C'mon back and let me watch you make the stencil."

"Good luck," Connor tosses at her as we move down the hall toward my station.

I'm shrugging out of my leather jacket when Ivy socks me in the shoulder, her fist tiny but mighty. "I can talk, you know."

"I'm aware," I deadpan.

"I could've answered Connor." Her eyes narrow on me in a way that makes me feel exposed. Like she knows that I'm a jealous prick hiding being ego and asshole.

"If you want to talk to Connor so bad, go talk to him," I growl, loathing how possessive and jealous I sound. I have no claim to those emotions when it comes to Ivy. Yet here I am, balling my fists at my sides as I blink down at her, heart racing, shoulders tense. I want her to want me, not fucking Connor.

Such a bullshit name anyway.

She blinks a few times, slowly, maybe even lazily. Her thick dark lashes hypnotize me, slowing my tachy heart, putting a stop to the anger bubbling in my veins. After what feels like too long, she asks, "You want me to make the stencil now or do you want to look at the piece one more time?"

Her lips are so plump. So perfect. I love that black lipstick she wears. I'd jack off to watching her eat a popsicle. "You're right," I say, my voice much hoarser than expected. "I should check the design one more time."

She reaches out, eyes still on mine, and slides my jacket off my arms the rest of the way. "I'll hang this up, get us some more coffee and we'll get going."

I nod. "Thanks."

She does what she says, hanging my coat near reception before filling two mugs with piping hot caffeine. I don't get anything ready while she's away. I just... watch her. I watch her and imagine how she looks in the first traces of daylight, without her purple eyeliner, black lipstick or ripped tights, her dark hair strewn over a pillow, her partially inked body covered by only a thin sheet.

"Here you go," she says, her amber scent wrapping my cock

as she sinks onto the swivel stool adjacent to mine. With the mug of coffee she poured me in my hand, I sit down next to her and sip as she sifts through my portfolio, finding just what I need.

She lays it all out and flicks on the lamp. Picking up my pencil, I blink down at the sketch, my mind a mess. *What am I doing?* I look at the flag rippling in an invisible wind, wondering what Ivy would look like wrapped up in a flag, in nothing but her birthday suit.

"Talk me through how you double-check," she says, getting the ball rolling. She presses her finger to the edge of the design, where the edge of the flag nearly meets the paper. "Would it be cool to add some wear to the seam? I mean, don't disrespect the flag or anything but... just show that it's been relentlessly up against the elements for a long time."

I nod. "That'd be dope." And with her suggestion, I tuck into the sketch and start working. With her by my side, I forget everything.

The fear, the pain, everything.

Only she has that effect.

It's not every day someone signs up to get a tattoo but shows up to the appointment horrified to go through with it. And I'm not trying to be sexist, but statistically speaking, the number of times men have been terrified of the needle? Not high.

It's part of the reason why I'm so puzzled this afternoon, half way through the long session. The client is a twenty-five-year-old man, one who of course knows Ivy.

The Bluebell energy of everyone knowing one another is

great. Cozy. But every man knowing Ivy? Eager to talk to her, desperate to hug her hello? Makes me want to take her to the biggest city in the world, get lost with her, so that no one will know her name and no one will think they have the right to hold or touch her.

"It's all right, Jere," Ivy soothes, using a side of her I haven't seen much. The softness of her tone and the way she calmingly strokes his shoulder with the backs of her knuckles...

I'm jealous.

Even though I'm the one training her, I'm the one helping her shape her craft, which is arguably the most important thing to her, I'm the man sitting at her side day in and day out for the last few months. Still. I am fucking jealous. The pen vibrates in my hand, color seeping through the needle, into his skin, and still, my eyes dart back and forth between the client and her knuckles, soothing him in repetitive, gentle strokes.

"Jeremy," I say as I turn off the machine, sitting up under the guise of stretching my spine. "You want a break?"

He peers down at me, positioned at his waist as his American flag tattoo is across his stomach. "I'm okay," he says, the sweat on his forehead glittering beneath the overhead lamps. He does this little wimpy, shriveled smile at Ivy, then says, "Her support is really helping."

Gag me.

I glance down at the finished ink. I've done the outline, I've done the stars and all the shading in and behind them. I had only planned on Ivy shading the red stripes and the shadow behind the flag, and I'd never put a client at risk but she can absolutely handle what's left.

"I hope my support is just as good," I tell him, eyeing her, lifting the plastic protected pen in my gloved hand. "You're up."

Her eyes widen for a moment before she recalls the jab I made about shock and insecurity. I hate that I said that because I know she was only excited. I know she isn't insecure in her abilities but more so, she just isn't fully comfortable with the pen yet. Which is normal.

Still, I broke her down as much as I could.

Without a single question, her blue eyes capture mine as she smiles, saying, "Perfect."

Jeremy props himself up on his elbows, looking a little pale and a lot woozy. Ivy offers him a Jolly Rancher casually, in a way that doesn't suggest she sees how bad he feels. She's got a bedside manner, and that's good.

I keep working. The design, for frame of reference, is about one foot wide and half a foot long. In the grand scheme of ink and pain, it's not a mountain. It's more like... a hill.

"You're... you're gonna switch?" he asks, struggling to be cool in front of me but also clinging to her battling inside him. I can see it. His gaze flicks between us, his chest moves a bit faster, and I have to pull my old cup of coffee to my lips and take a drink just to hide my satisfied smirk.

What kind of guy gets an American flag on his gut to show his badassery but whimpers when a beautiful girl won't hold him like an infant and whisper sweet nothings? A guy named Jeremy, that's who.

Most of the tattoos I got were without numbing cream, in silence, done by myself, absolutely sober. I invited the pain. Welcomed it when and if it came. The burn of the needle was always tolerable for me.

"Yep. Ivy here is an apprentice to the shop. She's working with me—"

"Hey" Jeremy sits up further. "I knew you looked familiar. You're Trace Calhoun, from *Needle Ninjas*, right?" He shakes his head in dismay, like he's just realized Tom Cruise is right in front of him. There may have been a time when I enthusiastically welcomed being recognized—basked in it, even—but now it just feels awkward.

"I am Trace Calhoun," I agree with a singular nod of my head.

"I watched your show all the time. You are so badass," he breathes, no longer looking at Ivy with puppy dogs eyes but now his focus is solely on me. "I saw the tattoo you did in Great Lakes, for that plane crash survivor. The phoenix rising from the plume of smoke," he recalls, making me also recall the ink.

I remember the guy. I remember the tattoo.

I also remember it was all bullshit. Something the show paid the guy to say and do. He was never in a plane crash, and the entire storyline was contrived for TV ratings. The ink, though, was real. And it was a great tattoo. One of the only borderless tattoos I've done.

"Thanks," I say as Ivy and I turn sideways, slipping around each other to change spots. I sit in the chair where she sat but I push away to the desk, watching. "Sorry, man, I'm not rubbing your arm."

He laughs, now that he knows who I am I can see he's more interested in me than her. And I'm happy with that, even though Jeremy has an unusually low pain tolerance and questionable taste in tattoo locations. Why? Because he's no longer wondering what color her panties are or if she'll stroke his chest the same way she touched his shoulder.

He focuses on me for the remainder of the session, asking me questions about various designs I did for a plethora of clients he saw on the show, prodding me about behind-the-scenes secrets, then moving on to Bluebell and how I ended up here.

I keep my answers vague, mostly because I signed a nondisclosure agreement with the TV studio. But also because I'm focused on Ivy. The way her hand moves with grace as she shades, how her brows pull together with focus and dedication —I could watch Ivy work all day. All night, even.

Tattoos are art. That's what's true in my soul, no matter what anyone else believes. To love something enough to want it etched into you for the better part of forever is a commitment, and people who commit to art that way are *my people*. Giving them that gift feels incredible.

But watching Ivy tattoo is like watching Monet paint. Like watching Mozart play the piano. It may just be red in the stripe of a flag, but the way she does it, the care she takes and the vulnerability she lends the art as she learns, is beautiful.

Lifting the pen, she glances my way, doing a double take as she catches me watching her.

Our eyes lock.

"And what about Goblin? He seemed so badass," Jeremy asks of a fellow tattoo artist that was briefly on the show for a while. "He's loaded, right?"

The corner of Ivy's lips lift, and my entire body grows hot. My cock thickens. My stomach clenches. My pulse skips.

"Yeah," I say to Jeremy, still looking at Ivy until she looks away a moment later. Her looking away feels like rising to the surface after a deep dive. "He's loaded. And... yeah," I say, processing his question. "He's a cool guy."

She doesn't look my way again for the next hour and a half while she finishes the shading, taking much longer than I would but taking the time she needs. I respect that. I respect people who take their time learning instead of gaining one ounce of knowledge and boasting they're a pro.

At the end of the session, I give Jeremy his aftercare

instructions and sift through the cupboard, looking for the baggie of stuff we send clients home with.

While I'm looking for his aftercare bag, Ivy tapes him up, carefully taping him up with plastic wrap. As she does, Jeremy does something very fucking annoying.

"You done for the day?" he asks her.

She must nod, because my back is to her and I don't hear her say no.

"Off at five?" he asks.

Again, she must nod but not hearing her drives a stake of discomfort through my back, and I grow rigid at the cupboard. Sifting through, I pull a bag out and add the last items—a pamphlet with approved antibiotic ointments, what to do and what not to do, etcetera.

When I get to my feet, I turn just in time to see Jeremy smile at Ivy, that familiar smile that every man knows about. I know, because I've given it many times.

It's the '*I want to stick my dick somewhere in your body and come*' smile.

Yeah, there's a smile for that. Trust me.

"Would you want to go to Goode's when you're off? I'd love to buy you a meal and catch up." His smile intensifies and I'm horrified to see her smile back at him. "Reminisce about high school or something."

Taking off her gloves, she pushes her hair behind her ear, exposing the dagger inked on the side of her throat. I love that she has a tattoo so visible and it's not like a fucking constellation or dream catcher but a fucking knife. I love her gauged ears and that she's the only one I've seen in Bluebell with them.

It's badass.

"Sure," she replies, helping stupid baby Jeremy up.

Sure? Ivy wants to go to dinner with the guy who needs

extra numbing cream and someone to hold his hand during a three-hour session?

Who is, by the way, a fucking *telemarketer*.

Yeah.

I slam the cupboard closed with my boot and drop the bag next to his hip. "Here."

I don't look at Ivy again, despite the fact her eyes prod me the entire time. I grab my phone off the side table and head for the hall, jealousy coursing through my veins like lava tearing through soil. Before I can take a second to breathe or think, I'm dialing.

"Yo," my buddy John answers, noises sounding off around him. I don't know if he's at work. I don't even know where he works anymore. Doesn't matter.

"Yo, you got plans tonight?"

"Nah," he sighs, "why? Wanna party?"

"Yep. In Bluebell, though. You got a ride?" I ask, unsure if he lost his license or not.

"Hell ya. You got booze and girls?" John asks.

I don't yet, but that's the easiest part of all. "I will." I glance over to the reception desk where Deuce is quietly talking with the new girl, the till on the register open. "Be here in an hour? We'll get it started."

"Sure," he says, "I'll leave now."

"Perfect."

He hangs up, and the next call I make is the one I feel the worst about. Jealousy makes us do ugly, stupid things, but I can't stop myself. Every time my finger hovers over the end call button, I see her smiling at him. I think of them across from each other at Goode's, the way we were, and I see red.

"Hey," I say softly, turning my back to the studio for a sliver of quick privacy. Then I proceed to invite a few people to Ink Time, telling them to be here the moment the shop closes.

Deuce lets me lock up. That means he trusts me with his space. I won't make him regret it, but I'll also borrow against the trust tonight.

My lips burn in anticipation, thinking of that first drink and the way it will burn through me, leaving my jagged edges fuzzy, my discomfort muted.

I want that.

I need that.

"Hey," Ivy hedges, appearing behind me, her hand on my elbow. I jerk out of her gentle touch, causing her face to scrunch. "What?"

"Nothing, just making a personal call." I keep my face expressionless. "What do you want?" The four words tumble out, cruel and pointed. My stomach clenches. I hate being a prick to her. But goddamn it, *why did she say yes to Jeremy?*

"I... uh... Deuce is taking care of Jeremy up front, then he's heading out to pick up Ace." Her blue eyes dance between mine, searching for why I'm being such a prick after we had such a good session together. Hell, it wasn't just the session.

We've been getting along. We've both been trying.

"Great," I deadpan. "I'm going in the back for a bit. Make sure the entire station is sanitized before you leave."

She doesn't say anything. She just stands there in that second-skin bodysuit that makes her tits look so fucking good and that skirt that shows her toned legs, glaring up at me like I just pissed in her cornflakes. I love that sultry, nasty look on her face.

"What? You're the apprentice. You stay and clean shit up. Why do you have that look on your face?" I shake my head, moving past her to the room in the back of the shop. Deuce mostly uses the room as a small office, but being Trace Calhoun, I have access to everything.

I don't give her the chance to reply. I walk past her into the stuffy little space and kick the door shut. Deuce keeps a bottle in his desk for what reason, I'm not sure. Tonight it feels like kismet. I grab the bottle by the neck, spin the cap off, sending it clattering against the corkboard, and take a long, slow drink.

I was a fucking idiot to think I had a chance.

So I drink half that bottle in one sitting, because that's what proper idiots do.

ELEVEN

Tantrum-y baby man whore

Ivy

Jeremy waits awkwardly in the reception area, browsing designs in laminated sheets as I clean the station.

Trace isn't wrong. This *is* my job.

But I knew that, and so did he. Which means we both know I had every intention of cleaning up before I left. It's the fact that he felt the need to remind me. Callously, too.

We were making such good progress.

I really thought we were moving forward.

This regression of his, lashing out, being an asshole and shutting down? It's got jealousy written all over it. Trace may not be aware but I'm smart and receptive.

Jealousy means he wants me to give him my focus, and not give it to Jeremy.

He likes me.

He may even *want* me.

It's not hard to believe. We're a perfect fit. We share passions and interests, but we vary in complementary ways, too. At different places in our lives, we offer different perspectives to one another and when he's ready to stop being a tantrum-y baby man whore, he can benefit from all the wonderful ways we'd be together.

Because we would be good together, I have zero doubt.

I know what I saw online. I know he's fucked as many women as he possibly could.

I'm more worried about him testing negative for sexually transmitted diseases than if I stack up to the other women he's been with. I don't do that to myself—I don't play that mental game.

I know who I am on the inside, and how I treat people. I know I am worthy of a good man, so I don't compare myself to anyone but prior versions of me. I strive to be better than the me I was yesterday and the me I was a week ago, but I don't get in the comparison ring with other women.

Swiping through the last of the disinfectant spray on the chair, I toss the cleaning rag in the trash. After tying it off and adding it to the can out back, I wash my hands in the restroom, grab my purse and head out.

Or *try* to head out. I skid to a halt in the hall at what I see.

Four women in the shop, two conversing with Jeremy, one on her phone in the reception chair (which makes my skin crawl) and the other? In front of Trace, her fingers hooked on the belt loops of his jeans, her face tipped up, lips in a pout.

She's...

"*Please?*" she begs.

Yep. She's begging Trace.

As if he's suddenly aware of my presence, he turns, his dark eyes poking me. "Have a nice time with Jeremy," he says, just low enough that I know Jeremy didn't hear. I could barely hear over the way this hooker is breathing all over him.

I can't muster a passive-aggressive smile despite the fact that I really fucking want to. Instead, I slink past them, not letting go of his gaze until I'm past.

I hook my arm through Jeremy's, the contact doing nothing to my veins, nothing to my spine. No electricity, no spark, but that's fine. I didn't agree to a meal with him because I thought it was a date. I agreed because I genuinely want to catch up with him. He's nice. We used to be friends not too many years ago and we lost touch.

Truthfully, I've been obsessed with Trace's work and my evolving art, and I shut off the world around me, except my sisters. I lost touch with so many, which is a feat in a small town.

Still, the lack of spark only reminds me how fiery Trace makes me feel. Though I don't want to, my eyes slide over to him and a crushing boulder of disappointment sinks my stomach.

His thumb is on her chin and he's slowly commanding her to lower to her knees. "Get on your knees and suck my dick," he rasps, causing my eyes to nearly pop from my head. Did he really just tell her to get down and suck his dick?

But her hands... they're on his belt, and her knees... they're on the ground. Obediently she works his pants, causing a wave of nausea to crash into the back of my nose and soar up my throat. I swallow it down as his eyes come to mine for just a split second.

A painful second.

"Let's go," I murmur to Jeremy, turning to push out of the shop and into Bluebell's perfect evening.

Except, it's wasted on me. The mid-seventies weather, the

sherbet sunset, the soft crowing of birds going home, leaves dancing together in the day's final wind—it's perfect.

And completely wasted because all I can feel is jealousy, anger and... hurt.

His dick is probably in her mouth right now.

"C'mon," I say, jerking Jeremy across the street, almost dragging him by the arm. I just want to get in Goode's and have the barrier of the street and another set of doors between us.

We choose a booth at the diner—I mean, I guess we do.

I don't know.

My mind is spinning, and all I can see is his thumb on her chin and her hands on his belt, the clatter of buckle on button making nausea sear my tongue.

"You know, he just did that to piss me off," I say, shaking my head as I stab a straw into the glass of ice water Lucy brought us. I didn't even hear her if she said hello.

This is so not fair to Jeremy.

"I'm sorry," I sigh, finally giving him the attention he deserves. "It's—"

"Complicated?" he offers, his chestnut eyes soft as he sinks back into the vinyl, draping one arm over the booth.

"I guess," I reply, just now realizing that Trace and I *are* actually very complicated. "I can't stand him most of the time. And tonight, you know, he invited those girls to the studio just because you asked me out."

Jeremy's smile doesn't reach his eyes and it's then I realize that maybe *he* hoped this was something more than friends catching up. "He was trying to make you jealous?" he asks, then nods. "Yeah, so, you two have feelings for each other, then?"

I lick my lips. "Nothing confirmed."

Jeremy leans forward, collecting the menu in his hands as he smiles softly at me. "The last person I got pissed at as much as you're pissed at Trace?" He glances down, his eyes moving along the printed options as he says, "I actually liked her a lot." He looks up at me. "Loved her, even. We dated for three years."

I chew the inside of my cheek a moment, processing his insinuation. He isn't wrong. If Trace can stop acting like a total clown, we could have something. A future. And that's what I want.

"You're right," I finally smile. "I like him." I don't add the 'a lot' at the risk of sounding twelve. "That's why he gets under my skin. Like, really gets under there like a... hot parasite or something. Because..." I sigh, glancing through the large window, across the street, to an ill-lit Ink Time. "I *really* fucking like him."

Jeremy sips his water. "Tell me about it."

Lucy takes our orders, and I talk to Jeremy. He listens, then he listens as we eat, and I never stop talking. And all that talking about Trace has me... worked up.

Emotionally charged, yes.

But, like.... *Worked up.*

I pay the tab when Lucy brings it, and Jeremy and I part ways outside of Goode's. Standing in the street, I stare at the gold ornate framing on the door of the tattoo shop, the place that has become my everything in the last few months. Nerves coil in my belly.

There's movement inside, but I can't make out what kind. Worried that Trace will get drunk and do something stupid—like leave the shop unlocked—I cross the street and walk inside.

What I see is... "What the fuck are you doing?" I hiss, my nostrils flaring as the door slams shut behind me, bumping my ass, sending me a pace forward. The blonde behind the reception counter jolts forward, lifting her hands from the register. The girl next to her, whose hair is black like mine, I recognize from being the girl who likely sucked Trace.

Realizing they were about to fucking rob Ink Time, I bend

down and grab my knife from my boot. Thank God I didn't change into slippers tonight—I don't carry my knife in my slippers because that doesn't make sense.

"Where are the others?" I question, a thrill rushing through my cheeks as they both stand taller, holding their hands up. I push the knife at them through the air. "Where are they?"

The blonde looks at the blade then up at me. "In the... little tattoo bed thingy," she says, her eyes going back to the blade.

I glance over, finding Trace completely fucking naked but for his jeans bunched up around one ankle, his shirt on the floor, socks and boots, too. I look back at the thieves. "Is he okay?"

The girl with the dark hair nods. "He passed out."

I hate that the words that come to me first are these, but I say them before I get a chance to think. "He's a heavy drinker, it's only been two hours. How has he passed out already?"

Then I see it. On the floor, next to his shirt and boots.

An empty whiskey bottle.

My eyes widen as I prod toward them, my knife the only thing keeping them quiet. "He drank the whole thing?"

Just then, the other two girls come stumbling from the bathroom down the hall, laughing as they both comment on how quiet it suddenly is.

"Did you get the money?" one of them asks right before she spots me. Stopping in her tracks, she grabs the other girl by her wrist, stopping her too. Pulling my phone from my back pocket, I dial the Bluebell police, using 911.

I proceed to tell the operator that four women were attempting to rob my employer and that I have them at knife point. They tell me, on speakerphone, that two officers are en route.

"If you try to bolt or make a move for me, I'll fucking stab you." I look at each one of them. "How many women do you meet with a knife in their boot?" I drag my tongue over my top teeth. "Not many."

I've never stabbed anyone. But I like knowing that if I need to, I could.

While waiting for the police to arrive, I force the girl with the dark hair to grab a medical sheet from the cupboard, and drape it over Trace's naked body.

She crouches next to him, tucking it under his bare ass. I don't want the police to see him like this, but I don't trust these little robbers enough to cover him myself. I think they'd bolt.

"Why is he naked?" I finally ask, scared to know the answer. I don't want him to have gotten head from this woman, but I really don't want to know that he had sex with her. Or any of them.

She shrugs. "Don't know. He just started freaking out and taking his clothes off, then he just... passed out."

The relief that hits me is indescribable.

Except, knowing he slammed a bottle of whiskey and called girls over pisses me off. A lot.

Attempting to calm myself, I breathe in through my nose and out through my mouth, letting my attention veer to my work station in the corner of the studio. On my desk, the chastity cage sits, next to my open sketch pad. Normally I'd have taken it with me because I'd been working on that design so much lately. But Jeremy asked me out, so I left work at work for once. The piece is important, though.

My first solo, and I really want it to be as close to perfect as possible.

The cage seems to glitter beneath the muted studio lights, and even though a light tap comes at the front door, a great idea hits me.

An idea I have to shelve for a few minutes at least.

I turn to see Dash Foster and his partner, Keanu *Reeve.*

Seriously.

And the wild part? They're both kind of... Bill and Ted, if you know what I mean.

"What do we have here, Ivy?" Dash asks, walking a circle around the women who are now huddled together nervously in reception.

"I came back to make sure Trace locked up and these two," I say, waving my knife at the culprits, "were getting into the till." I point said knife at the camera in the corner. "It's all recorded."

"Fuck," one of the women mutters.

Twenty minutes later, the women are at the Bluebell police station, and Dash is finishing up with me. He scribbles something in his notepad for what feels like eternity before finally clicking his pen shut and slipping it into his breast pocket.

"Does he need medical?" he asks, eyebrow raised.

I look over at Trace snoring beneath the blue sheet. I smile at Dash. "He's fine. Thanks."

Dash leaves and I snap on a pair of gloves, ready to give Trace the discipline he is so clearly fucking begging for.

TWELVE

I can't hold it back. I love the fire.

Trace

"Quit lying just to be an asshole and tell me the truth!" she shouts, the veins in her neck bulging, her eyes like fucking saucers.

I've seen her mad, but never like this. She reminds me of a little fuming devil in a cartoon, and with the way her upper half is jutting forward aggressively, I half expect to see plumes of smoke billowing from her ears.

I cannot help it, goddamn it, but a smirk lifts my lips as she rages. She's a little fuzzy, and I wonder if I'm drunk or even... *dreaming*. I smile, realizing that I'm dreaming of her. I like that I'm dreaming of her. And because I'm dreaming, I smile and allow myself to enjoy her freely.

Her sentence stops abruptly and she stands up straight just

as fast, her hands going to her hips. Those grabable, blooming hips of hers. God I wish I–

"Why the fuck are you smirking?" She steps nearer, so close that she's now standing between my spread knees, her eyes glowering down on me. "I'm going to make you regret that smirk."

My lips twitch, and the smirk grows without my consent. I can't hold it back. I love the fire. My dick is aching against my thigh right now.

She reaches down, wrapping her talented fingers around me, closing them, tightening her grip as her eyes intensely hold mine. "Smile," she commands.

I obey.

She squeezes my cock harder. "Again."

I smile yet again, this time with a tiny laugh tickling my throat. I see her game, and there's no way she's got the cojones to grab my cock hard enough to make me react.

I like it rough so there's no fucking—

"Fuck!!!" I screech, jolting forward, or... trying. It's then I remember I'm tied to it by my wrists and ankles. Her grip on my cock is so tight I nearly scream. I scream so loudly that the room around me vibrates, my vision goes hazy, the world goes dark... and then it's blurry.

And I'm lost deeper in my dreams.

THIRTEEN

Ivy

My gloved hand connects with his stubbled jaw, but all I get is a grumble.

"Hey," I partially shout, slapping Trace's face again.

His eyes open, but I can't tell if he's there or not.

"You're naked at Ink Time, dummy," I tell him, narrowing my eyes, inspecting him.

He mumbles something. Maybe Ink Time, maybe not. But his eyes fall closed again. I peer over at the door. Deuce will be down here in no time. He called a moment ago, telling me the security company called them. Said we never turned the alarm on and I explained what had happened.

I'm not sure if he's coming down here to help with Trace or to lock up, or both, but he's on his way.

My time is limited.

"I'm locking you up. If you don't wake up now, you're going in the cage," I tell Trace as I tug down on the blue sheet draped over his body.

It's not my first time seeing him naked and if that fact doesn't embody Trace Calhoun, I don't know what does. He stirs just slightly but his eyes stay closed. Standing mid-torso at his side, I slap his cheek again... but nothing.

"Okay," I tell him, "here we go. Last chance."

I'd feel like I was violating him if he wasn't naked in my workplace. If I barged in on him at home and locked him up there, that would be wrong.

But when you invite hooker thieves into your workplace and drunkenly pass out without clothes like an insane person, you get locked up.

Fair's fair.

I set the cage on his belly, knotted with muscle even when he's nodded off in a blissful haze. I've got to flex to make my abs pop and he just has them, lying there in a stupor. Men's metabolisms are a real fucking crime.

Carefully, I slide one hand beneath his sack, lifting his entire package just slightly. His soft cock falls onto his stomach, leaving just his balls in one hand. He's impressive in size even when he's not aroused, and there's something hot about that. Irrational, yes. But hot? Also yes.

Before he senses a woman is touching him, I take the cage from his stomach and align it with his head. Taking his shaft in one hand, I begin easing him inside, finally using a key to twist the device closed at the ringed base.

I stare down at his manhood trapped in the chastity cage, the gold lock contrasting the silver metal all around him. A smile curls the edge of my mouth knowing that while I have the key and he's in that, he can't do a damn thing.

Snapping off the gloves, I unlock the necklace I wear under my clothes. It's a silver necklace with nothing on it anymore. Years ago I thought it would be the necklace where I wore my engagement stone, but that didn't happen, and I didn't have the heart to take it off.

Now it serves a better purpose.

I slide the key onto the chain and put it back on my neck, immediately working Trace's pants up his body when I'm done. As soon as his belt is buckled, Deuce enters through the back door, his own big boots crowding down the hall.

He stops at the opening between the artists' stations, hands on hips, blinking at a passed out and now—thanks to me— clothed Trace. "What the fuck?" he says, then adds, "Not you, Ivy. Thanks for being here." Sweeping his hand down his face he lets out a heavy sigh. "What happened?"

I nod to the receptionist station where the iPad is pulled out and the footage is queued since Dash and Keanu just viewed it. "Watch the footage while I get his shoes back on," I say, finagling a heavy boot onto Trace's foot. The socks were easy but the boots are a pain.

"You're welcome," I tell him, dragging the words out even though he's been sawing logs for the last forty minutes.

After his boots are on and laced, I shimmy his shirt down, feeding his arms through one at a time before yanking it over his head. "Fuck, I'm sweating," I tell a still passed-out Trace as I wipe the back of my head with the end of his hoodie.

Deuce comes to my side, outstretching his hand across his body. I slip mine into his as he says, "Thank you, Ivy. You did good."

I chew the inside of my mouth, absorbing his praise. "Thank you."

We both stare at a snoring Trace before I quietly ask, "Did you watch all of the footage?"

I feel his eyes on me, and I look up at him. "What are you asking?"

I look back at Trace, making sure he's still passed out. Of course he is, but asking this definitely lets the cat out of the bag. I smooth my finger over the black nail polish on my thumb

"Did he hook up with any of those women?"

Deuce doesn't reply until I'm brave enough to look him in the eye. When I finally do, he puts me at ease. "No, he didn't." He looks over at Trace. "He just drank that entire fifth in forty minutes."

"Idiot."

Deuce nods. "You drive his car behind me? I'll take him in my pickup in case he gets sick."

"You're a good friend," I tell him, grabbing Trace's keys, wallet and phone from the drawer next to the table. "I'd make him puke in his own car."

Deuce smirks. "I don't want to be seen driving that ridiculous thing, even if it's at night."

At that, I snort, because Trace's car is ridiculous for a tiny town in the sticks. "You know, it doesn't really even suit him," I admit.

"You're right. It doesn't." Deuce bends, dragging Trace to the edge of the bench, curling his large body over his shoulder. Standing, he groans. "Not anymore anyway."

I follow behind Deuce, inputting the code on the security system that he tells me since his hands are occupied holding Trace's body over his. I help him get Trace in the passenger side, then slip into his little sports car, surprised to find the tank full and the radio off. The sports car definitely gave me *"leave it on E with the radio blaring 80s rock"* vibes, but I'm so glad to be wrong.

I follow behind Deuce until we arrive at his house. For a second, I almost forgot that Trace is living in the house next door now. I stay behind the wheel as Deuce gets Trace awake enough to stand, and guides him to the porch. He stumbles the entire way, but Deuce keeps a palm pressed to his stomach and his arm around his shoulders, helping him the whole way.

That's when I get out and run up, helping to flick on the lights and guide Trace inside.

We lower him to a couch, one that already has a pillow and blanket on it. "His bed is being delivered this week, so this will be fine," Deuce says, watching me eye the small home.

There's not much, and I can tell right away that Trace didn't bring any of the furnishings I spotted in the apartment that night, months back. What's here is new.

"He's starting fresh," Deuce says, and sometimes it's eerie how well he reads my mind.

"Is there, like... a puke bowl or something?" I ask, looking around the space again. But really, there's not much. A few pairs of boots lined up neatly against the wall, a case of water sitting on the kitchen countertop, a TV on a stand on the floor, some pillows strewn about, and boxes. Lots of boxes stacked along the wall in the hallway. None of them are labeled, but I'm assuming since he's just moved it's all of his shit. Or whatever it is he wanted to take.

"Nah," Deuce says, grabbing a few bottles from the pack on the counter. He tosses them, and we watch as they roll near the couch, next to Trace's limp hand. "Unfortunately, I've seen him drink more and not get sick. He'll be hurtin' for sure but he's okay."

I swallow hard as I watch Trace's chest rise and fall, his lips parted and his eyes fluttering. "He was doing good. From what I could see, he was doing good."

"He's still doing good," Deuce says, surprising me. I pull my hair off my face, sliding the elastic from my wrist to make a ponytail. Deuce smiles, watching me, and says, "It's a small setback."

I nod, bending down to unlace my boots.

"You're staying?" he asks, sounding surprised.

"Yeah," I reply cooly, "I know you said he'll be okay but..." The key hanging around my neck suddenly feels heavy, and I'm hit with the urge to lie down on the floor and rest, and watch Trace sleep. "I'm gonna stay a few hours. Just to make sure those women don't come here, or, I don't know."

Deuce's smirk fills me with uncomfortable, self-conscious-ness. He's onto me. I know he is. "Uh-huh." He nods. "Got that knife in your boot?"

I glance down at the shining handle sticking out of my boot. "Yep."

He scratches his head as he moves to the front door, resting his hand on the knob. "It was you going out with Jeremy," he finally says, and my mouth opens reactively so damn fast it makes Deuce chuckle. He lifts a hand to silence what he knows will be an angry defense.

"No, no—I'm not saying it's your fault." His wide eyes hold mine with clarity. "I'm saying, the idea of you with another man drove him back to his comfort vices."

My heart races uncontrollably as I tug on a sweater, feeding my hands through the sleeves, keeping them tucked at my sides as I nod. "I know," I admit. "Or, I mean, I put that together after I said yes."

"You gotta teach him, Ivy. You're the only one who gets through to him."

I laugh at Deuce as he pulls open the front door, letting in a steam of cool air. Smells like horseshit and grass, but I love the smell of Bluebell. "I get through to him?" I look at Trace, whose body is now fully slipping from the couch.

Deuce grips the doorframe. "Teach him better ways to get jealous than booze and—"

"Hookers?" I offer with a syrupy sweet smile.

"Right." He claps his palm against the doorframe to say goodbye. "You two will work it out. Good night Ivy. And thank you for everything."

"Night, Deuce."

After he closes the door, I get to work laying out pillows and blankets all over the ground near the couch, so if Trace slips off, he's as comfortable as he can be.

That stupid asshole.

I have zero plans to spend the night here, but I want to make sure this jerk is safe and comfortable. I feed my fingers through his sweaty hair, hating how soft it feels despite the perspiration. His eyes flicker open for a moment as I slip the pillow behind his head, keeping him propped up in case he gets sick.

"Hi," he breathes, all smoke and rasp, making my attention leap to him.

"Hi," I quietly reply.

His eyes search mine. Through the fatigue and fog, he really looks at me. A smile curls his lips, then mine. Then he's out again.

"God you suck," I sigh. After pulling off his boots and socks then nearly breaking my back getting off his hoodie and shirt, I leave him to sleep, tugging the old blanket up over his body.

The cabinets in his kitchen are so sadly bare that I *almost* feel bad, except I remind myself that he just moved in and he's got more money than everyone in my family combined, so his lack of a stocked kitchen speaks more to his lifestyle than anything.

Still, I dig around the one cupboard with miscellaneous items until I find a bottle of Advil. Leaving three pills near the bottles of water, I push his hair off his face and touch the key swinging at my throat.

"See you tomorrow, dummy," I whisper, before taking his car keys, locking his front door, and driving his sports car home.

He'll hate that I took his car.

But that won't seem like much compared to the fact that I have his dick, too.

FOURTEEN

A tiny torturous birdhouse for dicks.

Trace

The world comes into focus a moment later and I'm not in the tattooing chair.

Ivy's not gripping my cock.

Hell, I don't even think she's here.

But I am at work.

Wait, no, this isn't work.

Fuck. I was dreaming, and dreaming deep.

Groggily blinking, I try my hardest not to move as I mentally work out my surroundings.

I'm... on the floor, wherever I am. That much is obvious in the way my hips ache and my lower back throbs. Sleeping on the fucking floor is not a thirty-eight-year-old man's game.

My head swims, but I force myself to focus as I slowly roll

onto my back and blink up at the ceiling. At some point, I believe women were here. Or... I was with women.

Cheap perfume clogs my nostrils as I reach up to push my hair from my face. Turning my head, I take in the shiny floor, mostly covered in blankets.

I'm home.

In my new home, next door to Deuce.

But I can't remember getting here, and I sure as shit don't remember what happened before I got here, either. Solving my evening feels tiresome, so I close my eyes, trying desperately to get back to the dream. The dream where Ivy held my cock in her hands, where she was just about to control me.

But I can't find it. The dream is gone. With my eyes pulled shut, darkness engulfing me, in the distance, I hear the faint dripping of a sink not fully shut off.

The dream is gone forever, and I'm on the floor, sore and aching, hungover and... oh yeah, mad.

I got mad last night. If mad were a synonym for jealous rage, then yeah, I got mad last night. I groan as I bring my hands down my face, scrubbing away the lethargy. I need to get up and get a fucking shower and a cup of coffee.

Of everything I can't remember, what I can remember is being a prick to Ivy.

Sickness rushes through me, and I move to my elbows and knees like a sick animal scrambling to my feet. I make it to the sink in time to empty the limited contents in my stomach, blinking madly from shock.

I didn't drink that much. I mean, for me.

That sounds bad.

When I think of what I did, how I behaved last night... I'm so ashamed that a second wave of nausea hits. But I grab a bottle from the pack and twist the top off, drinking it faster than I can get sick. With the crumpled bottle rolling in the sink, I grip the edge of the counter and summon a deep, steadying breath, trying desperately to calm the sickness sweeping over me.

Ivy went out to dinner with the guy who needed extra numbing cream.

I could've watched her like a total creep through the fucking shop window. Seriously. Goode's is right across the street. And yeah, that would've been weird but it would've been a lot better than what I did.

A memory of a dark-haired girl flashes through my mind. "Your friend can't come," her voice knocks into me like a boulder, and I lean over the sink to prevent the dizziness from taking me out.

I called Tre, I remember that now. And he called me back right after Ivy took off. Couldn't find his keys? Was that what he said? I don't know. But it was too late. I'd already slammed the fifth and invited the girls to party.

"Jesus Christ," I bellow, shaking my head over the sink as a third round of sickness hits.

After cleaning out the sink, the most painful of all memories come thundering back.

Ivy's face. The sadness buried in her eyes as she watched me command another woman to her knees as if it all meant nothing. Right in front of her.

I've never told Ivy that I have an insanely fucked-up crush on her. I barely admitted it to myself until recently. How could she possibly know that everything I did last night was because of how jealous she made me? She'll think it's just the asshole being the asshole, yet again.

I picked the girl with dark hair so I could at least pretend it was Ivy. I grip the top of my jeans, trying hard to remember if anything actually happened.

Squeezing my eyes shut, echoes of laughter tumble through

my brain, and the taste of Jack burns the back of my nose. No—nothing happened.

After Ivy left, I couldn't go through with it. I couldn't do anything but think of her.

She gives as good as she gets, and I like that. She's challenging and smart, and drop-dead gorgeous. She wears what she wants, she says what she thinks and she follows her goddamn dreams.

Not to mention she's got roots. People who love her here in Bluebell. A small, quiet life but one still bursting at the seams with dreams and goals, passions and dedications.

She's what I want and she's got what I need.

Despite the booze and regret, my lower half awakens, throbbing at the thought of Ivy in that bodysuit and tiny skirt, all her ink exposed through the tears in those sexy tights.

Fuck. I may be more hungover than I thought.

I feel hard. Or.. I'm aroused but...

Panic slaps me across the face like I'm on *Maury*.

Did I finally break my dick? Did I drink so much that even in the light of day, hours of sleep and a bottle of water under my belt, and I still can't get it up?

My hands fly to my belt, which I struggle to unbuckle. It's like I'm trapped in a nightmare where I'm trying to dial emergency services, but my fingers won't find the right keys, or the keys won't press. That's this, only more urgent because this isn't a dream, I'm awake and it's my cock on the line.

The more panicked I become, the slower my belt slides from the loops, all the while, my aching cock is just that... *aching*.

"Jesus, finally," I crow, whipping my forearm with the edge of the belt as I jerk it free. "Fucking button fly piece of cocksucking..." I grumble and curse as my big fat thumbs struggle to pop open the buttons on my fly. Finally, after my forehead is covered in a thin sheen of boozy sweat, I shuck my jeans down, leaving them banded below my ass as I shove down my boxers.

"Fuck!" I scream, literally scream. Blinking, eyes wide, I stand there, staring down at where my cock normally is. And it's there but... "Ah!" I scream again, only this time, no words, only pure terror. "Ahh!!" I howl again, making myself jump.

And when I jump, my cock does, too, but within the confines of a tiny metal dick cage. Reaching down, I cautiously cup my balls which are shoved through the contraption by a ring that loops my entire package. I stare at my cock all compressed, the bulge and veins reduced to a handful, all shoved into a metal cage.

It's like a tiny torturous birdhouse for dicks.

I hate it.

"What... what the fuck?" I can't stop staring at my locked-up dick. Seriously. The last time I stared at my dick this hard was after the first time I ejaculated. I remember staring at my cock, thinking, what the fuck? I'd trade that what the fuck for this one any day of the damn week.

With my locked dick just hanging out because, again, what the fuck? I pick up my phone from the floor and dial Deuce, my heart absolutely racing.

"Welcome back to Bluebell," Deuce answers, making light of my drunken stupor last night.

"Are you mad?" I first ask, because even with my dick in a birdcage, I fucked up last night. But I'm at my house. The last thing I remember last night was being at Ink Time.

There are no half-dressed cowgirl singers around this place. Deuce has to be the one that brought me home. He has to.

"Mad? No. Disappointed, yes, but mostly for you," he says, thanking Ev quietly in the background.

"Wh—" I start my sentence but no words adequately fit the *what on God's green earth is happening right now* mindset that

I'm in. "What... happened last night?" I ask, still staring at my locked-up guy. Maybe whatever Deuce has to say will make my dick prison make sense.

Deuce sighs. "Thanks, baby," he says, likely to Ev, but I don't care to clarify. All I want to know is why I need a treasure map to take a fucking piss this morning. "Well, you got butthurt that Ivy went out to eat with Jeremy. Then you got shit-faced too fast and passed out, and the women you invited over to party tried to rob the shop. They were sticking needles in the side of the till when Ivy came back and pulled a knife on them."

"What—"

"Then," he continues, speaking more loudly to not let me get a word in edgewise. "She held them at knifepoint till Bluebell PD got there. Arrested them. By the time the security company called me to tell me we left the alarms off, the PD had it all taken care of. I showed up at Ink Time, watched the footage while Ivy got you dressed—"

"Ivy dressed me?"

Wait—I know I didn't fool around with any of those women. I remember when I helped her off the floor and told her I couldn't. She called me a pussy. And that's when the bottle entered the chat. Still, I don't understand.

"Why was I naked?"

"I don't know, big dog, you tell me."

I hold my eyes closed, trying desperately to remember last night. I can hear her calling me a pussy, the others laughing as she did. I sat down on the chair, the one Jeremy had been in and Ivy had sat next to just a few hours before.

"Oh fuck," I breathe, the unfortunate memory worming its way to the surface. "I, yeah, I, uh, I remember."

"Do tell," Deuce says, playfulness making his voice light. I guess I should be glad he isn't gonna fire me for almost getting his shop robbed.

"I was having a... drunken.. Oh God," I moan, grabbing my head as I sink into the couch, still with my jeans around my thighs. I look down at my caged cock and the mess of blankets and pillows on the floor in the new place. "Can you come over?"

There's a pause. "I ain't home," Deuce finally answers, likely calling into question his own idea of me living next door. "I gotta tell you something."

My stomach drops despite the fact I'm seated. "What?"

"I watched the security footage." He pauses. "I saw you strip and I saw you looking for Ivy."

"How do you know I was looking for her?" I ask, not denying he's right. I don't remember looking for her or saying her name, but she was the only thing on my mind last night. Add in some heartache and booze and what he's saying is wholly believable. Sadly.

"Anyway," he says, "she asked me after I watched the footage. Asked me if you and those women were intimate."

Silence eats up the line.

"You coulda got me robbed last night," he says.

"I'm sorry," I grovel truthfully, hating how in the span of one night I managed to upset the only two people I really care about. "I'm... it won't happen again."

More silence but I take the time to get to my feet and grab another bottle of water, pinching the phone between my ear and shoulder as I open it. Finally Deuce says, "Know what else I saw on that footage?"

"Oh my God," I breathe, relief flooding me. If he saw which one of those women did this, then we know where we can find the key or... code or... I grab my package and lift it, hissing as the cage pinches my ball sack. There is a tiny internal gold lock, the perfect size for a little key. "I'm freaking the fuck out right now."

His laugh is booming, and I deserve for him to take joy in this. I do. But right now, I don't give a fuck what Deuce deserves because my cock is IN A FUCKING CAGE.

"Well, get showered and come to work and freak out because it's a work day and the great Trace Calhoun owes me eight hours." He sniffs, letting the last of his laughter play out. "And maybe if you're lucky, Ivy will give you the key."

Ivy.

Ivy has the key.

That means... "Ivy locked up my dick?"

"Don't worry," he says, still unable to shake the laughter. I'm gonna sock him so hard when I see him. "She wore gloves." More laughter. "And she kept the key."

I let Deuce enjoy this because the only thing on my mind? Getting to my little Firecracker.

FIFTEEN

"Trace... But you can call me God."

Ivy

"It's your first solo session today!" Dolly squeaks, jumping up and down while holding her pregnant belly. "I'm so excited!"

"Me too!" Juni adds, both of them coming to my sides, making an Ivy sandwich.

"Okayyy," I draw out, shimmying from their grasps. My fingers inch their way around the collar of my hoodie, beneath the fleece. I sigh when I connect with the cool metal of the small key. "I'm excited, too. Nervous, of course, but... overall," I say, privately stroking the key beneath my sweatshirt. "Really excited."

"You're gonna crush it. Let me see the dick trap sketches again," Juni says, dragging a knife over a piece of toast, leaving Strawbarb jam in its wake. Strawbarb is her strawberry and rhubarb blend, and it's my favorite.

I snatch the sketch pad up and pass it off. Juni, while eating toast, and Dolly, while rubbing her pregnant belly, nod and coo as they take in my sketch of a male chastity cage.

Gotta love that support.

"Wow, it's gorgeous," Juni sighs, shaking her head, eyes full of pride. "Truly beautiful, Ivy."

Dolly dusts her fingertip over the sketch, biting into her bottom lip before she says, "It's so pretty, Ivy. It's going to be a beautiful tattoo."

Another hug is needed and while my eyes don't mist over, my heart threatens to explode. A knot clogs in my throat but I swallow it down, offering them a smile instead of tears. "Thank you, guys." I look down at the chastity cage, and imagine Trace this morning. The sketch is great—it's probably my best work. Ever.

The shading is perfect. The keyhole is subtly visible, starting an interest in how the device works. That was on purpose. The sleek dip of metal that curves a man's penis is shining brightly under lights. It's both ominous and curious, and the detail is hard not to appreciate.

I'm so proud.

Even with all of that... I've got dick on the brain.

I see through the sketch, into my memories, where Trace's aggravatingly beautiful cock is locked tight in that chastity cage. And again, I touch the key on my neck before pushing hair off my shoulder and grabbing my lunch bag.

"I'm gonna head in and print the stencil and get the station ready," I tell them, and while all that's true, I just need... a minute.

Alone.

"Let us know how it goes," Juni says, waving me off with a sweet smile.

"I can't wait to see pictures," Dolly adds, waddling her way across the yard, back to her and Hudson's place.

I get in Trace's car and slip the key in the ignition, hitting the main road quicker than ever. When I'm a mile away, I pull over, grip the steering wheel, and freak the fuck out.

"Oh Jesus. Oh my God." I shake my head, trying to remember all the tricks Juni has taught me.

Breathe in through your nose and out through your mouth.

Slowly, I take a deep breath in.

I touched his naked body. I put his penis in a metal cage and locked it.

I'm pretty sure in some way that's probably illegal.

Itchiness spreads over me as I cling to the wheel, whimpering about my own rash, aggressive stupidity.

I could go to jail.

Prison even, maybe.

Who the fuck knows.

My heart is racing so fast that my head grows spacy, and I lie back on the headrest and let go of the wheel, focusing on my breathing. My long hair clings to my sweaty neck as I force air out and suck air in.

It's going to be okay. *He's not going to report you to the police.* When you pass out nude and subject the world to your naked body, things might happen.

Okay, that's shitty.

I'll own up to it whenever I need to. Take full accountability that I truly had no real reason that I should have felt justified to put my hands on him.

I can only imagine the grin on his face when he realizes the lengths I went to touch him. He'd just *love* that I didn't let anything stop me, that arrogant asshole.

My lower half pulses and I draw my thighs together to ease

the sudden ache, just thinking of his smile and his cock in that cage.

It was wrong to do.

But it needed to be done.

He won't get me arrested, of that I can reasonably be sure.

Fired, though? Maybe. I hadn't thought of that until now. I shamefully spent last night masturbating instead of freaking out. In hindsight, those could have reasonably switched order.

I send a huge puff of air out of my chest, and take the steering wheel again. After a moment of smoother breathing, I roll down the window, turn on my blinker, and get back to it.

I don't want to be late today, and I have a sneaking suspicion that Trace will be on time.

Normally I like to have protein in my coffee but this morning, my stomach was so uneasy that I didn't have it. Now, though, I feel sick. Nibbling at the inside of my mouth as I take in nosefuls of fresh air, it hits me.

This is it.

I *have* to come clean about how I feel for him.

You don't put your nemesis in a chastity cage.

You don't stay at an apprenticeship with a man you honestly hate.

We bicker. He's an asshole.

But I know he's a good guy. His fractured, unhealed heart shows itself in every second glance, flared nostril and snotty quip. I see his defenses, and understand they were built from pain. I also know that he and I have something rare and precious. I feel our connection in every argument, every moment of pulse-spiking banter. I feel it in the way his eyes linger a moment longer than necessary, searching mine, like he wants to win when we battle but also needs to know that I'm okay. I felt it long before we met, when electricity struck my chest when I looked at his sketches. Truly. I knew it then.

Now I have to make him know it.

Ink Time comes into view, and I have no idea if I killed someone on that drive or not. It was one of those commutes where my mind was so hyper focused elsewhere, I couldn't tell you a detail of anything if my life depended on it.

I'm driving his car. Obviously my car is already at Ink Time, but I know he's already there. I can see him inside, standing with his back to the window, chatting with someone. Deuce, maybe. Or maybe the client. Some clients do that—come really early because they're nervous. Either way, I put the car in park next to my own, take a deep breath and step out. Carefully I place my boot on the door and just as Trace turns, his eyes meeting mine, I thrust, sending the door shut.

It didn't hurt his precious car, but it might look like it did.

Not a great start to the day where I'm supposed to admit how I feel but just being here again reminds me of last night and how he behaved. He didn't let that woman blow him but... he called her there.

He drank.

I make a choice for him: he's done with that bullshit behavior.

Now he has me. And I won't allow him to fall back to bad habits. He's too talented and too good for that.

But his car is meaningless. Just like the money. All that shit is only cool if he is. And lately, he's been a total turd.

I may have some ownership in that, too.

But he started it.

I pull open the door, my nipples hardening at the rush of his pine scent, and the faint notes of shampoo. His hair is down and damp, and he's wearing my favorite things: black jeans with his brown boots, and a slightly fitted and very worn crop t-shirt from Metallica in 1998. His chiseled, artful arms on full display, leading down to those sexy, massive hands of his. Hands that make me wet just looking at them.

I really wish we were alone right now. But I'll make do.

I'm glad I brought a change of panties, though. When our eyes meet, heat pours from my slick pussy, and I clench my thighs.

"Good morning, Ivy," he greets with no smile. He almost seems... detached. But then his eyes skim my bodysuit along the curve of my breasts and the pinch of my nipples. Stopping, I drop my lunch bag, and put my hoodie back on. I'd taken it off after my little meltdown but now, fuck this.

I pull the key on the chain out from the sweatshirt, dropping it over the top, garnering Trace's attention. He blinks a few times, transfixed by the key until his eyes lift to mine.

"I want to talk to you in private," he growls, nostrils flaring. I notice, though, while his nostrils threaten me with puffs of air, he steps apart. He shifts on his feet.

And that means *things* are happening inside that cage. Things that are making him squirm.

I lick my lips and drop my voice to a smoky roar. "I bet you do."

"Trace," Deuce says, setting in motion a pre-debated plan, clearly. Trace smiles at me, his eyes roaring with unruly heat, his lips tight with control. A wild juxtaposition but one he embodies well. It enthralls and terrifies me how much I want this man.

"I'm sorry for everything, Ivy. Last night was my fault, I take responsibility, and I'm sorry for putting you in a position where you weren't safe." His jaw twitches and his chest rises quickly, and I realize he means it.

"Thank you," I say, my words crawling out of me a weakened whisper.

Deuce clears his throat and I drag my misty eyes to him. He

blinks, making me blink, and it's then I realize he's buying me a moment. A second to gather myself before emotion slips and Trace sees. I take a short breath and nod, thanking him in a way he hopefully understands.

"I'm fine. I'm ready to get to my session today," I say, shimmying my shoulders, moving the conversation forward. Deuce seems satisfied that I'm satisfied, and I am.

It's not Deuce's fault what happened. It's Trace's fault. And he knows it.

"She's actually here," Deuce adds, tipping his head to the small set of chairs tucked next to reception. "Your client is waiting."

I smile tightly at Deuce, then at Trace. "Cool."

Internally, I want to squeal with joy and take a selfie because—my first solo client! Holy shit!

But another part of me is achy between my legs, soaking my panties, leaving my thighs covered in needy goosebumps, chilled from my unsated arousal.

That part of me is going a bit wild right now, knowing the key to his freedom is on a chain around my throat, nothing more than an accessory for the day. Like a mood ring or a scrunchie. A dick cage key.

Deuce walks my client, Rochelle, back and we spend the next ten minutes slowly getting reacquainted. She's been in twice before in preparation of today, but it's been a few weeks. We have coffee, catch her up on my apprenticeship status, explaining to her that I'm near the end. And that she's essentially my first client. Trace is quiet most of the time, adding a few encouraging words here and there when my client expresses her nerves for such a private thing about their lives to be made public.

He's great with her, but tense and standoffish with me. But I deserve that.

After she's in the chair, the stencil is printed and the design is on Rochelle, Trace decides to get chatty. My stomach clenches as I bring the needle to her skin and begin.

"So, Rochelle," Trace starts, sipping on a cup of dark roast black coffee. God that is so him.

But so hot, too.

"Yes?" she asks, and I love Rochelle so much for knowing who Trace is, and not giving a shit. She asked me privately if I could confirm that he is *that* Trace Calhoun and that it isn't a strange coincidence. Once I told her it's him, she waved it all off. "Eh, he can prove to me he isn't the stereotypical, self-involved, pseudo-famous hypocritical male before I swoon." We bumped fists on that.

"I don't understand men who don't want control." He nods to her upper thigh where I'm currently inking the design. Alluding to the chastity cage—the one Rochelle doesn't know he's currently wearing—he says, "I want control of my cock. And I want to be in control during sex." He shakes his head before taking a sip of his coffee. "All the control." I feel his eyes burning holes through me.

Rochelle smiles, her eyes soft and tender. "Are you single?"

My face falls. Holy shit. He's not going to like where this is going.

"I am," he grumbles.

"Relationship issues?" she asks, her voice still so soft that he can't help but answer honestly. He doesn't want to give in to this. He doesn't want her to be right.

"Yeah, maybe." He narrows his gaze and my pulse skips.

"So how's that control working out for you?" Rochelle asks, tipping her chin to the side just slightly, in a position that can only be described as a satisfied power player.

But he's silent, because he and I both know that Rochelle has a very good point.

~

M FIRST SESSION WENT INCREDIBLY WELL. WE TOOK
photos of it afterward—lots of photos. With the shop camera,
Connor got some on his phone, Deuce even on his, and Trace?
He took photos with my phone, making sure they were perfect.
He held Rochelle there an extra twenty five minutes taking
photos.

I called Juniper and Dolly and told them the good news,
promising that as soon as Dolly isn't pregnant, we'd all share a
bottle of champagne to celebrate. After I got off the phone,
Deuce, Connor, Trace and I went across the street and had root
beer floats. It was a glorious hour, and the rest of the day has
been a blur.

Avoiding Trace so that we don't have to have the serious
talk just yet has been... kinda fun, if I'm being honest. His
serious looks and chest-rumbling growls have me hot and both-
ered, but knowing there will be a time to come clean? I don't
know how he's going to react so I don't let myself think about it.

That's *future* Ivy's problem.

But my epic session with Rochelle this morning and my
horndog haze from last night is either about to pay off or make
me look like a complete creep. Weeks back, after presenting her
new tattoo design to her partner, Rochelle was so happy with
his reaction she came back and gave me a gift.

It's sitting in a bag in the supply cupboard, because I didn't
exactly know what to do with it. The note attached said,
*"Because you're good at cages, you may be good at other things,
too. XO, Ms. R."*

I knew exactly what it was by just looking in the bag.

And I have to say, that domme kinda saved me today
because I didn't have a great plan until now.

"Heading out to have sundaes with Ev and Ace," Deuce

says, clapping a proud hand across my shoulders. "Good job today, Ivy."

Trace appears next to Deuce. "Heading out?"

Deuce glances at his watch. "Yeah. The shop has another hour of daylight. Think you can manage not to get blackout drunk and get us robbed? Or should I stay?"

"Har har," Trace mocks. "Tell Ev I said hi."

"We're neighbors," Deuce reminds him. "You could come by and say hi yourself."

Deuce smiles at me. "See you tomorrow, Ivy."

"Later, Deuce."

From the back door, Connor and Sandi call their goodbyes. I tip my head their way as the door seals shut. "Everyone's taking off?"

Trace smiles, and my stomach flutters. "I told them to go. I told them," he says, stepping toward me, eating up my personal space. I'd give him the damn fork if he wanted. "I said, I need some alone time with *my apprentice.*"

I swallow thickly, my heart racing. "Yeah?" I'm suddenly aware of the key at my throat.

He outstretches his hand, palm up. His solid fingers wiggle as he silently coaxes me, but all that does is make my pussy clench, imagining those digits slipping inside of me. With one fell swoop, his face is mere inches from mine, and I don't know when he found the time to slip away and brush his teeth, but mint stings my lips. "Give it to me."

I fight the urge to finger the edges of the small key, to show him and torture him with how close his freedom is. But this is *my* time. I may never have Trace Calhoun as captivated as I have him now, with his cock locked and the key to it in my possession.

"Not until you're ready."

His eyes flick between mine but he stays close to my face,

unmoving. "Not until I'm ready?" he repeats, drawing the words out as if he'll find the subtext in them. But he won't because there is none.

I nod. "Yep. Not until you're ready." I lick my lips and love that his gaze follows the tip of my tongue as it slides along my mouth. "Not until you learn."

"Learn?" To his credit, his face only slightly bunches, his wrinkled nose calling attention to his piercing. My stomach flutters each time I notice another wild detail about Trace.

Putting on a shield of confident indifference, I smile at him as I get to my feet, bringing our faces and bodies even closer than a moment ago. "You'll learn that you don't use your cock as a weapon to hurt the woman you care about."

He opens his mouth but I press my finger to his lips. "No matter what she does, you don't use your body as a weapon." With my heart in my throat and my hands clammy as shit, I lean forward, take a breath, and press my lips to his.

They're soft, so much softer than I'd ever imagined. And I *have* imagined. Many times alone in my room with his sketches on my phone in my hand, my other hand pinching my clit as I ease the ache of wanting him.

I'd envision him dusting his lips against mine, pushing his way inside of me as he warned me of his size, warned me of the upcoming twist of pleasure and pain.

And even though my plan is a soft, slow kiss with the right amount of pressure and promise, I veer off course within the first few seconds, moaning into his mouth, past his soft lips.

He groans, reaching behind me, surprising me with a hand in my hair, his fingers gripping me passionately. His other hand falls to my hip, and suddenly, our kiss transforms from soft and timid to wild and frantic.

"You'll learn," I breathe as his lips slide from my mouth to my cheek, along the curve of my chin and down my throat. He sucks at my pulse point, causing my hands to fall to his shoulders, gripping and slapping him.

"Fuck, Ivy, you make me fucking crazy," he groans, pressing his groin against mine. Suddenly, he jerks back, his lips swollen from journeying over my body. My nipples ache beneath my bodysuit and sweatshirt as my pussy weeps for him. "Now's when I'd have you cup my cock and feel just what you do to me."

I tug my off my sweatshirt and toss it aside, grabbing the key at my throat. I hold it until he looks, and he growls his arousal and frustration, taking me by the hips. "You're fucking crazy, you know that?" he says, pressing his lips to my throat, sucking the key onto his tongue.

My head falls back and my legs spread, allowing Trace to take me by the hips and sit me atop the table. "Am I?" I breathe, fishing my fingers through his hair as he moves his mouth all over my body. His kisses trail my shoulders and down my arms, along my belly and thighs, too. Finally, he finds my breast, sealing his mouth over my covered nipple, making me moan.

"God," I breathe, loving the feel of his soft hair between my fingers as he sucks my clothed breast. It'd feel better with no clothing between us, but as it is, this is questionable enough for being on camera.

"Trace," he murmurs, moving his mouth to my other covered breast to suck that nipple. "But you can call me God."

"Oh, shut up," I breathe, my chest heaving as his large hands skate up my sides, causing another rush of arousal to gush from my core. "And stop—" I press against him, trying to get him to stop. I don't want him to stop, but I do want him to learn.

He rises, panting, still standing between my legs. "Stop?"

Pushing to my elbows, I blink up at him, our simmering eye contact dousing my nerves with cold water. "I had a great day here," I whisper, "and now I'm going to have a great orgasm to end it."

He reaches for his belt, but I shake my head, telling him to stop. My lower half vibrates when he immediately ceases on command. "I need the key," he breathes, and for a split second, I realize *he thinks he's getting out.*

He thinks that the words are the lesson, that simply telling him his cock isn't a device is where it ends. If he lets me, I will teach him. But that involves him staying in chastity.

"No, you don't. You need to get me the bag from the floor and take your pants off."

With his hair around his shoulders and his chest heaving, the sight of a horny Trace, lips swollen from kissing me, a feral instinct claws up my legs and grabs control. I get off the table and grab his hand just as he snatches the bag from the ground. By the wrist, I lead him into the back office.

The only place where there are no cameras.

"Get undressed and I'm going to lock the door and set the code," I tell him, happy that we're at least at closing time. Closing the shop up to fuck feels scummy, and not something I'd ever envisioned doing when finally at a studio. Then again, Trace is in chastity and getting naked for me.

After locking the door, I swipe the economy tub of petroleum jelly from the supply closet, and kick open the office with my boot. Trace startles but doesn't move to hide himself, which only turns me on that much more.

I like a bold man, one unafraid of new things, and one not ashamed to be vulnerable for someone he cares about.

I stare at his balls, pink and purple with strain, hanging from the metal cage. His cock swells beneath the frame, pushing out of the slats, and his large hands hang down obediently at his sides. His chest and groin, chiseled and covered in ink, flex as he twists his body, pushing aside the office chair to make room for me.

I close the door behind us and reach into the bag, pulling out the strap and dildo.

"Fuck no," he grounds out, shaking his head, pointing a wobbly finger at the toy. "You are not fucking me with that."

We stand in silence, the strap-on held out between us, a physical and metaphorical barrier.

After a moment he says, "You at least gonna be naked?"

A smirk curls my lips. "I'm not fucking you, I'm fucking myself." Stepping toward him I rise to my toes to steal a kiss from his lips, one he hungrily leans into. God, I love that. "But I will fuck you with this one day. And you'll be moaning for me to make you come in my hand as I jack you." I lick my lips, tasting our kiss. "*Fuck me, baby, fuck me and jack me,*" I crow, mimicking how he'll sound.

His eyes widen and one hand falls to his caged cock. "Fuck, Ivy. You're so... hot."

He glances down at the strap while watching me step into the harness, adjusting the nylon at my hips so it fits well. "You're... fucking yourself?"

I nod. "I told you, I want to celebrate my great day. But I'm smart, Trace. I'm a multitasker. I can come all over this dildo," I tell him, stroking my fist down the rubber cock bobbing from my center, "and I can teach you a lesson. Teach you that your cock isn't a tool to get revenge or to give you a temporary high. From here on out, your cock isn't even yours."

"No?" he asks, his voice a baited whisper.

I shake my head. "It's mine. And *my cock* is going to learn how to find pleasure without being a total whore." I slap his caged cock, making him jolt and groan. "Look at me," I tell him, but he wallows in the cock slap so much that I have to reach out and take ownership of his jaw, forcing his eyes to come to mine.

"It was a tiny slap, you're fine," I tell him, decidedly. "Now, look at me in this strap-on. Look," I command, heat blooming behind my ribs as his dark eyes roam over my body. "See how it fits?"

He nods.

"Good." I unclip the nylon straps at each hip and shimmy out of it. "Now put it on."

"Wh—" he starts but I cut him off by pulling down the straps of my bodysuit, revealing my naked breasts for the first time. I look down at my nipples, pink and plucky, and up at Trace. His mouth is parted, eyes hooded, locked on my breasts. I kick out of my leggings easily.

"Your tits are fucking perfect, Ivy," he breathes, raspy and tender.

"I know," I agree, cupping my bare hands to them. "And I'll let you hold them and suck on them if you learn your lesson." The strap is stagnant at his calves as he stays half bent over, eyes on me. I snap. "Stay focused, Trace Calhoun."

Saying his full name sends a shiver up my spine, causing bumps to sear my flesh. I can't believe this is happening. This is the first and only time I allow myself a moment to be starstruck. But after he secures the strap over his chastity cage, my mind goes to one thing: riding him and taking the orgasm I've been masturbating to for years.

I nod to the large table that's been turned into a makeshift desk. "Get on your back."

Trace begins moving the few items on top of the desk to the filing cabinet adjacent, stealing moments to take in my naked body. He drags the blunt end of his fingertip along my pubic bone, making me shudder. "Ink would look good here."

My mouth is dry, but I pretend that it isn't. I pretend I'm not nervous to climb on top of the man I've been dreaming about for ages and take a wet, messy orgasm from him. "What kind?"

His eyes lift to mine. "My name."

I smirk, knowing he's teasing but envisioning just how hot it would be to have his name on me. I nod to his cock before reaching out and cupping the heavy cage and swollen balls in my palm. "Or this. I'd love ink to remember this forever."

He groans. "Fuck, that feels... good. Aggravating because I can't get hard and I can't fucking touch my cock, but still... it feels good."

I drag my fingertip over his cock jutting from between his hips, using my other hand to gently stroke the seam of his balls.

"Goddamnit, why does it feel like you're jacking me off right now?" he rasps, sitting on his elbows as he watches me coat the dildo and tease his sack.

"Because you wish I was, so this is playing tricks on you," I whisper, coming off like an experienced domme. But I'm not. It's just... doing this with him feels natural. I feel as in my element with his caged cock in my hand as I do with a pencil in it.

"Tell me, last night when you told that woman to get on her knees," I start, climbing onto the desk, throwing one leg around him. I hover above the dildo, and Trace reaches out, touching my cunt for the first time.

My head falls back. "God that feels good," I groan, allowing myself just a moment of pleasure before it's back to business. I lift my head and meet his eyes. "Tell me how you had your way with her mouth."

His Adam's apple bobs as his hands move to my hips. Slowly, I work my way down his body, toward his groin. My face hovers over the glistening cock, which bobs as I stroke it. Smiling, I say, "Tell me, Trace. Tell me what you were going to say to her."

He eyes the cock just inches from my mouth. "Say it again," I command, my lips dusting the crown.

"Open up and choke on this cock you've been dying to taste," he whispers, and like a good girl hell-bent on reforming her broken boy, I lower my mouth until the cock slides onto my tongue.

He feeds his fingers through my hair, jerking my head deeper. Tilting his hips, the dildo fills my throat, making both of us groan. I lift my gaze from his groin, finding his eyes already on me.

"Choke on my cock, Ivy," he whispers, thrusting his hips impatiently, sending the cock down my throat, impaling me in short thrusts. His eyes widen as I choke, but I stay down on the cock, using my free hand to tease *his* balls. "Choke on me, choke on what I know you've been dying to taste," he murmurs, my lips forming a tight seal around the cock. He groans something feral and fierce, my throat bobbing with my first swallow of thick saliva. He holds my head and fucks my face for another minute or two, but the pressure is building, and I know if I don't get fucked soon, I'll come anyway.

And that's where I need *him*, not me.

I pop off and swat his hands away, making him grumble and groan, pushing back up to his elbows. Poor Deuce. I'm sure he doesn't want anyone's bare ass on his desk.

"It's time for me to fuck this cock you want me to choke on so badly," I breathe, biting into my bottom lip as I position myself at his groin, one foot on either side of his thighs. "So talk me through it, Trace," I whisper, aligning the glistening, spit-coated rubber cock at my swollen, slick pussy lips. "Tell me how you'd have fucked her."

Sweat glistens along his hairline as he reaches out, dragging his fingers along the seam of my cunt, exploring my arousal. There's so much of it, so many signs that I'm throbbing for him, for this. He groans, bringing his fingers to his mouth, driving them inside as his eyes flutter closed.

"Fucking hell, Ivy," he moans as his eyes open, finding mine, laced with need. "I could taste your pussy every day, you're so sweet."

I slap his face, making his eyes widen. "Did I say taste me or did I say tell me how you'd have fucked her?"

Leaning over, I grab the petroleum and unscrew the lid. Dipping my hand in, I scoop some up and slather it down the shaft of the cock.

Reaching down, I hold the cock steady and I drop down on it, impaling myself in one swift push. I gasp, I press a palm low to my belly, I moan, I cling to his chest and squeeze my eyes closed, willing myself to accept the swift intrusion.

"So. Full," I manage, wiggling my hips as I slowly open my eyes again. His are everywhere. On the place where the toy fills me. On my nipples. At my throat.

Holding my eyes.

"I'd tell her to bounce. I'd tell her to bounce on my cock until I was close, and then I'd tell her to grind hard when I come. Grind that tight, wet cunt against me to send me over the edge, to make me leave my cum urgently, deep inside of her," he says hoarsely.

With my hands on his chest, I grip him and move, working my hips in a slow pattern that makes his eyes roll back. He sucks his lip beneath his teeth as sweat slides down his temple.

"This is fucking torture," he groans.

I slap his face again. "Watch me as I torture you. Keep your eyes open, Trace."

I ride him faster. "God I love the way my name sounds when you say it."

My hips move, my thighs tighten around his hips and I drop a hand to my clit and stroke the swollen bud. "Why?" I breathe, my body flooding with urgent electricity, jolts of energy that press against my belly and pussy, an explosion growing.

"You make it sound good," he moans as I reach back, stroking his swollen sack with the tips of my fingers. "You make me sound good."

With his hot sack in my palm, I roll him around, all while gyrating my hips so that the dildo nudges the sweet spot. My stomach clenches and my thighs tighten as Trace sucks in a heated breath through his teeth. His jaw is tight, restraint etched into his handsome features. The knife-wielding octopus comes to my throat, his thumb pressing the key to my body.

He holds me there while I ride the dildo, fucking myself harder and faster as the sight of Trace beneath me starts to take hold. His nostrils flare as his fingers sink into my throat, touching my pulse.

"What do you tell them when you come?" I rasp, my orgasm spearing through my thighs, twisting in a knot in my pussy. I'm so close. Dangerously close.

"To take it," he utters, his dark eyes set on mine. His focus unfurls the orgasm inside me, bringing it to full bloom. With the hand behind my ass, I grab his caged cock and squeeze just as the first wave hits me. Clenching around the toy, I keep my eyes pinned on him as I moan, "Take it, take it, Trace."

Grinding my body against his, only a trace of the dildo can be seen as I fuck myself hard, coming in relentless, powerful waves.

"Fucking fuck!" Trace howls, still holding my throat, his other hand on my hip as a hot stream tears from the slit in the cage, coating my fingers, falling onto the desk with a thud. My eyes widen as I rock through my orgasm, realizing that Trace is coming as I fuck myself on top of him.

"You," I breathe, rocking and clenching, grinding and

moaning. I can't finish my thought because there's more warm cream coating my fingers and palm and for a million dollars, I can't take my eyes off of him.

Intensely, he holds my gaze as he comes, his body pulsing and thrumming beneath me as I drench the toy. He's breathing hard and so am I, but I don't try to finish that sentence, and he doesn't ask. When the last of the electric orgasm has torn free from me, and from him, I rise up, watching the dildo slide out of me slowly. It's coated in me, and before I even climb off of him, he's dragging his thumb against it, bringing it to his lips.

Once I'm on my feet, I take his hand and help him sit up on the desk. We survey the scene.

Thick, white ribbons of cum streak the desk, and I have the strongest urge to take a photo, to remember the way I made him explode. But I don't. Instead, I grab a roll of paper towels and wipe up the dildo, carefully cleaning up the desk with disinfectant, and he steps out of the harness.

"I'll wash it at home. Don't really wanna be on camera washing sex toys at work," I say to Trace, our first post-coital conversation.

He scratches the back of his head as he swings his legs off the desk. We take a moment to redress, awkwardly bumping our heads together as we both bend to put our pants back on. When we're redressed, Trace outstretches his palm to me.

My gaze ping-pongs over it. "What?"

"The key," he says.

I tuck my hair behind my ears, and adjust the crotch of my bodysuit before rolling the waist of my leggings. "Were you going to fuck her because you were angry?"

I shove my foot into one of my boots, keeping my eyes on him. He opens his mouth, dragging his hand over it, searching for words he can't find. But the answer is simple.

"You invited those women to Ink Time last night. Were you going to fuck one of them out of anger?"

He swallows. "Yes."

I walk my fingers up his chest, coming to grip the neckline of his t-shirt, dragging his mouth to mine. We don't kiss but we're close when I ask, "You were angry at me?"

He nods, barely. "Yes."

"Because you didn't like me going out with Jeremy."

Another nod, another "Yes."

"Because you like me."

This time, nothing. I reach down and twist his trapped balls through his jeans, still swollen despite the release. He sucks in a breath. "Yes."

I let go, rock to my toes and press my lips to his. "One lesson isn't enough. You really need to learn. Because we're worth more than pissing it all away if you don't get your way one night." I kiss him again. "You wouldn't let me tattoo someone after just one lesson, would you?"

He groans.

But he takes my face in both of his hands and kisses me so long and deep, I'm lightheaded. When he releases me he says, "You did good today, Firecracker. On your first session and with me."

I want to kiss him again, but the closeness of the moment is vacuumed out when he opens the office door and breaks the spell. "You get to me like no one else has, in the best ways."

I touch the key on my neck and he winks. "See you bright and early tomorrow." I watch him walk through the studio toward the door where he stops and turns, facing me. "How'd you feel in my car?"

I smile. "Pompous."

He rolls his eyes. "Liar."

SIXTEEN

But I'm keeping the key

Trace

"I'll take it to go, thanks, Lucy." I slip onto a barstool at the diner's counter in the back and rest my head in my hands.

I've been in a wild headspace since yesterday.

I spent a full day in this cage, and when I thought I'd be left to navigate a weird and tough conversation with Ivy, it turned into... more.

Staring at the line cook scrambling eggs, my mind veers to Ivy's perfect body, the way resting my hands on her naked hips feels like being home.

More than her being sexy as hell and fucking a dildo strapped to my body, she handles me in a way no one ever has. She didn't force me to wobble through a weak explanation, she didn't lash out or yell. There were no tears of hurt or betrayal.

She called me on my shit move, and made me pay. Simple.

But in the way she made me pay, we both got to come *and* come clean.

She likes me, too. What she did last night wasn't just to teach me. It's to claim me. Ivy Ellington wants to claim me and although I told myself I'd never let another woman stake claim to me again, I'm realizing how foolish it would be to make good on that jaded promise.

As much as it terrifies me to admit it, I want Ivy in that serious, permanent way. The desire to be near her, talk to her, get her opinion, hold her, taste her—the need has surfaced and I can't drink it down any longer.

It's growing, too. It started as a little burn deep in my bones in some unreachable place. I barely felt it, the hot little flicker of awareness when she came into the room.

But as time went on, that ember grew. Every salty comeback, every shitty smirk, every tender touch and subtle glance fanned that ember, growing it into what it is now. An all-consuming blaze, eating up all of my other hopes and dreams, swiping at my fears and insecurities. She's quickly becoming the only thing I think about. The only thing that matters, and if I'm being honest, I care about the art and tattooing much more with her around.

She reignites my passion, reminds me of why I'm here in Bluebell in the first place. Because I'm sick of that life I keep going back to and instead of sinking into toxic familiarity, it's time for me to grow a bigger pair and move past all that shit.

It's time for me to get the girl, the one that actually wants me.

I dig my phone from my pocket, and peer around me, making sure no one is witnessing the dumb-ass grin sweeping my face at the thought of texting that little Firecracker.

Mornin' Firecracker.

Lucy walks up with a mug in one hand and a carafe of coffee in the other. I point at it. "Actually, I'll take two." I set the phone down for a moment. "Hey, Lucy, I met your mom at the bowling alley."

She sets down my mug, reaching for another under the counter. "Did you get the cream soda float?"

I shake my head. "Root beer. But next time I'll try it."

She winks. "Here or to go?"

"To go," I smile.

She drums her fingers against the counter. "One of these wouldn't be for Miss Ivy, now would it?"

I nod. "Yeah, actually." I nod toward the back, where the cooks are working. "Part of that is for her, too."

"Well," Lucy says, leaning over the counter. "Ivy likes her coffee with protein powder. But you gotta blend it with a little milk first, then add the coffee."

I stare at the paper cups she pulls out from beneath the counter and watch her fill one. "I guess just... leave room?" I suggest, knowing I can't get my hands on protein powder so I can't bring her the coffee she likes best.

That vexes me.

Lucy nods, filling the cup. "Sure thing, sweetheart. Food will be out in a minute."

Once she walks away, I return to my phone, relieved to see Ivy has responded.

Hodwy.

I smirk at the screen.

You're never gonna let me live that down, are you?

Why would I?

I like that you call me Firecracker.

And *I* like that she's telling me what she likes. My thumbs work quickly, the morning commotion of the diner falling away as I focus on Ivy.

Tried a can opener on my dick this morning. You know. To get the cage off. Didn't work.

And don't think you're off the hook, by the way.

LOL. Can opener. You didn't tell me you're funny!

Off the hook?

In my periphery, someone sits next to me at the counter. But I don't take my eyes off the screen, the phone moving between my hands as I type.

You touched my naked body without my consent to get me in this device.

You gotta pay the piper for that one, baby.

Is the piper your dick? If so, I paid him yesterday, remember?

Or do you need a refresher?

I smirk.

I think the proper payment comes in the form of a tiny silver key.

I don't.

I'm bringing you breakfast.

Thank you.

But I'm keeping the key.

I watch as three dots bounce along the screen, and nearly jump when a hand comes down on my forearm. Flipping the phone screen down, I glance over to find Deuce sitting next to me, and Hudson on the other side of him. It irks me to leave that message unread. What did it say?

"Gentlemen," I greet, tipping my invisible cowboy hat.

I may live in cowboy country now but I am not wearing a fucking hat. Hudson lifts his from his head, resting it atop the bar counter as he greets me hello.

"Trace, good to see you," he says, then lifts his phone to his ear, reading the menu to someone.

Deuce turns to face me. "Morning."

I sip my coffee. "Good morning."

Lucy appears, sliding the plastic bag onto the counter, reciting my order. "Two short stacks, two eggs, four slices of bacon and two fruits, to go."

I nod and leave a wad of cash on the counter, far more than the total. "Thanks, Lucy."

Deuce grins. "You learned her name."

I pop my knuckles. "Yes, I did."

He hooks a finger in the bag. "Speaking of Ivy–"

"How'd you know this isn't all for me?"

He glances at Hudson, who is still engrossed in his phone conversation, then looks back my way. "Is it?"

I shake my head. "No. I'm bringing breakfast to Ivy at work."

He nods. "About Ivy."

My skin grows hot, and the weight of the cage between

my thighs causes me to shift nervously on the barstool. I pull my hair off my neck and wrap an elastic around it. "What's up?"

"I think she earned some skin for saving your ass." At that precise moment, Hudson ends his call, writing furiously on the back of some receipt he dug out of his wallet.

I cock a brow. "Skin?"

Deuce rolls his eyes. "Jesus, what did you do last night that you forgot the night before?" He shakes his head. "Ink. Typical rite of passage is inking herself at the end of her apprenticeship, but she's already inked herself plenty so... I was thinking it should be you she inks."

"Yeah," I say, holding back the smirk that threatens to peek through my curved-down lips as I picture Ivy straddling me, her little gloved hands working as she leaves her mark on me permanently.

Though I know she's already done that.

"She did great yesterday. And I think we both know she's got the experience to start her own client list." He sips his coffee and my pulse picks up, a sick foreboding edging in. "Thought we could wrap up her apprenticeship this week, let her get started on her own. Out of your hair."

Anger burns in my toes, rapidly gaining momentum as it tears through me, making my neck flush and my cheeks simmer. "One good tattoo doesn't mean she's ready to work on her own," I grumble, eyeing her coffee cup and the slow trickle of steam drifting from the mouth hole. If she's on her own, if she doesn't need me... she may not want me.

"She's not good enough to ink on her own full time," I finish, snatching the plastic bag of food off the counter. The truth is? She's beyond ready and more than good enough. It's me that isn't. I can't lose her before I have her, and for whatever fucked-up reason, that's what this feels like. I leave my coffee on the counter and grab hers, tip my head at Deuce and Hudson, and turn to leave.

I have a hot breakfast for my girl, and I want to take it to her, not hear about how she ought to do her own thing.

Only, when I turn, I find Ivy standing behind me, her phone in her hand. Her hair is down and straight, the onyx shining in the morning light pouring in through the door. She's wearing her boots, the handle of her knife peeking out, making my caged cock throb. In leggings and an oversized hoodie with a leather vest over the top, she looks like a goddamn wet dream. Like every fantasy I've ever had come to life.

Like my future wife.

From my pocket, my phone dings. I pull it out and look at it.

IVY

Look behind you dummy.

I blink at her, wind knocked from my chest as I notice her eyes.

They're misty and damp.

"Not good enough?" she questions hoarsely, her head bobbing. I hate that her eyes fall to my boots, and that she stares at them for a long moment before her gaze lifts to mine again.

A tear slips down her cheek, through her thick lashes. "I'm glad we still have time to work together," she finally says, taking a few steps backward, which feels greatly metaphorical.

"Ivy," I call, reaching out, the bag of food falling to the floor with a crash. "Ivy, wait."

But she's gone before I can do anything, and I only have myself to blame.

SEVENTEEN

Boss's orders.

Ivy

My rage is blinding me. Truly. I cannot see anything but epic darkness. Ringing fills my ears, so I cup my hands over them protectively and drop to a crouch, getting my bearings. It's just a panic attack, I tell myself, forcing deep breaths and rational talk. You're having a major moment, you're going into fight or flight. You got this. Just breathe, let it flow through you, and come back together.

A minute passes until I get back up, catch my breath, push my hair off my face and cross the street. Heading into Ink Time, I take a spot at my little table in the back, working on a redo for Connor's client today.

They're turning their old lover's name into a dagger wrapped in—fittingly—ivy. And I've been tasked with the sketch that ultimately Connor will ink.

That is all I focus on.

Turning *Stephanie* into a sharp, dangerous blade.

After last night, I thought we were in a new place. But then I catch that jerk saying I'm not good enough. With my head down, I let a tear slip out and don't take care to chase it. It plunks on my paper, sliding off the tip of my nose.

"That," Deuce says, startling me with his presence at my back.

I swipe beneath my eye and keep my chin held high. "What?"

"That wet spot on the paper. It's why I initiated ending the apprenticeship." His gaze settles awkwardly on me, waiting for a response.

"So you wanted to cut me loose and he said I wasn't good enough to be set free." I give him my bitchiest, most curt smile. "Really supportive workplace," I say, the sarcasm doing a shitty job of masking the hurt.

"Ivy," he says carefully, slowly, deliberately, like drawing out my name is giving me time to prepare for something bad. My stomach clenches, but there are no more tears. "You're falling for him, and I don't know that he's ready to catch you. Or anyone, for that matter."

I want to ask him how or why Trace might hurt me, but I also don't want to know. Maybe I'll find out, and maybe he will be right.

But maybe he won't.

My bottom lip wobbles annoyingly. "Where is he?" And by that, I'm crying, *why didn't he follow me?*

"I told him to take a walk. Catch his breath. He was upset and I know you're upset and that's... not a good combo for *work.*"

I bring my hands to my forehead, kneading the panic and tension, but it doesn't help. "God, I'm so sorry, Deuce, you gave me this apprenticeship and now everything is a fucking mess. I held women at knife point and because of me, the reason people come to Ink Time is now walking down the street."

"Hey," Deuce growls, "Connor and Rash held it down at the other location for years before Trace," he says, Rash being the artist that quit the shop in Riverside because he met a woman in Oakcreek. "Trace is my best friend. He's a great artist. But Ink Time will make it with or without him."

"Same goes for me. And I'm newer and need more help. Fire me, don't fire Trace," I exhale, still staring at my sketch, unable to meet his eyes.

"Nobody is getting fired, so let's clear that up. And second, you're right. I won't lie. I don't need either of you." He leans down, the scent of coffee and waffle syrup easing my sharp defenses. The smell of Goode's diner brings me comfort. Deuce brings me comfort. "But I *want* you at Ink Time, Ivy. And I want Trace, too."

I blink up at him as he rises, loving that he doesn't acknowledge the fresh set of tears stinging my cheeks. "I'm sorry I'm making things complicated."

Deuce scuffs his boot against the tile, shaking his head. "Life is complicated. Don't apologize. And..." He scratches the back of his neck. "Trace cares about you, he's just a little behind on how to show it."

My chest squeezes at his words. I know Trace cares about me. I've been confident in that truth for a while. But his demons are standing between us, and while I thought the cage would help, I'm realizing, I need to do more.

"Some men need more help than others," I say, smiling away the traces of tears left on my cheeks. "My feelings got hurt today. But he's right. I'm not ready to be on my own. And I'm not a quitter and equally, I don't want anyone to play favorites for me. I'll be done with the apprenticeship in six weeks like we planned."

"He didn't mean that, you know," Deuce offers softly. I peer around the top of my cube as Connor comes into the shop, a bouquet of roses in his hand. He reaches over the partition and lowers them to my desk.

"For your first piece yesterday," he says with a wink. He's a friend, and they were flowers for a friend. But all the same, I'm kind of glad that Trace isn't here to see it.

"Thanks, Connor," I say, getting to my feet in time to hug him over the partition.

"I hope you celebrated last night," he says with a wink before he returns to his own work, settling in.

I face Deuce, ignoring the flood of memories from last night that come rushing back. I came all over Trace and he came all over me, and we didn't even have sex. But we left that space closer than before, more understanding of our needs.

"He's scared if you ain't his apprentice, he'll lose you to..." Deuce nods to Connor. "Literally anyone else."

"How can he lose something he doesn't even have?" I question, though without a title, I'm his. I've always been his, I'm just waiting for his stupid ass to realize that.

Deuce shrugs. "He's taking the morning off to cool down, boss's orders."

I arch a brow. "Did you tell him it was the boss's orders?"

He smirks. "Yeah, he loved that. Not as much as he loved me suggesting you end the apprenticeship early but... close." With another consoling pat on my shoulder, Deuce leaves me to sketch.

And the entire morning, I brainstorm ways I can show Trace that trust and love are important.

Trusting and loving me? Necessary.

EIGHTEEN

Like a puppy

Trace

"Your daddy told you to stay put," Hudson says, glancing at his phone again.

"He ain't my daddy," I growl, pacing behind the row of barstools at the diner counter.

Hudson pulls a toothpick from his lips, eyeing me. "He told you to calm down, said you can't come to the shop till after lunch, and then said stay put." He shrugs. "I got two kids. That sounds a lot like you getting grounded by Daddy."

I roll my eyes. "He wants me to calm down, that's all. And stop saying daddy," I grumble while I continue to stomp back and forth, feeding my hands through my hair, wondering why I always gotta say the worst fucking thing instead of how I actually feel.

"And are ya?" Hudson asks, pouring the warmed maple syrup into a to-go container. He begins filling another one.

"Think you got enough syrup?" I question, taking out my frustration anywhere I can.

"Not for what Dolly has planned." He pops the lid on and pinches the top of his hat, resting it on his head. "Well, if you don't mind a word of advice from a man married to an Ellington sister–"

He lifts the plastic bags full of food from the counter, leaving a healthy tip for Lucy. I realize then that if things work out with Ivy, if I can get my shit together, this man may be my brother-in-law. Which would make Deuce... Well, nothing. But I'd be in their circle. I'd belong somewhere. Somewhere I think I actually enjoy being. With people I like.

Who, if I get my shit together now, may actually like me too. Not Trace Calhoun the has-been TV star but actually me.

Nodding, I welcome Hudson's advice.

"Well, from what I've observed, you seem a bit... tantrum-y."

I press a hand to my chest, still worked up from earlier. Now? "Tantrum-y?" I repeat. This cowboy boot-wearing, buckle-loving, hay-baling guy is gonna call me tantrum-y. "I am not," I retort angrily, stomping my boot.

Hudson's eyes veer to my boot, and my gaze follows. A moment of silence passes.

"You gotta have a level head with these women, okay? Because they're smart, and if you're all," he makes this face like he just licked a lemon, "all the time, then it makes it hard for things to happen." Gathering the second plastic bag full of food, he says, "I pushed Dolly away for stupid reasons. She stuck around. I'm just saying, don't think of stupid reasons to prolong the inevitable."

"Inevitable?" I repeat.

"You're a one-word master, aren't ya?" Hudson moves past me toward the door. "Ivy likes you. Ellington women get what they want."

"I like Ivy, too," I admit, feeling like a fourteen-year-old talking to my guidance counselor.

"So then, quit being a baby, get over whatever you got to get over, and accept that you're hers."

I can't help but chuckle at that. "Isn't that my line? Shouldn't I be the one calling her mine?"

He smirks. "Sure. Try that." He steps one foot onto the sidewalk. "Get over yourself. That's my best advice."

Then he takes his five thousand bags of food, his gallon of syrup and his coffee and goes to meet his pregnant wife.

And I find myself jealous of the cowboy boot-wearing, buckle-loving, hay-baling guy. And I'm inclined to *take* his advice.

"CAN I BRING YOU A SANDWICH?" LUCY ASKS, GIVING ME that half-tilted head, droopy smile that your mother gives you when she feels bad you got dumped again.

I smooth my hands through my hair. "I just had breakfast."

There's that sad smile again. "Honey, that was three hours ago."

I look at my phone and see it's nearing noon. Holy shit, she's right. I'm not hungry, but the urge to have a sip of whiskey to calm my nerves strikes. "I'll take a sandwich. Something with bacon. And french fries, too."

Lucy nods. "You want me to get something for Ivy, too?"

I hate that Lucy knows her favorite meal and I don't, but I've never asked. I've been the guy who answers questions, who soaks in a woman's focus and attention. But I have never reciprocated, and I dislike myself greatly for it.

"What's she like?" I ask quietly, twisting an empty straw wrapper around my finger. "For lunch, I mean."

She shrugs. "Her favorite is the chicken club. She likes sweet potato fries and coleslaw. But there isn't a single dish in this diner she won't eat."

I nod. "Okay then, I'll get her favorite."

"To go?"

I twist on the barstool and look through the glass, across the street, toward Ink Time. Deuce said I could go back about now, but something about rectifying what happened where it happened feels logical to me. "Here, maybe. Let me ask her."

Lucy smiles. "Good start."

I don't know if she's talking about lunch or relationships, but either way.

> Meet me for lunch across the street?

I hover over the send button, considering just walking across the street. But I want to talk to Ivy and I don't necessarily need an intimate audience.

I hit send and within a moment, she's responding.

> I don't have an appetite.

> C'mon, Firecracker. You gotta eat and I gotta talk.

> Fine.

> Got your crispy chicken sandwich with sweet potato fries waiting for you.

Thanks, Lucy.

She told me but now I know.

Gonna put that knowledge to use?

You wait and see. And get your ass over here.

A moment later, there's a swish of black hair and tights as Ivy pushes through the diner doors, greeting Lucy and two of the line cooks with a broad grin. And when her eyes find me in the semi-crowded diner, my chest aches.

My locked cock aches, too.

I lift an arm, waving her to me, and in return? She rolls her eyes.

Again, my cock aches and I let a quiet groan free. "*Fuck*," I whisper, my heart racing. She makes her way to me in long strides.

"Hey, Firecracker." I smile, slipping out of the booth to stand until she sits too.

Dropping her purse into the booth, she eyes me cautiously. She's got blue cat eye liner on today, and it's hot as fuck. Blue cat eyes, black lips, her gauges switched to black. My caged dick howls for her. "You stood for me," she comments, sliding into the booth.

"I didn't know I was gonna do that," I admit, sitting again. "But it felt right. With you." She stares at me as she plucks a sweet potato fry from the plate. "You want to roll your eyes at me, don't you?" I smirk.

Another fry, followed by a sip of water. "Kinda." And then I'm blessed with a smirk, the sassy one I've recently been thinking about in the shower when my hand is wrapped around my cage.

I stare down at my plate of food, unable to eat anything with so many unsaid things between us.

"I'm sorry," I admit, and as soon as I say it, make the admission, my chest lightens. I don't apologize often, and definitely not enough, but it feels good. I am sorry, and telling her feels like a massive leap in the right direction.

My greasy burger with crispy bacon poking out looks more appetizing. "I'm very sorry, Ivy."

She takes a bite of her chicken sandwich and the blob of special sauce at the corner of her mouth makes my balls pulse. God, I'd love to lick that sauce from her lips then cram my cock into her mouth.

"You're sorry because you want the key back," she says around a mouthful of sandwich.

"You talk with your mouth full, huh?" I tease her but I like it. I like how comfortable she is, and nothing is disingenuous either.

"Need I remind you that you passed out naked? Because talking with my mouth full," she says, making an apothecary scale with her palms. "Versus having my genitals out in public." The hand representing my naked penis sinks. She grabs her sandwich and takes another bite. "You really aren't in a position of judgment."

I can't help but smile. "I wasn't judging, I guess I just commented because I knew it would get under your skin, and I love seeing you riled up."

She rolls her eyes. "I thought you were apologizing."

My first instinct is to argue that I did, but I know there's more to be discussed. I clear my throat. "I am." I hold her eyes, hoping she feels my sincerity. I've never been more sincere. And that has my stomach tight and my palms sweaty. "I'm sorry, Ivy. I'm sorry for lying because what you overheard me saying to Deuce was absolutely a lie."

Her lips part and her hands, clutching half of her chicken sandwich, stay steady over her plate. "It was?"

I nod. "It was a lie. Because lies, for me, are easier than the truth. Alcohol and women have been another way to avoid the truth."

She sets her sandwich down and waves Lucy off as she appears with a pitcher of water, asking about refills. "What's the truth then?"

"Mr. Calhoun," a voice interrupts us, someone approaching from behind me. Ivy's eyes lift to the person approaching, and a smile curls her lips.

"Hey, Dash," she says. A moment later, a police officer appears, his uniform pressed, his hair neatly styled, one hand resting on his belt, the other tipping his shades up.

He says hello to Ivy then turns to me. "I hardly recognized you with your clothes," he grins.

Ivy leans over the table, lowering her voice so other patrons don't hear. "Dash came to Ink Time two nights ago when the— well, you know what happened."

I shrug. "Deuce told me but I didn't watch the footage." I wipe my hand on the paper napkin draped over my thigh and extend mine to his. He looks at my hand. "Thank you for your help. I was in a bad state, and I appreciate as a new citizen of Bluebell knowing law enforcement is solid."

Dash looks a bit startled by my words and just like standing when Ivy walked in, I'm a little surprised, too. But I mean every word. He came and helped and while yes, cops should always help, I've known some bad ones. In fact, in the next town over in Willowdale, I've met a few unhinged ones.

I know they're just people, and the badge doesn't automatically make them good. But Dash was good to Ivy, and Ink Time, and therefore, I like him.

"And by the way," I add, while I still have them both in

stunned silence, "Calhoun is my middle name. It's what I went by on the show because... well, they liked it better. But... I'm going by my real name now." I extend my hand again, for another shake. "Trace Wade."

Dash shakes my hand again, this time smiling. "Trace Wade," he repeats. "Good to meet you."

"You, too."

Dash looks at Ivy, and it gives me a moment to read his nameplate. FOSTER. It's important to take note of the people around me that matter. That's the recipe for laying roots.

They talk a little while I catch up on my burger. There is talk of Juniper, Ivy's older sister, and her jam delivery. Dash asks about getting an appointment with her to get some new ink, he compliments me on my boots, then he's gone.

"He's cool," I say, trying to control the flare of jealousy rearing inside me when she smiles.

"Super cool." She takes another bite, then adds, "And I'm pretty sure he's in love with Juniper."

Relief spreads through me and I glance at my watch to divert energy. Knowing I have an afternoon session, and seeing that time is running out, I redirect my focus. "You know, I think being locked up is somehow helping me... I don't know? Focus?" I'm not sure if focus is the right word, but the clarity I've had today, despite the hiccup this morning, is incredible.

"So... you're not horny?" Ivy whispers, eyes wide. God do I love her saying horny.

"Oh, I'm horny," I laugh. "Since you've been in this diner I've thought about fucking your mouth at least twice."

Her cheeks grow pink, and I love that I can turn my little Firecracker red.

"But not being able to act on it... well, it's different. But I like that it forces my brain to go other places." I discovered after holding in my piss for two and half hours, that the cage is indeed open at the tip, so all that agony was for nothing. And it's oddly comforting and I find my mind freed up since I no longer think about my dick half the day.

She smiles, and my entire chest radiates warmth. Fuck, I like her. I like her so much. "Hey, by the way, Deuce thinks you should ink me. Not sure if you caught that earlier."

She eats her last fry before responding. "Yeah, I heard."

"I think he's right. And not just because of what you did for me. But... I want your work on me, Ivy."

I don't know if she knows she does it, but right then, her hand rises, the tips of her fingers smoothing along the rough edge of the key.

"Thank you." I don't know if she's thanking me for the apology, or for letting her ink me, but her appreciation is as good as praise. With her flushed cheeks and my leaking cock, I pay the bill, and I trail behind her like a puppy across the street.

NINETEEN

"I'm all yours, Firecracker."

Ivy

"He's leaving it up to me," I whisper in the receiver to my sister, Juniper, whom I called for emotional support and squealing. Well, mostly squealing.

"And an apology!" she squeals back, because that's what sisters are for.

"I know! I don't know, Juni. Something is different. It's like... he's ready to be present in his life here and Bluebell, and somehow I'm part of that. And not just at Ink Time."

"I'm glad. I'm glad he's figuring it out. I know how much you respect him as a creator. And I know how you feel about him," Juniper adds, the sound of a jar being popped in the background. "So where's it gonna be? His shoulder? Ankle?"

I swallow, my excitement flaring. "His hipbone. He said he has a spot there for me."

"Ooh, beneath his pants. That's intimate."

Juniper doesn't have any tattoos. She doesn't realize that when it comes to getting inked, asking an artist to tattoo your hip or belly or even cleavage isn't really intimate. Not to the artist at least.

"Yeah, and you know what I'm gonna do?" I ask, looking behind me to double-check the office door in Ink Time is shut for the trillionth time. "Am I talking loud?" I whisper, massively concerned that Trace can hear every word I'm saying.

She laughs. "No, in fact, I can hardly hear you over the batch of jam I'm making."

My mind temporarily veers to Juni's jam, and despite having just had lunch, my stomach still rumbles. "Oooh, what kind?"

"Dragon Fruit. It's a... special order," she says, her voice veering off. "Dash's Dragon Fruit. Limited edition. Single batch."

I smirk. "Dash Foster?" I've seen him poking around our place for the last six months, and I know she's friends with him. But I'm pretty sure they're on the cusp of more. "We saw him at Goode's today."

"Oh yeah?" Her interest is piqued, but she veers the topic back to me. "Well, tell me what design you're doing on Trace!"

"We're putting a pin in this Dash Foster thing, got it?"

I can picture her saluting me. "Got it."

"Okay," I check behind me again. The door is still closed. "A Firecracker."

Juniper howls. "Oh my God. That's so cute!"

Both of my sisters know that I love when Trace calls me Firecracker. "It's cute. I'll take a picture of the sketch and send it to you."

"Is that what you're supposed to be working on right now

instead of talking to me?" she asks, the mother in her coming out. I can't wait until she has kids of her own, because she was great at helping raise Dolly and me.

"Yep," I admit. "But I've been sketching firecrackers since the first time he called me that. I've got the one I want to use ready. Just need to run it through the stencil machine."

There's a knock at the door. "You good?" Connor calls.

"Mm-hmm," I call back, closing my notepad, slipping my pencil through the loop. "Gotta go. See you tonight," I say to my sister. She says goodbye, and then I'm walking through Ink Time, on my way to tattoo *the* Trace Calhoun.

Err, Trace Wade.

Turning the corner, I find Trace laid out on the tattoo chair, his arms behind his head. "My afternoon session was canceled."

"Oh no," I reply, straddling the rolling chair as I take a seat. I open my sketch book and get to work getting the stencil made, my back to him. I want my back to him right now because the sight of him in that chair, knowing his cock is where I put it? My pussy is weeping. "Everything okay?"

"I canceled it."

My stomach bottoms out as I turn, blinking at him. "Why?"

He sits up, unbuttoning his jeans after undoing his belt. With a gentle tug, his pants slide down his hips and he leans back. "Thought I might be sore after my session with you."

"It's a small tattoo," I deadpan. "Your entire body is covered in ink."

He winks, and that simple gesture sends a wave of pleasure rolling through my lower half, leaving my legs wobbly. Glad I'm sitting.

"Want to see it or do you want it to be a surprise?" I ask, hoping he'll choose the latter. I really want to see his face when

I unveil it to him. I love that first look expression. I've seen him experience it with clients, I've seen Connor experience it, too. And I'll never forget the awe in Rochelle's eyes when she first laid eyes on her chastity tattoo.

The expression of seeing something so beautiful but also, so fitting for who you are, how it becomes part of your identity and your story, and today, I get to make that happen for Trace.

It's special. Tattoos are special, and I've always known it.

But now making it happen for other people is incredible.

I got emotional when I finished Rochelle's tattoo, mostly because it was her dream and my art and those two things came together to create a powerful moment for both of us.

Will I have that with Trace? I don't know. Maybe receiving tattoos aren't special to him anymore.

What I do know is no matter his reaction, I'm going to feel the same way I did with Rochelle.

Amazed.

"Surprise me," he says, after a thoughtful pause. "I'm not normally a surprise guy. In fact, the last surprise was a bad one, and kind of set me off on this trajectory..." He trails off a minute, staring down at the blank space on his body before his eyes find their way to mine again. "You know, the man whore, boozing one?"

I snap on my gloves. "I'm familiar."

He smiles, all white teeth and stubbled jaw, his long hair framing his face, partially curtaining the dark ink on this throat.

He'd make beautiful babies. And seeing those strong hands with his classic gold watch holding a baby to his bare, inked chest is almost getting me pregnant at just the thought.

"You ready?" I ask, crossing and uncrossing my legs to find the right position. Definitely not to ease the ache building inside me.

"I'm all yours, Firecracker."

~

The machine vibrates in my palm and my heart races, adrenaline spearing through my veins as I lower my hand to his body.

"You sure the stencil looks good?" he asks, causing my eyes to veer up to him. Trace is smirking and I responsively roll my eyes. "Kidding," he says.

He reaches out, fingering the key as I take my position. "Does this bother you?" he asks softly, somehow quieter than the machine, but I can still hear him.

I shake my head. "No."

He strokes the key a few more times before folding his arms behind his head. The needle hits his skin and my instincts take over, following the purple lines with precision.

"I can't believe what that key goes to," he says thoughtfully.

I snort, because when I think about the fact that Trace Calhoun is on my table—that I have a table at all—and his famous cock is in a cage and *I'm* at the helm? "Fuck, you and me both."

Another minute of tattooing and I add, "I think it's sexy, personally."

"What about it is sexy?" he asks, but not with condescension. And when I glance up at his face, I see genuine curiosity. As if he knows I'm checking to see if he's defensive or salty, he quickly adds, "I mean, I think it's hot, too. I just wanna know why you think it's hot."

"I like the idea of making things playful," I say, almost surprised by how easily the truth comes. "In my last relationship—and I'm not saying *we're* in a relationship—but with

Rhett, there was so much pressure on the sex to be a certain way. He really needed me to scream and moan and tell him he's the king."

"Did you?" he asks.

"I think the better question to ask was, was he?" I retort, smirking as I finish the edge of the fuse, swiping my cloth over it to make sure it's perfect.

He snorts. "Well, was he?"

I send him a pointed glare. "He was not."

At that moment, Deuce and Connor appear, their heads tilted to eye the design. "Don't say anything," I blurt out, "because it's a surprise."

Deuce winks at me before tossing a nod to Trace. "All right, Con and I are heading out early, got some shit to do. Trace, lock up and don't forget to set the alarm." He looks at me. "Ivy, don't forget to set the alarm."

"Hey!" Trace protests playfully. "I won't forget."

Connor squeezes my shoulder. "Great work, Ivy. See you tomorrow. Later, Trace." A few moments of baited silence pass where I wait to hear the door click, and then... we're officially alone.

"Okay, back to our talk... did you?"

I roll my eyes, hating the answer but knowing I have to tell him the truth. "I did play along. And that was part of it. I hated feeling disingenuous, and that made the sex... not fun."

"Sex should always be fun," he says slowly, his voice suddenly rawer and deeper than before. My skin prickles.

"I agree. And... that's why I like... it," I say, unable to say chastity cage aloud, afraid Connor or Deuce may overhear despite the fact I know they're gone and my fear is totally irrational. Plus, Deuce already knows. Still, I struggle a bit. "But I also like the exchange of power, too. I mean, Rochelle does it full time and they never swap roles. If it were me, I'd like to swap roles. But just knowing that's possible—knowing I'm with a guy who will relinquish control the same way he expects me to do... it's fucking hot."

I want to glance up at him, to study his face and pull apart what I think it means, but I don't. I keep my eyes on the prize, and continue to keep my focus on outlining. He's quiet, so I find myself rambling.

"I mean, it's not 1950. If women want their turn at being dominant, leading sex and exploring their own desires, why shouldn't they have that? Men get to do that all the time. They get to smack our asses in doggy style, they get to spit into our open mouths and slap our cheek to tell us to swallow it, they get to use our mouths like pussies, stick their dicks in our asses, hold us by the throat, tell us to take it—why shouldn't women get to experience that? Because we don't have a penis? I'm sorry, but I have a womb. I make life. I think I've earned the right to tell a man to suck my strap, for God's sake."

The outline is complete, so I let my eyes wander to his, and find them glazed over, hooded as he stares up at me.

"I agree completely," he murmurs.

"You have a... weird look on your face," I say as I switch the needle out from the cartridge, dipping it into the prefilled cap on my tray. I hope he's patriotic because this Firecracker is.

"I just... I agree. I mean, I've never been in a switch relationship—"

"Switch?" I question as I get started on the body of the firecracker.

"When you're both dominant and submissive, at different times, depending."

"Ahh," I reply, my eyes veering off to his crotch for a shameful moment.

A quiet moment passes between us before he says, "Can I admit something?"

I stop the machine and look at him, nodding.

"I'm... very aroused right now."

I'm suddenly breathless, my mouth dry as I struggle to respond. "It's... probably the location. The vibration through your hip bone, down to your groin. With the cage, the pressure... that makes sense."

"Yeah... that makes sense." He rolls his bottom lip between his teeth. "It's mostly being with you, though."

I keep my focus on the tattoo, filling in the effervescent candy apple red. It's my favorite red, rich with blue undertones, vibrant and breathtaking, but crimson too in some light. It looks perfect against his slightly sunkissed skin tone. Then again, I don't think any color would look bad on Trace.

"Ivy," he murmurs. "I mean that."

Heat dances over my cheeks, sliding down my neck and back. Beneath my bodysuit, my nipples crest as my arousal ramps.

I glance behind me, and then around me, knowing what I'm doing is a risk. Knowing it's disrespectful to Deuce.

But no one is here anymore.

It's just us and some cameras. With footage we can *technically* erase.

I pull off a glove and slip my hand beneath his t-shirt, rubbing my fingertips around his nipple, flicking and pinching the tip. He sucks in a breath, then exhales, huffing out a rugged groan.

"Fuuck," he sighs, squirming a little in the seat.

"Hold still, Mr. Wade," I reply, using the name I know he wants to go by now. I respect that he wants to turn over a new leaf, and I will support him in any way I can. That's what you do for the ones you love.

Stealing my hand away, I put a glove back on and return my focus to the tattoo, happy that I'm almost done. Not that I want it to end—I think I could live in a happy bubble of tattooing him forever.

"Almost done," I tell him, keeping my voice steady and calm, as if I'm unaffected by his squirmy state. After a glove and needle change, I use the last cap of ink for the explosion, using Barbie pink for the fade. Beneath me, he stays still, but when my eyes move to his, I find him in a state.

Droopy eyelids, lips parted, nostrils flaring, one of his hands now needlessly stroking his chest. "Ivy," he breathes, my name rolling off his tongue like smoke on the water.

When I make the last pass, I begin the process of cleaning him up, ignoring his calls for my attention. The more time that passes, the more I feel the shift in dynamic.

He's so used to women bending to his will, falling to his feet, giving him anything he wants. But with the key to his cock around my neck and him lying beneath me, my name on his lips, him begging for my attention, I know this is exactly what he needs.

Freedom. Freedom from being Trace Calhoun.

"I like that you dropped Calhoun," I tell him as I make the final cleaning pass over his new ink.

"I'm ready to move on, to move forward," he says, my gaze sliding to his as I snap off the black rubber gloves and toss them in the bin. "With you."

Taking advantage of sitting in a chair on wheels, I roll myself up the length of his body, and lean over him, stroking my hand through his hair. With our eyes locked, I sift my other hand up his shirt, and find his nipple again.

"Fuck," he groans, "I had no idea I liked that until now."

"Until me," I correct.

"Until you," he agrees hoarsely. "Kiss me," he groans as I

make slow, sensual circles around one nipple, sliding my hand along his carved, warm chest to find the other. "I've been thinking of kissing you for two days."

With a tough pluck of his nipple, he groans and I smile down, slowly lowering my mouth to his.

Dusting my lips against his, I close my eyes, absorbing the warmth radiating from his mouth, and the electric buzz in my veins of being so close to him. His breath is mint and coffee scented, and when I finally let my lips crush against his, the stubble on his chin grates my skin and sends a pulse between my legs.

Opening my mouth, I let my tongue discover his, taking in all that coffee and mint, my legs clenching. He squirms in my chair as I drag my thumb over his nipple, my heart pounding as a feral groan tears out of him, flooding my mouth.

I break the kiss and smile down, loving the needfulness in his eyes, the gentle swell in his lips.

"Ivy," he groans.

"You already said that," I tease softly, flicking his nipple again as his core tightens. He attempts to move beneath me but with a soft yet stern shake of my head, his body relaxes.

"I can't—" he breathes, the ring in his nostril gleaming as he struggles for breath, his forehead glazed in sweat.

"Can't what?" I ask, licking my lips, my cunt pulsing as his eyes follow the tip of my tongue.

"I'm losing my mind here," he groans, urging us both to look down at his crotch.

"A firecracker," he breathes, finally taking note of the new ink on his body. With his pants pushed down, the curves of his lean hips exposed, the thatch of dark hair poking out, I'm hit with a wave of arousal so hard that wetness blooms between my legs, flooding my panties.

"A firecracker," I repeat, moving my eyes back to his as I

take my hand from his nipple, shucking his jeans down past his cock. My thumb grazes the cage, skimming his hot flesh that pokes through the metal, causing him to curse and growl.

"Fuck, Ivy, Jesus Christ, I don't think I—" He loses track of his sentence as I replace my hand beneath his shirt, on his chest, and get back to work teasing his nipples.

"Trace Wade," I murmur, dusting my lips against his in the most teasing kiss, "are you going to come for me?"

"Ivy," he sputters, his core clenching, his rapid heart pounding against my palm as I give his nipple a final flick.

A moment later, he groans, and it's so feral and wild that my chest vibrates from it, and then heat—so much heat—is splashing onto my arm.

He's coming, and as much as I want to see his trapped cock spurting everywhere from my subtle teasing, I keep my eyes on him. He returns the contact, his jaw falling apart only slightly as he orgasms from the tease.

I could come from this. From bringing a man like him to his proverbial knees from so little physical touch and so much mental control.

An array of emotions swarms me as I finally lower my mouth to his. His tongue lunges into mine, discovering every part of me as I process the moment.

I'm proud of him for letting himself have this. For not needing control or booze. I'm proud of me for doing it—for having the courage to do it. For being brave enough to show him that I can help. For doing something I myself have never done, but having the confidence to try it.

And the last thought that crushes me as I break the kiss and finally look at the mess on his belly and chest? I'm beyond wanting him.

I have to have him.

Forever.

"I can't believe I just did that," he rasps, pushing up to his elbows as we both take in the beautiful mess.

With our eyes idling together, I lower my mouth to his belly, and kiss my way through the mess, licking my lips every few inches. He groans as I taste his cum, slowly showing him my appreciation and love while cleaning him up only slightly.

After a minute of cum-filled kisses, I sit up and smile, a pearly drop still in the corner of my mouth. He curses his pleasure as I push the last drop of him into my mouth, and reach for a paper towel to clean him up.

"Ivy," he says, taking the towel from my hand to wipe himself up.

"You keep saying that," I tease, reaching behind me to release the key from my throat. He outstretches his palm and I lower the key there. "Try again."

"Thank you," he replies quickly, his brow pinched in thought as he tosses away the paper towel, reaching behind himself to tug his shirt off over his head. Watching his elbow jut out, his bicep flex as he pulls it off tests me—I've never been this wet and swollen before. Ever. "And... I need to taste you. Watching you fucking do whatever it is you just did, making me rocket the fuck off without a touch—I need to get my mouth on you. Right now. Please."

He sits up, swinging his legs off the chair, reaching for me.

I pull back. "Not here. This is my workplace. That would be hugely unprofessional."

His nostrils flare. "My house. Now."

I rise, grabbing my things from my cupboard, handing him our standard tattoo aftercare bag.

"First, you need to unlock," I nod to his caged cock which is still exposed, and God is that fucking hot. "Then you need to lock up," I smile, referring to the shop.

"Wait for me. Ride with me," he says, his tone bordering on desperate and begging. I love it.

"No." I smile, despite the fact I want to ride with him. He has to work harder. He needs to learn that things worth having require hard work. "I'll meet you." I smile, and so does he, and in my whole life, I have never, ever seen a man move so damn fast.

TWENTY

I'd do anything for this woman.

Trace

I have looked in my rearview mirror more in the last ten minutes than a man on a high speed getaway from the damn cops.

She's still there, you idiot, my brain chants. I've never had this shiver of worry in my bones, this flicker of panic in my chest that maybe she won't show up.

At the next stop light, I straighten in my seat behind the wheel and picture the small tattoo on my hip. Even new and raw, the thought of it makes my heart thump. My lips tingle and I realize I'm smiling.

A horn sounds from behind me, causing me to jerk my gaze up, seeing the light is now green. Glancing in the rearview, I see Ivy pointing at the green light, shaking her head.

I hit the gas, eager to get her to my house, lay her on my

bed, spread her wide and feast on what I now know is undoubtedly the most beautiful, perfect cunt ever.

I haven't been able to stop thinking about her lips, how soft they were, how sexy her moans were as she rode me. How fucking flushed and gorgeous she looked as she fell apart all over that toy, in my lap, teasing and pleasing me unlike ever before.

Flicking on my blinker, I nudge myself to think of things I have historically avoided.

The hard shit.

Like the fact that I really like Ivy. Not a fleeting thing where I use her energy to feed my endorphins and adrenaline, only to kick her to the curb once it passes.

I want Ivy.

I want her to be my girl. I want to show up at Ink Time every day with her, sit next to her, talk to her over the partitions, eat lunch with her at Goode's, go to that farmers market everyone is always talking about. I want the life I envisioned years back, before fame and money.

I want to be a dad. I want to wear a wedding band and have a back seat full of groceries and a house full of responsibilities waiting after a long day.

I long for that.

And now that I've met Ivy, I'm no longer afraid to say I want that. I'm not afraid to chase it as fast as my legs will go, arms out, palms open.

But I'm afraid I'm not ready. I'm afraid the old me will claw his way through me and take over if I'm under any stress. And I don't want to hurt Ivy.

I want to be good enough for her, brave enough to ask her to live our dreams out together. Strong enough to know she may say no, and I might have to live with that.

I don't want to turn back to the booze and babes. If I quit

lying to myself, I can admit that I never really wanted that. But I wanted to appear better. Bigger. Nonchalant. Unhurt. Unfazed.

And the stupid part is? I don't even know if it worked, if I fooled the ones that hurt me, because I never checked to see.

They hurt me, and then I did everything in my power to hurt me, too.

I put my car in park and when I step out, the gravel crunching beneath my boots, dusk settling around us like a warm blanket, I realize this car has to go. It doesn't fit this life, and it doesn't fit me.

Ivy's door slams closed and I turn to spot her, walking toward me through the purple glow of the setting sun, fireflies popping off in the haze, a gentle breeze lifting the ends of her hair.

She's a masterpiece. Inked perfection in torn tights.

"You came," I murmur, my voice hoarse and raw.

"Actually, *you* came," she smirks, her slender shoulder bumping mine as she passes by. Stuck in my spot, I watch her hips sway as she climbs the steps to the front door. Wiggling her fingers, she peers over her shoulder at me, the porch light painting her in soft yellows, accentuating the wide curve of her lips, making her Cupid's bow almost edible. "Now let us in so I can come, too."

Leaping up the stairs, I fumble with my keys, and she laughs, the toes of our black boots kissing on the concrete. I drag my phone from my pocket and hover it above.

"What are you doing?" she questions, her hand on the door-knob, waiting for me to let us in.

I take a picture of our feet, and show her. The dusty tops of black boots, the melting sky and dim porch light making the scene look like a watercolor come to life. "Our feet look good together," I tell her, realizing after I say it that it's kind of weird.

But Ivy taps the screen and a moment later says, "I sent that to myself. I love it."

Our eyes idle as a bug flits between us, reminding us we need to get inside. I need to get inside her, but for now, inside the house will do.

A jiggle and turn and we're inside. Twisting the deadbolt, I flick on the lights and face her. But she's not even there anymore. She's already headed down the hall, to the bedroom in the back.

Stopping in the doorway, ten feet from me, Ivy's long dark hair cascades down her back, making my poor balls ache. "You're beautiful, Ivy. All the fucking time. You know that?"

Her smile spins me out, as the cage seemingly shrinks in size. "Of course I know." Her wink has me running down the hall, and she dips into my room with a playful giggle as I chase her.

Standing shirtless and breathless in the doorway, she holds my eyes, unlacing her boots one by one, sifting a long finger through the laces.

"Did you take off the cage or leave it on?"

I dig the key from my pocket and let the chain dangle from my middle finger. "It's on."

"I told you to take it off," she says, kicking off her first boot, moving to the second.

"I'm not a good listener," I reply, "and I was hoping *you* could take it off."

With one boot off and one on, she makes her way toward me, pressing her fingertip between my pecs. "If I wanted to touch your cock, I would have touched it. If I tell you to take it off, it's because I want you to take it off."

She steps back, kicks off her other boot and shucks off her leggings, standing before me in a skimpy little bodysuit. Her nipples pierce the fabric, one arm and one leg inked, her long hair curtaining her face. She's a knockout. It's criminal how hot she is.

I'd do anything for this woman.

It takes the same time as a sneeze for me to undress. Grabbing my swollen, sticky package, I fumble until the key slips into the tiny lock, and I give it a twist. The device splits open and falls into my palm.

I let it all drop to the floor with a thunk and begin massaging myself, kneading out the grooves in my cock left by the metal, but Ivy says, "Don't touch."

My hands drop to my sides like I'm at gunpoint.

Or in Ivy's case, knife point.

Her hand comes to her shoulder, pushing the strap off the soft slope of her body. She repeats on the other side, and I watch with rapt focus and a dry mouth as she removes her bodysuit.

I've seen her naked. I've watched her come.

But knowing that she's in my house and I'm about to put my mouth on her sweet pussy, seeing her naked now is almost fucking painful.

"Fuck me, Ivy, you're so perfect." My eyes roam her curves, her pinkened and plucky nipples, the pieces of art she's chosen for her body in a variety of styles, and the white of her painted toenails. Need sears my chest from the inside out.

She's watching my cock, so I look down at him too, my fingers drumming my thighs at my sides. I'm so goddamn hard. I haven't been hard like this in years. Booze, drugs, lack of sleep, age—all reasons I told myself why I never got rock hard anymore.

But in the moonlight, the most beautiful perfect woman in front of me, a smirk curling her lips and my sheetless bed behind her, my cock stands hard and thick, a pearly bead of precum waiting at the slit. Against my belly, the heat of my erection makes me feral, and I move toward her.

She backs up, making me groan. "Stay there," she breathes, "stay there until I'm ready for you."

I nod, my mouth open and my chin coated in drool.

After dragging a random quilt from a moving box and fanning it over my newly delivered bed, she crawls in the center, her back against the wall. Slowly, her legs part, and I can't look away from the way the mattress dips as she digs her heels in, preparing for me.

My gaze travels from her leg to her pussy, glistening even in the ill-lit room. "You're wet," I croak, my cock now painfully hard, aching and throbbing. I think if I even touch it right now I'd rocket off.

"You in your cage was hot," she says, reaching down, her fingers spreading apart her cunt. "And now you're going to lick up the mess I made because of you, then you're going to wash my panties because you made me get those wet, too."

"Okay," I reply, faster than a speeding fucking bullet. Seriously, I think the new order is: speed of light, South Korean internet, $S4714$ star in the galaxy and horny, teased man in love with a woman who is bringing him back to life.

Kneeing my way onto the mattress, Ivy snaps, motioning me down. "On your belly, with your hands on my inner thighs."

I do as she says, no part of me grappling for control, no part of me even wanting it. And that's the first time in years I've felt happy in existing with a woman, not caring about the power dynamic, not needing to hold the reins.

I just want her.

"Can I?" I ask, my mouth hovering and watering above her bare cunt. God I can smell her. Sweet and subtle, like amber and patchouli, slightly tangy too, like arousal and desire. I swallow as my cock presses painfully against the mattress. I haven't touched myself in two days, and I'm hyperaware of that now as precum smears into the quilt, my balls fucking pounding between my legs.

"You may," she allows, biting into her bottom lip with the tiniest dip of her head.

Peering down, I take in the sparkle of her wet cunt beneath me, the way her lips peek open partly, her arousal making her bloom. Her clit is swollen and pink and after a moment of taking her in, she lifts her hips from the bed, causing my mouth to crash into her.

"Eat me, Trace, don't make me say it again."

Jesus Christ. My cock leaks, and I'm not even sure it's precum anymore. I think I'm actually leaking *cum*, but I ignore the signals in my own body and focus on Ivy.

Snaking my tongue between her lips, I delve inside of her, exploring more of what I now know is my favorite flavor. She's sweet like jam, salty with arousal, and when I move the tip of my tongue around her clit, the sound she makes is pure heaven.

My bedroom comes alive for the first time ever, her gentle crooning echoing off the emptiness, filling the space with the perfect mix of desire and frantic need. Her fingers sweep through my hair, pushing it away from my face as I blink up at her, past the terrain of her full breasts, into her deep blue eyes.

She doesn't say anything, but her gaze speaks to me. It urges me on, telling me she wants more, she wants more of me, my mouth, my body, all of it. A storm of emotion tears through me, leaving my chest full and aching. I press my mouth into her, ignoring it, lapping at her sweetness, sucking on her little clit.

"Oh God," she murmurs, her head rolling against the wall, a tangle of beautiful black hair everywhere. I dig my thumbs into her thighs, using my nose to nudge her clit as I stroke my tongue inside of her. She's open, wet, her body ready for my cock. But I fuck her with my tongue, my own body sending me the same signals.

I'm ready to be inside of her, my cock savagely swollen and hungry against the bed. Each lunge of my tongue into her sweetness causes me to move a little against the mattress, my own orgasm coiling tighter as I do.

"Suck on my clit, and stick your finger in my ass," she hums, telling me what she needs, her cheeks flush, nipples puckered. God I want to eat her pussy but equally crawl up her body and suck one of those little tips into my mouth while I drive my cock deep inside of her.

But I do as she says and suck her clit into my mouth, gently rolling it between my teeth as I sink my thumb into her ass. She tightens around me, and I nearly lose it. "Ivy," I groan into her pussy, hoping to God that her scent lingers on my stubble.

With her fingers still in my hair, she tugs me, stealing my mouth away from her body. "If you don't come when I come, I'll let you fuck me."

Jesus Christ. I didn't know sex was on the table. But I hadn't planned on coming on the bed and myself like a fucking teenager, either.

"Easy," I grin, loving her stickiness on my lips. She smirks but rolls her eyes, pressing me deeper into her cunt. I love the way her nails grate my scalp, reminding me that she is in possession of me, not the other way around.

Her legs widen as I suckle at her clit, my thumb making circles in her ass. She moans and cries out, and my cock weeps and weeps. Fucking crybaby. The coil in my gut winds tight, and my legs get the telltale trembles, and my toes begin to curl.

"Oh fuck," I groan, sucking her clit deeper, moving my thumb quicker.

"Yes, yes, yes," she chants, her thighs trembling around me in the periphery. She's close.

I just need to make it another thirty seconds, and then I get to sink into this silky, velvety heaven. I can do this.

"Trace, are you gonna eat me until I come? Hmm?" she asks, her tone laced with unbridled need. "Make me come, Trace Wade, make me come all over your face." Her head hits the wall as her gaze drops to my mouth on her cunt.

"That's right," she urges as my stupid hips grind mindlessly into the mattress.

Fuck. I have to stop moving. *I have to stop moving.*

Suddenly she lifts her legs off the bed and wraps them around me, her heels digging into my back as she erupts, moaning my name in a way I've never heard.

"*Traaace,*" she draws out, her hands coming to her breasts, thumbs moving across her nipples. "Trace, you're making me come, you're... oh God, Trace," she breathes, her sweet little asshole clenching around my thumb, sucking it up as her pussy pulses—that's all it takes.

Her sweet orgasm flooding my mouth, my name on her lips, her legs keeping me locked into my bed with her—"Fuck, Ivy!" I growl in between sucks and nibbles, my orgasm spilling free as I grind and feast.

I'm throbbing, each ribbon of pearly relief trapped between my belly and the quilt, creating a pool of warm mess. I can't help it. I can't stop. I move my hips, trying to find more friction for my cock as I unload yet again, all the while eating her through her orgasm.

When she's nothing more than a bumbling mess, her legs slide down from my back, trembling around my face. I stay there, against the mattress, prolonging heaven as I dust kisses over her used, swollen cunt.

"Firecracker," I groan, licking the insides of her thighs, unable to leave my new favorite spot.

"Trace," she breathes, pushing her hands through her hair,

exposing her flushed cheeks and bright eyes. "That was so good," she says, her compliment landing ten thousand times more powerful than any compliment in the studio. Being praised by Ivy makes my skin hot and my groin tight. She lowers a hand to my face, cupping my cheek as much as she can. "Get on your knees, on the bed," she whispers.

"Ivy, I can't—I can't fuck you," I admit sheepishly, because motherfucker. I have never wanted to be inside of someone so badly.

She smirks. "I know. I knew you came. I knew you were going to come. But I want to see it." She sits up farther, scooting her pussy away from me. "Show me the mess you made."

I get to my knees, finding the pool of cum on the quilt, smeared along my stomach, rivulets hanging in my happy trail.

After surveying the mess, I look up at her, finding her smiling at me. "You fucked up your quilt."

"Actually," I smile, grabbing a towel from the floor. I think this was yesterday's shower towel. I get to work cleaning up the mess as I eye her on my bed. "I fucked the quilt, but fortunately she's not looking for anything serious."

Ivy laughs, bringing her hand to her collarbone. "So corny."

I cock a brow as I finish wiping up what I can, off my body and then hers. Her orgasm was messy, and fuck if I don't wanna get hard again just thinking about it. "You like my corny," I reply, outstretching a hand to her. She takes it with a questioning look.

"Where are we going?" she asks as I drag her off the mattress. I gather her clothes from the floor, and she puts her hand out, ready to take them.

"I'll dress you," I reply. That's the first time I've said that. "But you're wearing one of my shirts."

"Okay, but don't forget, you need to rinse my panties out in the sink." She folds her arms over her chest, nodding toward the open bathroom door. Without question, I do as she says, getting hard again as I stroke my thumb over the damp strip of white cotton centering her thong. Why is this so hot? I don't know, but as I rinse them beneath the tap, I catch sight of the firecracker on my hip.

My eyes burn and my chest tightens. I lift my gaze to the mirror, finding my reflection in a powerful moment wherein I realize... This tattoo means the most.

I love Ivy.

TWENTY-ONE

I've never met anyone like you, Firecracker.

Ivy

Bringing the shirt to my nose again, I suck down another noseful. And like every time I've smelled it before, needful bumps spread along my skin, and my pulse picks up.

"Smelling your man's shirt again?" Juni asks, popping her hip against my bedroom door frame, her jam-stained apron tied to her body.

I nod, holding it to my nose again for one final hit of the good shit before I get dressed. "Just call me Dolly," I tease, but before Juni can laugh, my pregnant younger sister bustles in, a hand on her belly.

"Speak of the obsessive beauty," I tease as Dolly comes to my side, pulling me into a hug.

"Good morning and hey, if you're taking after me," she rubs her belly again, "that's a good thing. Look at how my *obsession* paid out," she says, using air quotes around obsession as if it were alleged.

"That's true," Juniper says, braiding her long blonde hair. "Do you think it's headed that way? Ring and bump, I mean?"

I shrug, knowing the little twist in my gut is praying for those things to happen. "I never thought that the man I admire most would ever even know I exist. But look, now we work together and he's my mentor and—"

"Your plaything," Dolly adds, wiggling her eyebrows.

Yeah, my sisters have the full rap sheet on what's happened so far. They're my best friends, and if I don't share the high level details with them, it feels like a betrayal.

Obviously dick size and the copious amounts of cum that Trace expels are for me only. But admitting to them that I've been playing around with him, trying to make him work for me, work for something that fulfills him and leaves him happy when he puts his head on the pillow each night—that's sharable. Because I'm proud. I'm proud of the patience, the forgiveness, the power, everything I've done with Trace, short of lying about a contract, gives me confidence.

Laughing, I feed my arms through his t-shirt and agree. "Yeah, my plaything. But I mean, if all of that happened, anything can happen."

Juniper comes into the room and takes a seat on the edge of the bed, handing me my black pair of leggings. I jump into them. "What do you want to happen?" she asks. Dolly tips her head to the side, her blonde hair falling over her shoulder. "Yeah, Ivy, what do you want with him?"

I shake my head, because it's so much but also so simple. "Everything."

After the night at his place where he gave me the most mind-blowing orgasm I've ever had, we went out and got burgers, eating them in his sports car. We talked, covering films and albums, discussing favorite and least favorite meals, and we even went into boots—thick sole, thin sole, leather, patent—anything a boot could be, we talked about our preferences for it.

At his house, we shared a slow, sizzling kiss. He held my face with one hand and wove our fingers together with the other. It was intimate and romantic, and not at all expected from Trace.

When I got home, I had a text message waiting, asking me if I'd arrived safely. After responding yes, he sent me one more message. One that I have reread more times than I can count.

> There's so much I want to talk to you about, Ivy. But tonight changed me. I want to move forward, but I have to move slowly.

In that message, I read everything I'd hoped and suspected.

He wants me but he's clawing his way from a boozy and pussy-filled depression, and he's scared that if we move too fast, he may slip back into old ways.

I get that.

We've worked together at Ink Time the last couple days, grabbing lunch with Connor and Deuce at Goode's one of them, and on another of them, we ate together on the curb out front, splitting a hoagie the size of my forearm.

We text at night. Casual but sweet.

But today, after admitting to my sisters earlier that I want everything, I can't stop focusing on everything.

I've looked his way approximately six trillion times during his afternoon session, and now, as the client is paying and giving out compliments, I feel like I'm going to explode.

"What are you up to tonight?" Deuce asks Trace after the client walks out.

"Painting," Trace answers, "your house, asshole."

Deuce grins. "I'll be sure to check the molding and base-boards, make sure you don't make any mistakes."

Trace rolls his eyes as I approach. I spent the day watching him, taking notes on his technique, filling ink caps, sanitizing his space and generally just being his apprentice.

I don't know how much Deuce knows, but no sooner have I walked up than he's saying he's on his way out. Something about Ev and Ace, but I'm not listening.

My eardrums are pounding. My heart is threatening to break my ribs. My panties are drenched.

I know we're moving slow, we're building and we're not defining things.

And I'm fine with that. Really. Whatever gets us to our finish line, I can roll with it.

But I need to fuck him. He's riled me up by just existing as a sexy, talented man, and it's time he eases the ache he put inside me.

"Would you like me to come help you paint tonight?" I ask, tucking my hair behind my ear.

A growl rumbles through his chest. He's wearing a faded crop black t-shirt with a torn chest pocket, black jeans and brown boots. His hair is down, sitting on his shoulders, and his jaw today is clean shaven. I love how his belly shows, just a little. He smells like pine and heaven, and I want to push him down onto the floor, crawl over him and eat him alive.

"I do indeed," he crows, hunger rippling in his voice.

My mind spins. I'm going to his house again... and while I want to fuck his brains out, I also want to play... and make him work for it.

I deserve a reward for edging myself so damn much.

"I have to run home first but I'll come over right after."

His eyes drop to my mouth, and I love how his tongue sweeps his bottom lip as he studies me. "Perfect," he finally says. Then, stepping nearer to me, so close that his breath flanks my nose, he adds, "I've missed you, Firecracker."

I snort nervously. "We've been together all week."

He arches a brow. "You know exactly what I mean."

My palms grow clammy. "I've missed you too," I admit, shedding the coy act instantly. I reach out and cup his cock, surprised to find it partially stiff. "See you two soon."

I grab my things and head out, already making plans in my head. Because Trace may not know this yet but he wants more than sex. He wants to earn it.

And he will.

I DON'T EVEN GET THE CHANCE TO KNOCK. TRACE OPENS his front door as I'm taking the porch steps, letting out a rush of distinctly Trace smells. Pine, shampoo, deodorant and now? Coffee.

I'm glad it's not whiskey anymore.

"Hey, Firecracker," he says, the rough timbre of his greeting wrapping me like a sexy hug.

"Hey you," I reply, surprised when he loops his arm around my waist and bends to kiss me. It's not short, it's not on the cheek and it isn't subtle.

Our mouths open as his fingers dig into my back possessively, his moans filling my mouth. After a moment we pull apart, and he peers over to Deuce's, the lights on, blinds open. "I told him you were coming over, just so he wouldn't look out the window and find out." He searches my eyes. "You cool with that?"

I shrug. Something about knowing that Trace told Deuce that I'm going to be at his place makes me feel... as corny as it sounds... special. "It's fine."

After slipping inside, Trace locks the door, just now noticing the black bag hanging from my shoulder. He points to the cans of paint lining the wall near his boots, the stack of blue tape and tarps, and the bucket of new brushes. "I have everything... I mean, unless that's, like, your overnight bag or something," he says, dipping down to kiss me, holding my face by the chin as he does.

I lick my lip when the kiss breaks, and smile. "Oh no, it's not an overnight bag."

He moves to the kitchen, pulling two glasses from the cupboard. "I got glasses delivered while at work today. And a bunch of other house shit too." He wiggles the glass for me to see before filling it with water. "So what's in the bag?"

I smile, my heart racing. "The dick you're gonna suck for me."

Water sprays across the empty counter, in my glass, all over his wallet and keys. "The fuck?"

I drop the bag to the floor and cross the room, raising my hand to sift my fingers through his soft hair, dragging the heel of my palm along his cheek and chin. "I think you heard me."

He blinks. He keeps his eyes on me as he tries another cautious sip of water. "Ivy," he says, and it's clear he isn't sure what to say. Despite the nervous flutter in my belly, I stand strong. Because I do think this is what he needs.

"Trace."

"Ivy," he tries again, stretching my name out like a piece of taffy.

"Will you excuse me? I need to get changed," I smile at him, snatching the bag from the floor before stopping next to the cans of paint. "Don't worry, we'll paint. *After.*"

"That *after* sounds ominous," he says as I smile at him over my shoulder on my way down the hall.

"Don't get scared. Get naked."

With my heart racing, I close the hall bathroom door and flick on the light. There's nothing in this bathroom, which is unsurprising since I know he just moved in and only uses the one in his room. I plop my bag on the counter, over the sink, and a thrill runs down my spine at the sound of the metal zipper peeling apart as I open it.

Inside is everything for a perfect night.

Quickly, I kick off my boots, shimmy out of my leggings and peel off my t-shirt, then slowly pull the elastic bands from the ends of my braids. Reaching into the bag, my fingers find lace and elastic, and a burst of excitement lightens the tightness in my chest.

Pulling on the lace teddy and garters first, I grab the strap and harness next. It's the same one we used before, only now it's going to go in *him*, not me. For a moment, I take in my reflection, loving the wild waves of my dark hair and how they contrast the red lingerie. The strap-on is black, the harness, too, and as I spin and check my silhouette, I realize my boots would look so hot with this.

I put them back on, take a deep breath, and pull open the bathroom door. I'm surprised to find a completely nude Trace standing right where I left him, a puddle of clothing at his feet.

I keep my fist wrapped tightly around the dildo as I stroll out, chin down, eyes locked on him and that fat cock of his. God he's sexy. A man with piercings and ink is obviously hot, but add in a big dick and a willingness to change? Impregnate me now.

"Fuck, Ivy, you look so hot," he groans, pulling at the back of his neck as his eyes skate up and down my body, over and over. "You are hands down the hottest woman I've ever met. The lingerie and boots..." he trails off, shaking his head.

I know he means every word he says. Because he's naked.

And his cock is fattening up, turning pink and greedy,

rising to the occasion. My stomach flutters at the sight, and it gives me the confidence to keep on going.

"Thank you." I smile, my pulse beating wildly in my throat, my nipples piercing the delicate filigree of the lingerie. "Want to play with me?"

"I don't know what that means but... fuck yes, I do," he rasps, his eyes still coursing over my body like a piece of fine art.

"Let's play *mirror*," I say, coming to stand a foot in front of him. "You mirror me."

Despite the fact he looks a bit confused, he nods his head as his eyes veer to my breasts. I know what he sees. Greedy peaks poking through, begging to be sucked. Not yet, though. He'll have to earn that.

I reach out and wrap my hand around the rubber cock, and pump myself once. He reaches out, copying me, and I can't help but let a little breathy gasp free as his veiny, thick, tattoo-laden hand stretches the length of his thick cock, already hard, making it harder.

"I don't know what the fuck we're doing, baby, but this is hot," he groans.

I pump my cock again, and he pumps his, sending a rush of wetness into my beautiful lacy lingerie. "This is making me wet, Trace," I breathe, my voice unexpectedly low and seductive. "Maybe if you're good at following orders, I'll let you feel how wet you're making me."

"Jesus Christ," he utters, gripping the slick cap of his cock as I make him wait for another order.

Moving my fingertip to the end of my toy, I begin swirling it around the rubber head. He does the same, smearing a bead of opaque liquid around his tip, his head falling back in tortuous delight as he does. His throat bobs with a feral groan and my eyes move to the sheer size of his neck and the tattoos; a rose blooming through a patch of violent, sharp thorns and a snake partially coiled.

I bring my finger to his mouth, and push it onto his tongue. He groans, knowing just what I'm doing. "Mirror," I command, nudging him through his hesitancy. I take my finger back, and he brings his hand up. Opening my mouth, I stick out my tongue, causing him to release a string of muffled curses before plunging his precum-coated finger into my mouth.

Sealing my lips around his knuckle, I suck and moan, enjoying his salty taste, but more so, enjoying the untamed pleasure in his eyes. My tongue curls around his digit, and though he's the one whimpering and dripping for me, I'm just as aroused.

I wrap my hands around his large one and slowly pull his finger from my mouth, loving the way he watches my lips.

"Now... I once heard a really handsome but kind of egotistical man use a line... and I'm dying to try it."

His jaw falls apart and his eyes slowly peel from my mouth, crawling to my eyes.

I tap my chin. "I think he said.... *Get on your knees and suck my dick.*"

A flush hits his cheeks, and he blinks. We both know when I heard him say that. The night at Ink Time when I agreed to go out with Jeremy. When he called those women to the studio, and he wanted to hurt me.

"Ivy, I—"

I stop him. "I think you mean, *yes, ma'am.*"

We share a heated gaze, and then Trace smiles. "Okay, Firecracker."

Slowly, he lowers to the floor, his body still large while on his knees. And that's got my pussy seizing, too. My orgasm has been building since I unzipped this bag, and now that my fantasy is coming to life, my core is tight with need, my cunt swollen. I'm so wildly hungry for him I can't stand it, but I love teasing him and teaching him too.

"Hands behind your back," I tell him, making sure he doesn't stroke himself. "The next time your cock is touched, it will be by me, so keep those hands behind your back unless you want to find out what your punishment is like."

He nods. "Yes, ma'am."

I take his square jaw in my hand, the chisel and set of his handsome features making my pulse flutter low in my belly.

With his hands pinned to his hip bone and his beautiful jaw in my palm, I step toward him. "Open."

Something passes over his features for a moment, short and fleeting, but I jerk his face up to mine, his mouth still closed.

"Trace *Wade* is open to new things. Trace *Wade* is evolving. So open your mouth, Trace *Wade*, before you regret it."

I love that he smirks before he obeys, opening his mouth. Still holding his face, I push the cock onto his tongue. "Seal your lips and suck," I state, my breasts aching at the erotic sight before my eyes. God, I want nothing more than to be ravaged and destroyed by him. For him to grab my tits so hard they hurt all the while he hammers into me until I'm screaming my orgasm for God to hear.

But first, this. He needs this.

Maybe we need this.

"Suck my cock while I tell you how I'm gonna suck yours," I rasp, watching his cheeks hollow and his eyes blink up. Fuck, this is way too hot. Why don't more people play like this? "Mirror," I remind him. He nods on my cock, and I press on, eager to play.

"I'll be on my knees, completely naked, with my hands behind my back," I whisper, moving my hand from his jaw to the back of his head. I sift my fingers through his hair until I find the right spot, and grip his scalp, gentle but rough enough to make him groan.

"You'll put your hand in my hair, you'll say, *goddamn, Ivy, you look so good taking my cock.*" I lower my voice further. "*You look so good on your knees for me.*"

With a gentle push, I move him down on the cock, his lips sliding along the rubber, making my core tighten with fiery need. This is quite possibly the hottest thing ever.

"You'll tell me how good my tongue feels and I'll pop off, sucking the tip, letting all that cocksucking spit dribble down my chin, coating my tits," I moan, letting my tongue slowly traverse my bottom lip as his dark eyes stay focused on mine. He bobs slowly, freely, without my nudging him, and I move my hand back to his chin, stroking his neck as he sucks me.

"You'll reach out and you'll rub spit into my nipples, and I'll like it so much I'll go deeper, suck you harder, and moan all around you," I croak, jerking him off the cock and using his throat as a grip. "Keep your mouth open," I whisper, using the dildo's wide head on his tongue, slapping it there to make spit slip from his mouth, down his chin.

"Fuck," he breathes, while he has the chance. But I slide the cock back into his mouth, and like a good boy who doesn't want to be in trouble, he seals his lips around it and continues sucking.

Finally, I allow myself to look down, between his spread thighs. His cock is an angry hue of pink, the head nearly purple as he bobs on my strap, spit falling to the floor between us. "You'd say, *you're doing good, Firecracker,*" I whisper down, slipping my hand beneath the dildo, finding my pussy.

I'm so swollen and slick that just the slight contact of discovery has me whimpering. I'm so turned on right now it's insane. Using my fingers, I smear my arousal on the part of the cock he's not sucking, then tell him what every man tells every woman sucking his cock.

"Deeper, suck me deeper," I urge, slipping my hand beneath the cock to find my cunt, stroking myself as he immediately plunges deeper on the dildo, a gag erupting in the back of his throat, spit bubbling around his lips.

"Stay down in it, baby," I coax, loving the way his eyes flutter closed and he moans around the cock as he tastes what I left for him. "I taste good, don't I?" I question, my fingers rubbing slow, small circles on my engorged clit.

He nods and the cock bobs, putting additional pressure on my already sensitive cunt. I keep my eyes peeled as I rub myself, watching as he bobs on the cock, his own now steadily leaking. A ribbon of pearly liquid swims down his shaft, curving delicately around the throbbing veins, disappearing into his plump balls.

"I'm close," I admit, both as myself and as the character I'm playing. Because if I were on my knees like this for Trace, I could probably bring him to his knees in a few minutes.

"*Are you going to take my cum, Firecracker?*" I ask, biting my bottom lip as I pinch my clit, urgent need pounding down my spine. "Swallow my cum for me, show me how bad you want me, show me you want everything I have to give," I finish, just as the undeniable zing of an orgasm echoes up my legs, landing in my pussy.

My knees shake as sweat slips down my spine. Trace's eyes are wide and drunk at the same time, his cock bobbing wildly, some of his own spit dripping from his chin to his slick head. He groans around the rubber as my hand works faster, my orgasm right around the corner.

"I'm gonna come now, and I want you to keep your eyes open while you take every drop, got it?" I ask, my eyes moving between his, his mouth, and his beautiful weeping cock.

He nods, bobbing on the dildo and moaning, the same way I do when I know a man is close. I love how good he is at this, at the game, at pleasing me. He's not perfect, but he's perfect for me. And with that thought, I lose control entirely.

"Fuck, baby," I groan, "you're making me come." My fingers slide through my stickiness, my clit the most sensitive it's ever been as my orgasm peaks, my cunt spasming relentlessly. Trace groans, his eyes going to where I'm fingering myself beneath the harness, and as I cry out that I'm coming undone, that his mouth has unraveled me so perfectly, he comes too.

Ribbons of white soar through the space between us, landing with a thud against the floor, rope after rope, moans comingling with moans as we come in unison, our eyes still locked.

When I've rubbed so much I can't touch myself a second longer and my pussy is nothing more than a quivering mess, I finally break our eye contact and look down at his cock and the mess he so beautifully made.

Hard, cum dripping down his shaft, painted on his abs, coating the floor—it's the hottest thing I've ever seen. Slowly, I back up, taking the dildo from his mouth. Unstrapping the harness, I step out of it and set it on the kitchen counter, then return to my man on his knees.

"Fuck," he sighs, a shudder racking his shoulders as he lets his head fall forward in respite. "That was intense. That was hot. That was..."

"You can use your hands now, you know," I tell him, noticing that he's still got them behind his back.

He releases the position and I outstretch a hand, helping him to his feet. Once he rises, standing at least three inches over me, he brings his hand to my face, cupping my cheek. "I've never met anyone like you, Firecracker."

I smile, feeling the loss as he releases me, kissing my lips quickly before disappearing into the kitchen. He returns with paper towels and begins cleaning up his mess.

As he wipes, he looks up at me. "I need to fuck you right this second, Ivy."

I laugh. "You just came. Don't you have a refractory period?"

He shakes his head. "Not with you, I don't."

I cup my breasts over the lingerie, garnering his attention as he wipes at an already clean spot on the floor. "Okay," I say, feeling like we're ready, like he's earned me. "We can have sex. But I choose the position."

Trace gets to his feet, abandoning the paper towels and sticky strap-on sitting next to his coffee pot. He tosses me over his shoulder, my boots dangling against his back. "Goddamn it, Firecracker, I cannot wait to get inside you."

I can't wait either. Because I have another surprise for him.

TWENTY-TWO

It is my favorite. She is my favorite.

Trace

Flinging her onto my bed, I don't bother with the lights. Moon-light spills into the room, illuminating the space with mood lighting. My Firecracker in that lacy thing with her badass boots on? *Fuckin' A.*

And what's with me blowing for her without touch, over and over? She's changed my DNA, I swear. She crawls up the bed, wearing a smirk that tells me she isn't done having her way with me.

"God," I groan, stroking my hardening cock. "I want to get inside you so bad. That was so hot."

"You liked it, then?" she asks, pulling down the straps to her outfit. My cock jumps like it's the first time he's seen tits, but in truth, it's her. She rewires my brain, short-circuits reason and makes me abandon thought. When Ivy is naked in front of me, all I can think about is greeting cards with hearts and poems, wedding bands and forever.

I nod. "A lot."

She smiles, pushing wavy dark hair behind her ear as she yanks the lingerie from her foot. "I have something else for you to try, and I'm making an assumption that you've never done it."

"You keep me on my toes, baby, so you know what, I probably haven't done it." Grabbing a condom from the box in the bathroom, I sheath my cock then knee my way onto the bed, hovering over her as she slides onto her back. With her blinking up at me, the house quiet and my brain still, I have the strongest urge to coil my hand gently around her neck and press my lips softly to hers. To ease her into a slow, meaningful kiss where I share how I feel without words. The last time I kissed a woman with those intentions, I was in love.

I gave her a ring.

"There's so much we don't know about each other still," I breathe. "But you have me in a choke hold, Ivy Ellington."

She bites her bottom lip then says, "I'm about to have you in amazon."

My brows pinch and before I know it, she's hooked her legs around me, and flipped me to my back, my chest pounding from her wild laughter.

"Bend your knees," she says, her laughter fading, smile evolving into something more sensual.

"Like this?" I ask as I curl my knees to my chest. When she nods her approval, I feel like a dog getting an atta boy from his owner. If I had a tail it would wag.

"Now, I'm gonna fuck you," she whispers, leaning over my curled legs to find my lips for a kiss.

"With a strap?" I ask, wholly confused as to how we're having sex with me in this vulnerable position. And when I envision Ivy exploring my prostate with a strap-on and fucking me? I don't hate the idea. In fact, I look down to find my cock happy and hard along my belly.

She shakes her head. "Nope, this is amazon position. I'm in control, so I'm fucking you, but with your own cock."

"I don't know if I get it," I admit. She's the one above me, the one who knows what she's doing, the one teaching me, and the contrast to us in the studio versus bedroom is something I never thought I'd like, but I'm beneath her in awe.

Aligning her knees on either side of my rib cage, she smooths her palms over my knees, and instinctively I drive my heels into her lower back. Slowly, she sinks down on my cock, taking every inch slow, all while telling me to watch.

"See that? See the way I'm taking your cock, how I'm in control?"

I can't decide where I want to look because I want to look everywhere—at the way her soft pink lips clench my veiny cock as she sinks down on it, at the way she peers down at where we connect, at her velvety tits with hard little tips, at the silhouette of us drawn against the floor. When she glances up at me, I lock onto her eyes, and with that, she starts riding me.

Hard.

Harder than I expected, harder than I envisioned for this position, harder than I was prepared for.

How can I feel the burn of another orgasm coiling in my groin after what we've already done? I don't know. But within a few seconds of her full tits swaying, her dark hair spilling down her back, her hands gripping my knees with force, I feel it. I feel the swell of release growing in my balls, making my cock ache and my taint burn.

"You like it when I fuck you? Hmm?" she questions as she rides, her eyes growing hazy and hooded, just like mine.

"Yes," I answer, my mouth cottony as I struggle for better words. Dirty talk. Filthy talk. Shit talk. Anything.

But I can't.

All I can do is lie on my back and watch the most beautiful woman in the world slide up and down on my cock and pray my fuse is long enough that I don't come before she gets her pleasure .

With a jerk of her hips, the angle changes, and my eyes squeeze shut, the last bit of self-restraint draining from me as my ass clenches and my cock throbs. "Ivy, you're so tight, so good," I praise, a stark contrast to my usual sex talk. The truth falls from my lips without thought, and I reach up, twisting my finger in loose strands of onyx silk, tugging gently. "Firecracker," I rasp, and though she rides me hard and fast, bed squeaking, tits swaying, my world spinning—the moment is still intimate. My heart beats louder than the room around us, my mind shouts even louder.

Make this woman yours.

Though as she chants she's on the brink of coming, her nails marking my knees as she gains momentum on my dick, I think she's making me hers.

And I want that. As much as I wanted to ink, as much as I wanted *Trace Tats* and *Needle Ninjas*. No, that's a lie. I don't want it as much. I want it more.

"Trace," she cries, her head falling back, exposing the smooth column of her throat and the underside of her jaw. Future memories and possibilities flash behind my eyes as my orgasm tears up my legs and sears through my shaft, making my cockhead throb deep inside her cunt. A smile on her lips, her body curved over my chair at Ink Time, my gloved hand at her throat, inking our initials into her velvet skin.

My eyes snap shut as I explode, filling the condom in shuddering, powerful bursts, the feel of her cunt squeezing and milking me only making me come harder. Groans and moans tumble together around us, hers and mine, skin slapping skin, finally, I open my eyes. Her head is tipped forward, the ends of her long hair dusting my knees as she smirks that same fiery smirk she gives me at work.

"I fucked you," she smiles, slowly rising up until she's empty, my partially stiff cock slapping onto my belly. Using her hands under my knees, she lowers my legs to the mattress, laying me flat. Reaching for the condom, she stops, her fingers at the ringed base.

"You come a lot," she says, poking the full tip of the rubber.

I shake my head against the bed. "I think I'm still coming," I tease, my cock twitching slightly in the sheath, another drop of cum slipping free. My balls are still thrumming, too.

She laughs, slowly rolling the condom off of me before tying it and sliding off the bed. In the en-suite bathroom, I hear the toilet and sink, and when she returns, she's got a wet cloth in her hands.

Slowly, she moves the cloth over my cock, swiping away the stickiness, cleaning me up entirely. Tossing it to the floor she flops down next to me, stroking her hand over my chest as she rests her head on my shoulder. I reach out and grab her leg, bringing it to rest over mine.

"You a cuddler?" she asks with a yawn.

"Nah, haven't cuddled in years." I twist my head, peering at her through one open eye, my heart racing at the sight of black hair strewn over my bed. "But I like being tangled up with you. In my bed."

"Hmm," she sighs, "so if you don't cuddle, what do you do after sex?"

My face tingles. "Drink."

She rolls and rocks, positioning herself on her elbows as she peers down at me. "Let's go paint," she offers, and while I had no intention of jumping up and grabbing a bottle, I like that she's trying to protect me.

Off the bed and on her feet, Ivy pokes through an open box on the floor, dragging out one of my t-shirts. She holds it up and without asking, slips it over her head, pulling her hair out of the collar. Finding her panties, she puts those back on, too, then claps her hands at me.

"C'mon, this place isn't gonna paint itself. And I'm hungry." And with that, she's traipsing down the hall, and I'm smiling at my ceiling like a damn fool.

TWO EMPTY CANS OF GRAY PAINT AND WE'RE TAKING A break to eat the takeout from Goode's we ordered. Ivy sinks into the couch, her Styrofoam clamshell in her lap, her long hair on top of her head, secured with a pencil.

"These walls drink paint. I can't believe we already went through two cans and we only did the dining area," she says, popping open the lid, the smell of sweet potato fries and chicken hitting my nose. My stomach rumbles.

In my jeans and nothing else, I take a seat next to her, placing two cans of Coke on the table in front of us. I pop hers open, then mine, and sit back with my own food.

"I know. I think we'll be painting for another week at least, even though this place is pretty small." I toss a French fry into my mouth and groan. Food has tasted better lately, and I know that could be the lack of booze in my veins, but I also know it could be the pretty lady next to me, too.

"I like it, though. I mean, I grew up in a pretty cozy house and... I don't know. There's something about being able to shout from your room to the kitchen and hear someone. I like it," she says, taking an enormous bite of her sandwich.

"Yeah?" I ask, taking a bite of my own sandwich. I went with a club this time, and fuck if it's not the best sandwich I've had yet. I groan and she nods, pushing a rogue piece of lettuce into her mouth as she gloats, "Told you Goode's is... good."

We smirk at one another with our mouths full, and she twists on the couch, legs crossed beneath her tray. "And yeah. I mean, part of living in a small town like Bluebell is liking things small, right? That goes for trust circles, house sizes and—"

"Not cock size," I interrupt with a wink.

She rolls her eyes. "If I loved a man, and he had a small dick, it wouldn't matter."

I nudge her with my elbow as I take another bite. "Good thing you're not in that situation."

She pauses, and our eyes idle as I stop chewing. The insinuation hangs between us, unspoken but understood. My skin prickles with heat, and the back of my neck burns.

"Good thing," she finally says, taking another bite.

I change topics, not allowing myself to bask in the fact she didn't challenge me on that. And we both know it's not about my dick size.

"And what else? What else is small in small towns that you like?" I ask, wishing there was a book called ABOUT IVY that I could binge, just to know everything.

"Dreams," she says, holding up a finger to stop my immediate protest. "Hear me out. I can have a dream—becoming a tattoo artist was my dream, you know? But the way I can fit that dream into the right setting in a small town, and work where I love while doing what I love, without any sacrifices, that's perfect. But if I wanted to be a doctor or, I don't know, an astronaut, well, I couldn't do that here."

I pick up the other half of my sandwich and pull the frilly topped toothpick out. "I get you."

"Would you have stayed in your hometown and been

happy tattooing if you hadn't gotten the show?" she asks, reaching forward to take a sip of Coke.

My hometown comes to mind, and my ex follows right after. Her face is hazy now, all these years later, but the splinter of pain that comes at the remembrance isn't. It's sharp and glinting, even now. I shake my head. "No. Too much shit there I didn't want to be around."

"Your ex?" she asks softly, as if testing the waters. I wasn't even aware she knew.

"How do you know about my ex?" I ask. Listen, I'm not proud but I've googled myself. It happens when you rise in fame overnight. Of all the terrible and dope things I've seen, her name isn't one of them. Successfully, I moved on without anyone tying us together. So Ivy knowing is... a first.

She pushes a piece of hair from my face, but it rocks my groin the way she casually takes care of me. Digging into her sandwich, around a mouth full of sweet potato fries, she says, "The circuit. Everly kind of told us a little at girls' night."

My interests rise. "Us?"

She nods. "Me, Juniper and Dolly."

My throat is sticky. "What did she tell you, exactly?"

"Honestly," she replies, "not much. Your ex cheated and broke your heart, and then you got the deal with *Needle Ninjas* and left." She gives me an empathic look. "I was cheated on too. So I completely get your desire to split."

"Someone cheated on you?" I ask, choking a shocked laugh.

"I could say the same for you," she says, "but yeah. My ex-boyfriend Rhett." She waves a dismissive hand between us. "Back to you. Rhett truly isn't worth talking about."

"Neither is she," I add quickly, then say, "I don't want to waste a minute of my time with you talking about people that don't deserve our thought or words, baby."

She stills, and blinks at me, her eyes misty. "Yeah," she croaks, clearing her throat, "I mean... yeah, I get that."

We finish our meals, all the while discussing the best horror movies and soundtracks. When Ivy tells me Michael Myers can't be beat, I twist on the couch and tell her to check out the TV screen tattooed on my left shoulder blade, where Michael Myers himself is on-screen.

Ranking everything that falls below the greatest, we agree that Freddy Kruger is kind of weird in hindsight, and that *Jaws* needs more recognition as a true horror flick. After that, we rank caffeinated drinks while moving on to our second cans of Coke. From there, the chat never stops, because talking to Ivy is the easiest thing I've ever done.

But when the sun slips behind the mountains and drapes my small home in shadows, the spell shatters, and she slips down the hall and puts her clothes back on, reappearing in the living room without my shirt. "I left your shirt on the bed," she says, picking up her black bag, stuffing the strap inside.

"You didn't have to take it off," I manage, my internal alarms sounding as she gets ready to leave. But I can't ask her to stay. I can't ask her to spend the night. I don't know what we're doing, and without a label, it makes it hard to ask her not to go. But when she rocks to her toes, presses her lips to mine and sucks my tongue into her mouth, sadness washes over me.

Not because I don't want to be alone.

I don't want to be without her.

But I let her go, not without peace of mind that she gets home safely. I drive behind her the entire way, all the way down the long dirt road that leads to her place and Hudson's. I flash my lights as she pulls open her front door, my way of saying goodbye.

And on my drive back, my phone lights up with a text.

Hope you like your tattoo. Thanks for a great
night.

Stopped at a red light, I text her back.

It's my favorite.

I'm sure she won't believe me, since I'm pretty much
covered from head to toe, but I'm not lying. It is my favorite.
She is my favorite.

TWENTY-THREE

"Explosive."

Ivy

Sunday morning breakfast is quick since we help Hudson set up the farmers market. But over a bowl of Corn Flakes with blueberries, my family and I have a quick catch-up.

"How's it going down at the tattoo shop?" Hudson asks, bouncing Honey on his hip as Dolly pulls a comb through Bear's hair.

Juniper shakes the box of cereal, tossing some into her bowl. "More so, how's it going with Trace?" she asks.

Looking between them all, I cannot help but grin. Cheesy, I know, but that's who I've become. A big ball of cheese with black buns.

"The apprenticeship is nearly over. I've got two weeks left. And it's going great. I'm already building a following, my portfolio is coming along nicely, and I have a few more solo appointments next week," I reply, looking directly at Hudson.

He nods, kissing Honey's open palm as she reaches for his lips, cooing "Dada" a mile a minute. "That's great, Ivy. You've always been so talented. I'm so happy it's all coming together for you."

Dolly, sitting across from me, stares up at her husband with stars in her eyes, sighing at his sweet response. That's probably going to earn him a blowjob in the near future.

"And things between me and Trace," I start, drawing the sentence out slowly, gathering Juni's and Dolly's focus. "They're... really moving along." I stare into the bowl of milk before getting the courage to admit the rest. "I'm falling for him, and it doesn't feel one-sided."

It's scary to admit that. If I'm wrong, though, my family won't make me feel foolish. They'll be here to turn my broken pieces into a collage of beauty, and bring me back to life if I need it. But I don't think I'll need it. I don't think Trace will hurt me.

He wouldn't.

"Yeah?" Dolly asks, rubbing her belly as her eyes widen with interest. "How so?"

I cast a sidelong look at Juniper, who knows I haven't been home as much. "Well, we've been hanging out more. Lunch breaks, after work, in the studio. I mean, last night I was at his place till nearly 10, helping him paint and just... talking." I clear my throat and pass Hudson a wince, knowing he won't be wholly interested in this. "Well, not just talking but a lot of talking. A lot of bonding."

Juniper claps her hands together and squeals. "Ooh, Ivy! Did you sleep with him? Oh my gosh, you sleeping with Trace, the man who you've followed online for ages? That is just," she shakes her head, bringing her hands to her mouth in disbelief, "perfect. It's a love story of all love stories."

Dolly agrees. "So romantic. Just think of the story you can tell your future kids one day!"

"Whoa," I groan, holding up a palm. "No babies yet. Right now, we're just... in that blissful state of falling. I think."

The room goes quiet but for Bear's tablet chirping as he plays a spelling game, and Honey still babbling about Hudson. We all know the feeling, because everyone here has fallen in love. Including Juni, though she's currently single.

"And yeah, we slept together," I add, breaking the sweet spell.

"And?" Dolly prods.

I shake my head. "Explosive."

"Ivy," Hudson starts, passing Honey to my sister. "You're aware of Trace's past, right?"

I love Hudson for Dolly, and I love having him as part of my family. He is always looking out for everyone in equal measure, and doesn't hide how protective he is.

Nodding, I sip my coffee. "Yeah, I know his ex cheated on him. We've talked about that. Rhett cheated on me, so we share that trauma."

Hudson shifts in his boots, his face hard to read for a moment. "He was really betrayed," he says, brows pulled together, eyes focused, as if he's trying to impart something more.

"I know," I reply, and I love that Hudson is so concerned but this is something his sister told me weeks ago. "Betrayal is one-size-fits-all in my book. The way a sin is a sin, betrayal is betrayal."

I look at my sisters, who nod because they agree.

Hudson doesn't say anything else, and Juniper makes me

promise to keep them updated on our relationship, and of course I agree.

I finish my cereal and start setting up white tents outside for the market.

I know Hudson only wanted to make sure I was aware of Trace's betrayal because of how much it affected him—he as much admitted last night that he left town because of the heartache, and that the show wouldn't have changed his decision to leave.

I didn't leave Bluebell when Rhett cheated on me. Hell, I actually haven't heard from Rhett in well over a year, and the last time he was spotted, Juniper saw him. She said he was on his way out of town, feeling bad about what had happened. Either way, I know he's been betrayed, and I know that changed him.

It changed me, too.

But as long as we're honest with each other, we can move past his hurt. Together.

And I think we're on our way to doing that very thing.

TWENTY-FOUR

Howdy, hodwy.

Trace

I haven't been nervous about a design in a long time. Years, even. When you have the name recognition that I have, with that comes trust. But being in Bluebell has instilled a sense of need in me.

I want to make them happy in a different way than I wanted for my other clients while traveling.

If someone in Bluebell isn't happy with their ink, I'm gonna see them day in and day out. At Goode's, at the farmers market, down the street at the credit union, or at the baseball field for Bear's T-ball games.

We're going to know each other because Bluebell is small and intimate.

After the stencil comes off the printer, I hold it up, bouncing the idea off of Ivy. We've been working together now for so many weeks, I look forward to her take on my designs. She's got a keen eye for detail, but more than that, she offers a perspective I can't. She knows these people, so when she tells me I'm missing a great opportunity on my new design, I listen. Because I trust her.

"I mean, Kenny's mom owns the Big Bun Bakery down the road, so here," she says, leaning over me, her dark hair swishing over my shoulder. I grab it, holding the silky strands as she talks, an intimate gesture that Deuce couldn't pull off with her. Only me. Only I know her this way. Ivy points to the spot in the mandala where the design will curve, since he wants it on the back of his bicep. "You can hide a little piping bag here, or maybe even just a whisk? Either way, we all love that bakery, and Kenny's so proud of his mom."

Still leaning over me, she turns her head, our faces close together. "She was a single mom and built the bakery from the ground up with two recipes."

Her plump lips have my cock hard. "That's incredible," I breathe, trying to stay focused on the task at hand. "Kiss me," I whisper, unable to fight my desires for her. It's getting that way now. The more we're around one another, the more I need to touch her, hold her, laugh with her, kiss her. She gives me a small peck as the front door jingles open.

"Do the piping bag," she whispers with a wink.

Kenny checks in at reception, and Deuce walks him over. Ivy is busy setting things up: my tray, the ink caps, my pen, restocking my cartridges, and reprinting the new stencil with the Easter egg added into the design.

Once we've got the stencil placed where Kenny wants it, the music is low and the lights are on him, I get started, Ivy in the corner watching.

"My girlfriend didn't really want me to get this tattoo," Kenny says as I begin the delicate work of outlining his design.

"No?" Ivy asks, and I can't help but let my gaze flicker in her direction, stealing a glance of her tucked away in my space. "Isn't she tattooed, too?"

Kenny sighs, and I continue working as I listen to people who've known each other forever have a nice chat. Bluebell is comforting in that way.

"She does have tattoos but it's not about that. I think... well, she's wanting to move forward and if I spend my money on anything but a ring, she won't admit it, but it bugs her."

"How long has it been?" Ivy asks, getting to her feet to steal a photo of me working for the Ink Time website.

"Six years," Kenny sighs.

I clear my throat right as Ivy groans, "Oof."

"I know," Kenny drones, "I know, I need to propose. It's just... I don't know. I always thought I'd have my life together more than this when I became someone's husband."

"You have a job that you work hard at. A home you love in a town you love," Ivy says, "what else is there?'

"I guess a better job? More money? A bigger place? I don't know. I just... didn't think I'd still be in the same place I was at eighteen." He sighs, turning his head to face Ivy.

"But you love her?" she asks softly, her eyes staying on his despite the fact I've changed needles and moved to shading the design. She always finds the right mix of engaging with clients and shadowing me. Deuce wasn't wrong—she was ready to be on her own weeks ago.

"Love her? God, Ivy, there's gotta be a bigger word."

"Tell me," she says.

"She helps me even when she doesn't realize it, you know? She's one of those souls where life is easier when she's in the room. When I'm on the brink of doing something stupid, she nudges me away. If I'm being an asshole, she'll give me a look and without scolding me, I'll realize what I'm doing. She never makes me feel bad, ever. And she's taught me so many new things. Small things when you think about it, like trying new foods and giving things a chance. But all of those things add up to a much more fulfilling life. I used to think I was too big for Bluebell, but she's shown me that there's so many layers here, and my mind was too small to see it. Now I see Bluebell is the perfect place for us. And she showed me that without judgment."

The rest of their conversation becomes a soft hum, like an air conditioner running in the background, or a ceiling fan spinning. I tune it out but still hear it, and lose myself in my own thoughts as I focus on shading the design.

I was a prick to Ivy. And when I was, she gave it right back to me. But not without a lesson. She saved my ass that night when those girls planned to rob Ink Time. That would've done some serious damage to my relationship with Deuce, not to mention, how could I work here every day as the guy who got the place robbed? And she did all of that on the heels of me purposely trying to hurt her—after we had a good day together. All because my feelings were hurt. And why? Because I didn't communicate my feelings to her.

She is helping me stay off the booze without rubbing my nose in the fact that I have a problem. And when it comes to the lifestyle I was leading before—she knows. She knows I've been sleeping around for years, and she doesn't remind me of it every free chance she gets. She doesn't compare herself to those women and make me tell her she's better. With Ivy, the past is in the past. She's so sure and confident, in a way I've never experienced. It's refreshing and bold, and when I'm with her, I'm the best version of myself because I want to be, not because I feel like I have to be.

And the sex.

Fuuuuuck. I never thought I'd get on my knees for

anything. In my past life, I was the man people swooned over. Waited in line to see. Asked to take photos with. Begged to fuck.

Something about being told how to please her all while pleasing myself is heady and addicting. The way she seamlessly controls my cock without effort is damn drunkening.

And every time I go down this road, whether it's over a cup of coffee or on the drive home, I always want to come to the same conclusion.

I want to start a real life here, with her.

My mind hasn't veered from that conclusion in weeks, and if anything, the need to get her off the market and officially make her mine has only grown, like wildflowers between concrete.

Another hour and Kenny's tattoo is finished. Ivy prepares his aftercare kit and hands him the mirror, pointing out the tiny spot where we paid homage to his mom.

He praises me over and over, and despite the fact I did the work, I share the praise with Ivy, because I know Kenny wouldn't like it as much without that little Easter egg.

After he pays and we stand around in the lobby, making small talk with Connor, he takes off. I find Ivy in my space, sanitizing my station. Her ass is fire in those little jean shorts with the torn tights underneath. And when I see the silver handle of a knife poking up from her boot, my cock thickens.

"Hey," I say, slipping in behind her, grabbing a towel to help her clean. She pauses, peering at me over the tray of supplies.

"I got this, you don't have to help," she says, smiling.

"Yeah, I do," I say, swiping over a patch of cleaner. "I shouldn't have let you do so much. I'm sorry about that."

She pauses her cleaning and says, "Deuce made it clear that the apprentice helps the mentor." She lifts the rag. "This is helping, don't go feeling guilty just because I've seen your *come face*."

Laughing, I shake my head, my ribs tightening. "I like your sense of humor, have I told you that?"

She rolls her eyes. "Obviously. It's awesome."

"Mmmhmm." I smirk, still looking at her out of the corner of my eye. "So, how long have you known Kenny and his girlfriend?"

"Forever," she sighs. "I went to high school with Kenny. I think he's between my and Juniper's age, but I can't remember. His girlfriend, Addie, is my age, though."

A knot rises in my throat. I've never been good at saying the important shit but with a woman like Ivy, it would be a crime to be dishonest. Truly. "You know all that stuff he was saying about his girl?"

She presses her hand to her chest as she stands. "So sweet."

I stand too and we toss our rags away. "He described you, you know."

She swallows and it's so quiet between us, I hear it. I step toward her, taking her elbows into my hands, drawing out her arms, linking our fingers together. "Yeah?"

I don't care that Connor is laying a stencil for a bald eagle not more than ten feet away. That we're on camera. That she and I haven't discussed "us." That Deuce is here and Sandi, at reception, is probably watching us.

Don't care about any of that.

"Ivy, all those things he said, the way his girl makes him feel," I start.

"Addie," she says nervously, and I think it's the first time I've seen her nervous. I glance at her lips, painted in black lipstick, and my chest squeezes.

"Don't care what her name is," I admit, my voice thinning with desire. "Ivy, I would be a fucking moron if I didn't notice all the ways you make me a better man. And even stupider if I couldn't see what a fucking catch you are."

That dark bottom lip wobbles a little, but she sucks it back in. My girl prides herself on being strong. I squeeze our waffled hands, giving her a little wink. "Do you know what you are to me?"

Her blue eyes bounce between mine. "Your apprentice."

Dipping into her space, I bring my lips to her ear, the back of my neck breaking out in bumps at her patchouli scent. "You're my girl, Ivy." I press my lips to her cheek, over and over, until I make my way to her lips. I don't care if mine end up black; I'd paint my body in her lipstick if it meant getting to taste her.

"You want to be my girl?" I ask, dropping my forehead to hers. Her fingers tighten around mine.

"Girlfriend?" she quantifies.

"Girlfriend," I confirm.

She squeals, and I crash my mouth to hers, eating up those noises of delight. I fucking love this woman, but I'm not ready to say it. Right now, I want to show her that I can be to her all those things she is for me.

Supportive, encouraging, guiding, caring, helpful. I want to show her that I deserve to love her, because I've shown her my ugly side plenty of times. Now it's time to give her the best I can; she deserves it.

I break the kiss and step back, shaking our hands free. Her eyes widen in confusion but I cup mine to my mouth, tip my head up, and shout, "Ivy Ellington is off the market!"

Her cheeks flame and she laughs, grabbing my forearm, tugging my hands down. "Shut up, dummy," she hisses, a smile from ear to ear.

"I can't," I tell her, looping my arm around her waist. "I

gotta make sure everyone is clear," bringing our mouths together, our lips barely grazing, I groan, "you are mine."

She arches her brow. "Fine, I'll let you believe that. But I think it's the other way around."

"You love disagreeing with me." I smile, kissing her lips then down her throat. She shoves me back.

"Not at work!" she protests, but those tight little nipples tell me she wants it.

Later. Definitely later.

"You're mine, I'm yours, potayto, potahto," I say, sinking in the chair as another client comes in.

"Howdy, hodwy." She grins.

I shake my head. "I'm gonna pay you back for that tonight, Firecracker."

And I intend to.

TWENTY-FIVE

"I wanna smell you on me tomorrow."

Ivy

"I'm definitely locked in the bathroom right now," I whisper, my cheeks aching from the smile I've been wearing for the last two hours. "And I'm pretty sure my last appointment thought I was high because of the stupid look on my face."

"Stupid happy!" Dolly corrects jubilantly, Bear and Honey laughing in the background. "That's great—being official is a great step!"

"Next up—a ring!" Juniper adds.

"I'm so happy he came to Bluebell. Deuce was right, this was the best thing for him," Ev chirps. "Actually, you were the best thing for him. He's really changed, Ivy, and I think we can all agree—that's because of you."

Pinching the phone to my shoulder, I reach into my pocket and dig out a tube of lipstick. Using my mouth, I take off the cap and spit it in the sink, twisting it until the black pigment appears. "We've been good for each other," I agree, but to say it's all been me that's helped Trace turn things around... I don't think so.

Not drinking takes more than a strap-on and a tease of sex. It takes willpower and dedication, all the while being in a new environment, training someone, and adjusting to the world around him– "I'm proud of him, though. He's really pulled out of the dark space he was in when he came to Bluebell."

"Well, what now? Are you coming home tonight?" Juniper asks, but before I can answer, Ev and Dolly give a unanimous "*Psshhh.*"

"She's getting dicked down to celebrate, aren't you, Ivy?" Dolly asks.

I tap my chin, mulling over some plans I've been brainstorming for some time. "Yeah," I reply, "something like that."

"Something like that," Ev repeats. "That sounds kinky."

"Oh, Ev," I smirk, putting the tube of lipstick away as I plop my lips together. "You have no idea."

TRACE'S MOUTH HAS TASTED EVERY SQUARE INCH OF ME. Seriously.

His tongue dips into my belly button while his hands skate my ribs, gripping me. "*Shit,*" he groans, "If I could bottle you up and drink you, I still don't think it would be enough."

Appreciation flutters through me, heat flaring in my cheeks and blooming in my chest. After I stopped by my house to get a few things (*ahem*), we came to his place and this man had me stripped naked in under a minute.

In the midst of painter's tarps and boxes, he's got me on the floor, nothing on but open, unbuttoned jeans. His lips carve a trail of heat along my stomach as I peer down, spotting the wet tip of his cock aggressively surging from his open jeans. My pussy blooms at the prolific sight, and it has me moaning for him, pleading with him.

"Trace, I want you to fuck me, fuck me, *fuck me*," I beg, each time my voice rising higher, need rattling in my throat. The more I cry out, the harder I dig my nails down his bare back. When he groans, I torture him by sucking his fingers into my mouth. And the more I want him, the crazier he becomes, pressing his erection into me as he leaves a mark on my neck.

He gets to his feet, finally shucking off his jeans. Trace moves toward the hall, no doubt toward the bathroom in his bedroom, going for the ridiculously oversized box of condoms he has stashed in there, but I grab his wrist.

"You said you got tested after that night," I whisper, refer-ring to the infamous night in the lobby of Ink Time where I finally got to put my boot-knife to use. I knew that thing would come in handy eventually.

One day in the studio, when Trace and I were working quietly side by side while his arm grazed mine repeatedly, the chemistry between us a silent blaze, he made a confession. He said that after that night, he got tested because he knew he wanted to turn things around. That if he would ever have a chance with a woman like me, he had to make changes. And that started with his health.

"Ivy," he breathes, boomeranging back to me, lowering his body over mine. The feel of his carved chest and round muscles, his warm skin painted in beautiful art telling stories of his soul—it will never not be the hottest thing on the planet. Maybe in the entire solar system. Honestly.

While we've established he's clean, there's one thing *I* haven't told him.

I've been on the pill for years. I didn't tell him before but now, it feels right.

"I'm on the pill, Trace," I tell him slowly, our eyes idling in the slow dance of processing. I lick my lips. "If you want to spread my legs and sink your fat, veiny cock inside me, I'll milk you," I say, nodding gently, licking my bottom lip, thoughts of his cock inside me flitting through my mind. I want this man so much. "I'll clench all around you if you fuck me hard, and then when you can't take it, you can come in me, bury all that hot, thick cum deep inside my hungry, swollen little pussy. And when you've filled me full, you can pull out and watch your cream spill from my pink lips, and drip down my ass. Don't you want that, Trace? Don't you want to see your cum oozing out of my pink, swollen, used cunt?" I bring my head off the floor, pressing my forehead to his. "*Your* used cunt."

His broad chest heaves as a virile, feral growl tears through. "Shut up, Ivy," he groans, nudging my face to the side to take a bite of my pulse, making me moan.

"I love your lips on my neck, and I can't wait to feel your bare cock slipping into me at the same time," I tease, trailing my fingertips lightly up his spine, edging him.

"Shut the fuck up, Firecracker," he warns, lifting his head from where he was blissfully sucking my neck. Our eyes tangle in the midst of our heated desires, his nostrils flaring with virile need. He wants me back, and that makes my pussy weep. What else makes me soaked? The feel of his cock heavy against my belly, leaving an eager mess. So sexy.

"You're dripping, leaking for my pussy, desperate for me to say the word," I whisper, dragging my tongue through the split of my lips.

"You're going to make me blow all over you, is that what you want?" he growls, dipping his head to my chest, sucking one of my nipples into his mouth. A deep groan tears through him, his teeth clamping down, making my spine arch from the ground. I love the way he gently grinds his body into mine, his cock gliding in precum against my stomach.

"Are you gonna hump me and cum all over me before you get to fuck me? Hmm?" I suck his earlobe then give it a nibble.

"I told you to shut your fucking mouth, Ivy," he groans, rocking to his knees, death gripping his cock.

I smirk up at him, the flare in his eyes making my chest tighten. "I like it when you talk shit to me," I tell him, collecting my tits in my palms, strumming my thumbs over my pointed, thirsting nipples. He watches, gripping himself something fierce. "It's gonna make it all that much better when you finally take control, and fuck me just the way you like."

"Right fucking now," he breathes, stroking my clit with his thumb. Arching my back, I push against his hand, seeking more friction, ready to deploy the next part of my plan in driving my new boyfriend absolutely batshit crazy.

"Before you fuck me, I have something I want to show you," I mewl, reaching for the bag I brought.

Trace follows my arm, seeing what I'm grabbing, and shakes his head, now stroking his erection. I could masturbate to the sight of him stroking. I probably will later.

"Oh no, no *suck the strap* shit, I'm getting in that pussy of yours on *my* terms," he states, reaching for the bag. But I yank out a dildo, one he hasn't seen yet.

"That wasn't my plan," I tell him, bringing the dildo to my stomach, moving the head of it through the mess he left on me.

He's all heaving chest and rumbling moans mixed with a string of curse words as I bring the dildo to my mouth.

"I can deep throat, did you know that? Have I told you that?" I ask, batting my eyes. I kiss the tip of the cock and show him the black lipstick imprint left on it, making him snarl.

"Ivy," he warns, but I'm not stopping. I have him just where I want him.

"Put your hands behind your back," I advise, and when he doesn't immediately do it, I add, "*now.*"

Once he obeys, I smile and take the six-inch toy down my throat in the first push.

"*Fucking shit mother freaking fuck,*" he sputters, his fist barely pumping now, using caution that arouses me. I love how I bring him to the edge.

Plunging the dildo deep in my throat a few times, I take it out. "I want you to put your hand on my throat and feel how that toy fills me, and imagine it being you," I tell him, adding, "imagine being that deep in my throat and coming."

He pushes my hand toward my mouth playfully, urging me to continue my show. Sinking the cock onto my tongue, aiding the deep throat with a swallow, my pussy nearly explodes at the sight of him reaching for me, at my favorite octopus-covered fingers wrapping my throat, his palm pressed against me as the cock spears me.

"Shit," he growls, his other hand stroking his erection, still weeping freely onto my belly. "Ivy, you're so goddamn beautiful."

Pulling the cock from my throat, I smile and say, "It's almost time to fuck me, but there's one more thing I want to do."

"I need inside you, Firecracker, I'm dyin' here," he moans, but like an obedient lover, he helps me up when I stretch my hand toward him.

"Stand up with me." I smile, bringing my saliva-coated lips to his.

We get to our feet, and I press the dildo base to his groin, forcing his erection to stand horizontal, parallel to the toy. Taking my time, I get to my knees and bring my mouth to the dildo, wrap my fist around the shaft, and begin pumping it while I tease the rubber crown.

"What are you doing to me?" he breathes, sifting his fingers through my hair, keeping it all off of my face.

With his cock pressing against my throat, I suck the dildo into my mouth, blinking up at him through tears of strain. My hand twists and my nostrils flare as I bob relentlessly on the toy, his hand still reluctantly obeying by holding it to his body.

The feel of his slick cockhead sliding against me as he watches me devour the toy, both of us pretending it's him, has my own orgasm building.

Wetness coats my thighs, but I suck the rubber cock and stare up at him, determined to make him nuts.

"Ivy, I can't take this, baby," he groans, sucking in a sharp breath, pulling his bottom lip under his teeth, he battles for control over his cock. The one that is hardly even being touched.

I pop off the toy cock and blink up at him. "Come on my tits, Trace. I want your cum all over me."

Curling my tongue underneath the head of the dildo, I suck it into my mouth right as his hand tightens on my head. He forces me deep on the toy as heat splashes against my neck, hot jets spraying me repeatedly as I'm flanked by his curses and groans.

Shooting his cum all over me, the pearly slide of it dripping down my tits, my cunt throbs. I've never needed a cock inside me as bad as I do now. I physically need him inside me, and because of it, a wicked shudder rolls through me and my body erupts in needy trembles.

He tosses the toy aside and takes my chin in his hand, tipping my face up to him.

"You're shaking," he breathes, still catching his breath. I

spread my hands through the mess on my body, trembling for his cock.

"I need you," I admit, still playing with his cum. "More of you, please."

He's got his hands under my arms and I'm wrapping my legs around his waist, his still hard cock pressed between our bodies he storms us down the hall, to his bedroom.

Tossing me onto the bed, he stalks over me, a predator no longer fucking around with his prey. It's consumption time, and I'm about to see how Trace Wade fucks his girlfriend when he's in control.

My stomach clenches as shivers continue to roll through me, leaving me a sticky, trembling mess for him. Hooking his hands under my knees, he rolls me up slightly.

"Watch," he commands. "Watch me get inside you bare."

My eyes threaten to flutter closed at his promises, but I keep them open because I want to memorize this moment. Our eyes lock for a moment, and he winks, causing a new wave of shudders to roll through.

Then, his thumb aligned with his crown, he pushes inside me, sinking into me inch by inch until our bodies are thoroughly joined. At the same time, we sigh, content, as if this is the moment we've both been needing. This is different than when I fucked him.

This is Trace taking control of me, showing me what I mean to him with his body. Dropping to the mattress, he keeps himself over me with his palms on either side of my head, our bodies sticky with his cum.

He rocks his hips slow at first, drawing his length in and out, taking his time as he studies my features.

"You look beautiful taking me," he rasps, making me clench all around him. "Whoa, whoa, none of that, not yet. Not until I pound you out and make you fucking scream for God."

"Trace," I whimper, needing him to pick up his pace, thirsting for his mouth on me, hungering for more.

His smirk lights my soul on fire. "Who's begging now, baby?"

I arch off the bed, seeking out more of him, but he stops me, pressing a palm flat on my groin. The arm holding him up torques as he applies pressure to my lower half. "No, Firecracker. No. You get what I give you. Got it?"

I nod, loving the role reversal, my mind a scorched mess from his commands.

"Now, are you ready?" he asks, eyes dancing with mine.

I nod.

"Reach behind you, grab the headboard, and don't let go until I'm dripping out of you, got it?" he questions quietly, his tone gentle, as if he's not delivering the hottest orders.

I nod again as his hand comes back to the other side of my head. Reaching up, I curl my hands around the wooden headboard.

His strokes build momentum, each slick glide of his hard cock through my soft flesh builds intensity. His eyes never leave mine as he pumps and thrusts between my splayed legs. "You want my cum, don't you, Firecracker?"

Briefly, his eyes flash to the sticky cum drying on my tits. "You want it on you and in you, but mostly in you, isn't that right?"

The headboard slams into the wall as I cry out, screaming *more! Harder! Faster! Yes! Please!*

"You want me to leave you so full that you can't take a step for a week without my cum dripping down your thighs," he groans, swiveling his hips, the head of his cock nudging something deep inside me.

I clench around him, throwing my head back, basking in

the building pressure. My heart flutters and my toes curl. "Trace," I moan, reading the signs. "I'm gonna come."

"Yeah you are," he says, rutting into me harder, his hips aggressive between my legs. My pussy burns from the roughness in which he fills it, over and over. "You're gonna come on your man's big dick because you've been wet for it all day, haven't you? You needed my cum on your tits and on your fingers because you just couldn't wait, isn't that right, Firecracker?" He groans, and then it's over. His cock and his mouth take me out, and my world goes dark as my pussy seizes, exploding all around him in heady bursts. Clenching and throbbing, my hips buck off the bed, my words jumbled in chaos as I writhe and come.

"Shit, Ivy," he grits, and then I feel it.

The first time I've ever felt it. And with the only one I ever want to feel it with.

Cum flooding me. Thick, hot waves of his release, inundating my abdomen, riding back up his shaft and down my ass. His cock pulses, and the twitch of his orgasm inside me has me bucking again, finding a second release.

"Yes, Trace, come deep," I urge and moan, thrashing beneath him as his cum spreads through my hips. We come, and come down together, leaving me a stuffed and sated heap.

Finally, when he's grunted for the last time, he slides out, peering down between my legs to watch his cum follow. Reaching down, I dip into the mess, fingering myself to feel what he left inside me, watching his face while I do.

"Ivy, you are just—" He shakes his head, still watching his orgasm streak out of me.

"Your girlfriend," I finish, giddy as I say the word *girlfriend*.

His eyes travel my bare, sticky body and come to mine. "I was going to say the sexiest woman alive but I guess that's interchangeable with girlfriend." Trace wastes no time in scooping me up, setting me down on the bath mat before starting the shower.

"There's soap and shit in there, probably not the good-smelling shit you use but—"

"It's fine," I tell him, waving my hand beneath the spray to test the temperature. "You wanna get in with me?"

He shakes his head, pressing his lips to mine. "I'm gonna change the sheets and get us some water." Scratching the back of his head, he looks into the spray a moment then at me. "You, uh, you want to sleep here?"

I reach out and pinch his nipple before stepping under the stream of hot water, letting him watch me for a moment with the curtain pulled open. "Let me ask you this," I start, grabbing the bar of soap from the ledge. "Do you want me to sleep over?"

He nods. "Fuck yes."

"Me too."

Then we stand there smiling like total dipshits before I yank the curtain shut and smile alone in the shower stall, where it's far less corny. "You really don't want a shower?" I ask again as he brushes his teeth at the sink.

"Nope," he replies. "I wanna smell you on me tomorrow."

"Gross," I reply, but I'm still smiling.

Thirty minutes later, his leg is tangled with mine and I'm lying on his chest, listening to his heart beat as we find deep, restful sleep together.

And no matter what I dream while asleep, nothing is better than my current reality.

TWENTY-SIX

Can we keep this between us?

Trace

"Open up," Deuce hollers, throwing his fist into my door over and over.

Stumbling out of bed, I grip the wall as I traipse down the hall, my head killing me, my mouth full of cotton. Yanking open the door, I bring my arm over my face, blocking out the egregious morning sun. "Jesus Christ, man, is the house on fire?"

"Why aren't you answering the phone?" he questions, peering around me into the house. Opening the door, I let him in and close it, still waking up.

"Because I was asleep." I motion to my fucked-up hair and near-naked body.

He looks at his watch. "It's ten a.m."

I rub my eyes. A painful whomp radiates through my head. "I was up late."

Leaning in, he studies me. And it takes me a moment before I realize what he's doing.

I shove him back, more awake now that I understand. "Fuck off, I'm not hungover."

He studies me another moment, his dark eyes roving over me like a parent to a child. Finally, his shoulders sink and he huffs out a deep breath. "Thank God."

"You really thought I'd go back to all that shit?" I ask, moving around him to get to the kitchen. Rinsing the carafe, I fill it with water and pour it into my Mr. Coffee. I like this coffee maker. It's simple, makes 12 cups, nothing fancy. Ivy got it for me. And when she sleeps over, we have enough for both of us. I got her protein powder, too.

"I don't know, you asked for the day off today and Ivy didn't sleep over last night. Those two things..." he trails off with a shrug. "I'm just making sure."

I scoop out some grounds and dump them in the basket, slapping the lid closed. "Okay," I say, considering his words. A breath in through my nose and out my mouth, another one, and I meet his gaze. "I can see where you may have thought that."

Deuce's head swivels back, his eyes wide, a real dumb look on his face. "Wow. You're not gonna be butthurt for an hour because I dared to check on you." He lets out a low whistle, shaking his head. "You better marry her."

I don't respond to that, because I'm still working things out in my head when it comes to Ivy and marriage. Instead, I tell him exactly why I'm home on a workday, why my beautiful girlfriend slept at her place when she's basically been living with me for the last few weeks, and why my head is killing me.

"I lied to her and told her I didn't feel good—told her I didn't want to get her sick since Dolly's pregnant and she's around her so much. So that's why Ivy didn't sleep over. She thinks I'm sick." The coffee's slow drip makes my skin tingle. Fuck, I need caffeine.

"And... you're not sick?" He narrows his eyes. "You look kinda shitty."

"That's just what I look like, asshole," I reply, getting out two pieces of bread from the box on the counter. Ivy said I needed a bread box to keep things off the counter, but to keep my bread fresh. It doesn't make sense to me because the bread box sits on the counter, but I got one anyway. I'd get a fucking bread box tattooed on my cock if she told me. "But no, I'm not sick. I stayed up all fucking night planning a party and because I've never planned a party, it was a lot harder than I thought."

"Dude, my brother-in-law hosts the town farmers market every week. He's great at planning shit. You coulda called me." He sinks into the couch, stacking his boots on my coffee table. "What party you plannin'?"

A smile curls my lips as I dig Juni's jam and butter from the fridge. "Well, Ivy's last day as the shop apprentice is next week. And I thought we'd have, like... I don't know, a graduation-style party? But just for her, for ending the program."

Deuce just stares at me. I stare back.

"What?"

He shakes his head. "I just... I don't know. You're so different." He smiles in a way that tells me I'm about to get annoyed. "I was right about you coming here. Admit it."

I roll my eyes. "Does Ev never compliment you or what? You gotta come over here and get me to make you feel good?" The toast pops up, and I snatch it, laying the pieces across a plate.

A real plate, not a paper one.

Ivy is to thank for that too. Well, Ivy and Amazon.

"I'm guessing the party is a surprise," Deuce says.

"Yeah," I agree, slathering the jam on thick as my stomach

rumbles. "And I guess it's a good thing you did your compliment crawl because I wanted to ask if we could have it at Ink Time."

Deuce nods. "Course we can," he agrees easily.

I bite the inside of my cheek as I smear butter over the jam. Yeah, that's the order. "There's something else." I look up and find his eyes on me.

"What?"

"I want to buy this place from you."

He snorts. "You know you could buy a better place. Or build your own place."

I roll my eyes, and I get why Ivy does it so much. Sometimes an eye roll covers what words don't. "I know that. But..." I trail, summoning the man courage to say feely things to another man. "This is the place where I got better and figured out what I want, and who I want that with," I admit, my voice rough. "And I know you and Ev bought it as a fixer-upper investment but I'm willing to buy you out, and buy you guys any other property in Bluebell."

"We'd be neighbors. Can you be my neighbor?" Deuce asks, a grin teasing his lips.

"I don't know. Will you be over here begging for compliments all the time?" I prod.

"A few days a week, max," he says. He gets up from the couch with a grunt. "Let me talk to Ev, all right?"

I nod. "Yeah, and the party, can we keep this between us?"

He salutes me. "You thinking Friday for the party?"

Pouring my cup of coffee, I agree, telling him more of the plans. "Yes, and I have a bunch of black balloons, black crepe streamers, you know, a ton of gothic party shit being delivered here in a day. After I figured out I wanted to do a gothic theme, I drew up a little design for her, and I'm gonna have that printed onto a banner today to hang in the entry of the shop."

"Show me," Deuce says, reaching past me to swipe a mug, "and fill it."

I pour him a cup then shuffle down the hall, sipping the much-needed caffeine, grabbing my sketch book. Flipping it open, I show him the design. "It's kinda stupid, the play on words. But I couldn't bring myself to do a dumb congratulations sign, you know?"

We look down at the sketch taking up the page. The words Ivy Inks are written in gothic print, the knife in her boot replicated through the I in *Ivy* and *Inks*. "It's gonna be black and white, with this here being a spot of red," I say, pointing to the little drop of blood dripping off the end of the blade on the knife that makes up her name.

"She's gonna love it," Deuce finally says, and I release my breath, relieved he approves. I've never planned anything for anyone, so around three in the morning I questioned if all of this was stupid or not. Deuce knows Ivy, irritatingly it can be argued he may know her better than me in some ways, so if he says it's good, I'm on the right track.

I clap my hand on his shoulder and squeeze. "Glad to hear you say that because after six hours into this I was worried it may be... I don't know... too much."

He laughs. "Proposing on the first date is too much. Throwing a party to celebrate your girlfriend's hard work and accomplishments is not too much."

I nod, taking a bite of my toast as I stare at my sketch.

"She's gonna know, though," he says, finishing his coffee.

"Know what?" I say around a bite of toast.

"That you're in love."

"You're right," I reply, "she'll definitely know the next day, because I'm going to tell her."

"Don't wanna tell her that night? I mean, hell, she's gonna see the work you put into this and know, man."

I take another bite and talk with my mouth full because it's Deuce, and I ain't wasting manners on him. "Na, that night is about her. Celebrating finishing the program. Not about how I feel about her. It can wait until the next morning." I bend down and pull from the cupboard another Amazon buy.

"You're telling her with that?" Deuce says, chuckling.

I look at the heart-shaped waffle maker. "Yeah, asshole, I am. Because it's *cute*." I take another bite of toast. "And I'm making the batter black."

Deuce laughs. "That's better."

We make some more small talk and work out a few details for the party, and Deuce finally heads out. I send Ivy a text, telling her I'm all better, but it's probably best if we spend the weekend apart.

I hate it. I want more than anything to see my girl. But I need to get to the printer in Oakcreek to get the banner done, and pick up some silk black roses from the flower shop, too.

I can't wait to celebrate her. To see the look on her face when a room of people she loves cheers on all that she's done.

She deserves the best night ever, and I'm going to give it to her.

TWENTY-SEVEN

"There's always a blonde."

Ivy

With the towel draped around my shoulders and clipped under my chin, I tip my head forward, peering at my blonde roots. I give the bottle another shake and start applying, the dye is cool through the rubber gloves, and cold against my scalp.

Today is the last day that I'm an apprentice at Ink Time. Tomorrow? I'm a resident artist.

That fact still gives me chills.

I'm excited—Juniper and Dolly want to take me to the art supplies store after work and treat me to a whole slew of new pencils and pads. Deuce texted me this morning saying he's got a bottle of champagne with my name on it. Ev came by the house this morning with celebration donuts. Hudson had Bear and Honey hold a congratulations sign and text me a picture.

Trace says he has a surprise for me.

And I'm excited.

I am.

But my stupid, overthinking mind can't let go of the fact that there were three days and nights this week where we didn't see each other. He even missed a day of work.

He said he was sick and that he didn't want me to catch anything and give it to Dolly, and at first I thought that was incredibly thoughtful.

I know I don't have a reason not to trust Trace. Since the first time we fooled around, he's been loyal to me, emotionally and physically. We drew the relationship line a few weeks ago, becoming an official couple. He shouted it around the shop. And the day after he took that photo of our boots on his porch, he posted it to his social media. The first time he's posted in over a year.

The caption read "It's not the where, it's the who" with a smiley face emoji. He changed his profile name from Trace Calhoun to Trace Wade, and now, in his bio, it says "Livin' the dream somewhere in Cali."

I shouldn't have questions in my mind. But as I slather the eclipse shade onto my hair, I can't help but wonder, did he slip up and drink on one or all of those days and is he ashamed to tell me?

Don't think that way, Ivy. Don't let your belief in him falter, because he'll see it. He knows you well by now and he will see the doubt in your body language.

Juniper pushes into my room with a yawn. "You're up early," she says.

"Want to look good for my last day. I know we'll take pictures," I tell her. "Why are you so tired? Weren't you in bed by 7?"

She blinks at me, her hands tightening around her mug of tea. Her hair is messy, like she tossed and turned all night, which is unlike Juniper. Once she goes to bed, I don't hear a peep.

"I, uh, had company last night, after you got home from Trace's and went to bed."

I didn't sleep over last night, knowing I wanted to do my roots this morning. And if I'm being honest? I can't stop wondering about those three days, so the decision to sleep at my own house felt even worse.

"Company?" I stop dying my roots and look at my older sister who, for as long as I can remember, has been single. At thirty-one, she's got a thriving business and has never seemed interested in more than exploring nature, hikes, long drives and making jam.

Her cheeks turn to bubble gum. "Yeah..." she trails off, sipping her tea to buy time. But I'm five minutes into a forty-five-minute hair dyeing session at six in the morning so I've got time. Lots of it. And I'm also starved for a distraction.

"Juni, you realize you need to spill, right?"

She sets her mug down next to my bottles of perfume on my dresser and takes a seat on the foot of my bed, behind where I'm sitting at my vanity.

"Promise to not judge me?" she asks, biting her thumbnail.

I twist in my seat and face her. "If we didn't judge Dolly for all the crazy shit she's done over the years, what makes you think I'd judge you?"

She tucks her messy golden hair behind her ears, nodding. With a huffed-out breath, she says, "I'm actually seeing two guys, not just one."

I blink. Somewhere in the distance, a cricket chirps, I swear it does.

"You're fucking two guys?" I breathe, both surprised and proud. "Damn, Juni, *get it!*"

She brings her hands to her face, hiding away as she shakes

her head. "No, no, we're not... *fucking*." Spreading her ring and middle finger apart, she blinks at me through her hand. "Yet."

I slap her knee and return to facing the mirror, adding more eclipse to my ends. "Who are they?"

Over the top of her mug, in the mirror reflection, Juniper smirks. "Actually, you know them both. You saw them here once, returning empty jars to me."

A few faces run through my mind. A lot of customers come out here to return Juni her jars—she offers a discount off her order for reusing them. But it's mostly old ladies and churchgoers.

My eyes widen as that morning from a few months ago rushes back. "Dash Foster and Sterling Ford?" I ask, remembering how Bluebell's favorite police officer and only garbage man stood out front, whispering and... well, bickering. "Aren't they roommates too?"

She nods. "Yeah."

Where blonde pokes through the old dye, I smother it in new dye. "Dash is my age," I state, as if she doesn't know. "And Sterling..."

"He's thirty-four," she adds, her voice a little lower than a moment ago. I meet her eyes in the mirror.

"Juniper!" I squeal. "You're with a younger *and* older man!"

She smiles. "Well, we're not, like, official or anything. But I have a connection with them both."

I lick my lips. "Do they, you know, do stuff with each other?"

She shakes her head. "No, I mean, I don't know. I don't think so? It's still new. I mean, it's... complicated," she says, going distant for a moment.

"When you're ready to share, I'm here," I offer.

"Thanks," she adds, getting back up to retrieve her tea.

From the doorway she says, "I can't believe it's your last day already. I'm so proud of you, Ivy. You did it."

"Thanks," I reply, squirting the last bit of dye onto my head.

Juniper leaves, and instead of focusing on the fact that today is my day, a day to celebrate all that I've done, my mind goes back to those same three days and the same thought—*was he really sick?*

EXPECTING TO WALK INTO A SLOW STUDIO WITH CONNOR tucked away in the corner with a client, Trace and Deuce chatting over coffee, I'm blown away with what greets me.

Trace, dressed in his usual dark jeans and black t-shirt, his hair down and damp from a shower, brown boots on his feet. Waiting at the door, he weaves his fingers through mine and pulls me into the studio, crowded with my family and friends.

Hudson and Dolly are here, Honey in Hud's arms, Bear running around the place. Juniper is here, and now I know why she was up despite having not slept. Connor and his friends stand in one corner, lifting their mimosa cups to me as I take in the space. Rochelle is here, with her partner/sub, and so is Jeremy. Between clients and friends, there's hardly room for me to move, but Trace pulls me through until we're at reception.

"Look," he says, motioning to a banner hanging from the eaves.

My eyes immediately blur with heat, and a knot forms in my throat. Ivy Inks is drawn out, clearly by Trace because I'd recognize his work with a blindfold on. The I in my name and Inks is a dagger, ornate and detailed, the same one I keep in my boot. "I made it for you, to celebrate your last day," he says, his lips pressed to my ear as he wraps his arms around me, lifting me up.

"I'm so proud of you," he adds, and I don't get the chance to say anything because I'm on my feet again and he's whistling, garnering the attention of everyone in the space. I spot Deuce, who winks, and points to Trace, mouthing, "He planned all of this."

"Listen up," Trace shouts. "Ivy's here, and we're all here to celebrate her, so please, first, a round of applause for Bluebell's most talented artist," he says, clapping as the room follows suit.

When the cheering settles, he looks down at me and amidst the hushed room, says, "Ivy, you are talented and hardworking, and you're good with clients. Watching you grow into a role you were destined to fill has been an honor and a privilege. Thank you for letting me be your mentor, for teaching me things when I should've been teaching you." He lifts a champagne flute full of juice as someone nearby shoves one into my hand. "To Ivy."

The room echoes "To Ivy" and then we're sipping mimosas, and Juniper is wheeling out a cart covered in plates and napkins, with fruit, muffins, scones, cookies, cupcakes and jams everywhere.

I turn to face Trace. "You did all this for me?" A knot of emotion lodges itself beneath my words, and I'm afraid to say more, because I don't want to cry. I just... I can't believe it. Trace did this for me, and everyone is here, for me.

He lowers his mouth to mine, kissing me as his hand takes my chin. "Ivy, you deserve all this and more."

I blink up at the banner he made. "You made that for me," I breathe, taking in how accurate the knife is to the one in my boot.

He smiles. "I had to sneak out of bed a few nights and study your knife so I could get the sketch just right," he admits with a wink.

I point to the gold and black balloons around the shops, and the crepe paper draped from station to station. "You did all this?"

He nods, his chest puffed with pride. "I did. If you felt a little distance over the last week it's because I was doing this." He looks around at the decorated space full of people before his gaze lowers to mine, wide and shining, full of sincerity. "And it still doesn't feel like enough. I wish I knew a better way to celebrate you and all the amazing things you are."

"Trace," I start, unable to speak.

"Thank you for being my girlfriend, and congratulations." He pulls me into the fairly empty hall and hands me a box with a red bow. I flip it open, but tears blur my eyes so fast I have to blink to see. Inside is a tattoo machine, the handle wrapped in pink, ready for me to use. "It's the same one I use," he says quietly.

"I know," I breathe, turning the machine over in my hands. It's the best. One I couldn't afford or wouldn't be able to afford for years. "Thank you, Trace."

I wrap my arms around his neck and sink into his chest, closing my eyes at the feel of his palms skating up my back.

"You're welcome, Firecracker."

We break apart and he smiles. "The party's all day. Everyone will be here all day. And guess what? You have a full schedule. Every hour you have a dealer's choice session booked."

New tattoo artists are rarely left to their own devices, instead assigned to do the client's choice. But today, they're letting me do my own thing, and that's a huge deal. I know Trace is to thank.

I rock to my toes and kiss his cheek. "Thank you," I tell him, feeling overwhelmed by all that he's done. And he was planning this while I was thinking he'd relapsed, or worse. "I'm sorry," I choke out, the guilt gnawing at my toes.

"For what?"

"I don't know," I say, glancing up at the door as a petite woman filters in. "Being distant last week, I guess."

"You had a lot on your mind. Graduating your apprenticeship is a big deal. Being able to ink freely is huge. Don't worry, Firecracker, I understand."

He places a kiss on my forehead and steps back, motioning to reception. "Today ain't about us, it's about you, so I'm gonna let you mingle and work. Your first session is here. I had Juniper bring your sketchbook." His grin makes my stomach tighten and my heart bloom behind my ribs. I love this man, of that I have no doubt. "Lunch is coming from Goode's, but me and you? We reconvene tonight. When the party's over." He presses his soft lips to mine. "Then we celebrate." He dances his eyebrows.

I rock on my feet, holding my new tattoo machine in my hands. I'm giddy with all this excitement and what he's done for me, so with a grin from ear to ear, I say, "Thank you."

I AM EXHAUSTED BUT IN THE BEST WAYS. OKAY, MAYBE NOT the best because the best way to be tired is from sex, but tattooing? Close second.

Today I've inked a skull swamped by wild vines, a shooting star, a treasure chest, a pirate's map, a mermaid, a pistol and a Care Bear. It's been the most professionally fulfilling and emotionally uplifting day of my life. A day I'll never forget.

Nearing five o'clock, I slip into the bathroom to touch up my lipstick, smothering on another layer of black. After finger-combing my dark waves, I adjust my tits in my black bodysuit, turn to make sure my ass is still looking fire in my cutoff shorts, and pluck at the tears in my tights, making sure they align to show off my tattoos.

Looking good, feeling good, I head back out to the studio to find a fresh wave of people there to celebrate. Lots of friends from the farmers market, the woman who owns the art supply store, my eighth grade art teacher, and so many other familiar faces.

Today is the best day ever. And I cannot wait to show my gratitude later.

After another few hours of visiting, taking photos, giving out tiny tattoos, my very pregnant sister decides she needs to get off her feet, so with my nephew's hand in mine, I walk her out. Hudson straps Honey in the car seat as I kiss Bear goodbye, hugging Dolly last.

"I'm so excited for you, Ivy," she says tearfully, her hormones getting the best of her. "You did what you set out to do, and you're in love!" She shakes her head, swiping beneath her eyes at the unending stream of tears. "Everything turned out so perfect. Like a fairy tale," she hiccups.

I stroke my hand down her hair, smiling. "Tattoos and fairy tales," I reply, "it all worked out."

"Tell Trace we said goodbye. I couldn't find him in there," my sister says before pulling me into a final hug.

Hudson collects her, helping her into the cab of the truck. The four of them wave through the windows, and drive off into dusk. I watch until their taillights are gone, and stay beneath the streetlamp an extra minute, soaking up everything that was today.

Sucking cool fresh air in through my nose, I exhale, blinking at the red lettering painted on the window across from Ink Time. Goode's Diner. I smile at the diner, knowing that my favorite place in Bluebell is now just steps away from where I work. That I can go there anytime and get my hometown comfort food and see Lucy whenever I want. Twisting, I peer into the busy and bustling tattoo shop, full of friends that are there to celebrate me.

A year ago I was chasing after a dream I wasn't sure I could catch, grappling with the idea of giving up Bluebell for a cityscape, thinking it may be the only way to become a tattoo artist.

And now I'm here.

In the town I know and love, across from my favorite place, a building full of the people I love just feet away, the man I love at the helm of this massive celebration.

I don't know if I deserve it, but tonight, it feels like I have it all. And I've never been happier or more grateful.

One last lungful of fresh country air and I'm spinning at the curb, ready to head back inside and finish the last hour of the party. As much fun as I'm having, the nearer the end of the night becomes, the more eager I am for this to be over.

So I can go home with Trace and thank him for everything. Jesus, my pussy clenches at the promise.

Two paces from the front door, my arm outstretched, I stop in my tracks.

Through the glass, my eyes lock to the very back corner of the shop. People move about the space, temporarily blocking me from what I know I saw. My heart in my throat, I stay there, on the sidewalk, my eyes burning from how hard I'm staring.

With a shaky breath rattling my chest, I rub my eyes, needing to be sure of what I'm seeing.

I drag a closed fist up my sternum, desperately trying to knead life back into my chest. But my breath is caught, suspended somewhere inside me, keeping my throat tight and my mouth dry.

Here of all places, after inviting everyone I know and love, he's doing this here.

"Oh my god," I murmur, catching the words with my hand as I bring it to my face, cupping it there, hiding the shock. My eyes are wide and as much as it would serve me to look away, I can't take my eyes off of them.

My brain taunts me, going back to those three questionable days where Trace told me he was unwell, then told me he was planning this very party. God I'm so stupid. How could I honestly think a chastity cage and some back talk was going to fix him? Did I seriously think I could heal his broken heart, and cure him of years of struggle?

My body sways as I blink, gaze still fixed on them. Fire stings the backs of my eyes, and I stammer around on the sidewalk a minute before gripping the wall.

And then I torture myself and watch as a former tattoo client—one of the first clients he had at Ink Time—slides her fingers through his hair, which I guess at some point he put in a knot, and rocks to her toes, pressing her lips to his.

His arms are around her, but I can't see his hands, they're blocked by the partition the two of them are standing behind.

She isn't thanking him for the tattoo. Their mouths open and even from back here, on the other side of the glass, I see the pink of their tongues thrashing together as the overhead light shines against his nose ring.

Finally, after watching for what feels like an eternity, I turn, my hand still covering my mouth.

A visceral shudder racks my core, making me cry out and gag all at once. "You fucking idiot!" I scream, the dam broken, tears streaking my cheeks. I don't know if I'm talking to him or myself, or maybe both of us.

But the knife in my boot burns against my flesh, calling for me, begging to deliver retribution. Reaching down, I pull it out and stalk down the sidewalk about ten feet, right to where Trace's stupid car is parked, shiny, fancy and fucking pretentious.

With my knife firm in my fist, I slip between the parked cars and stare through the windshield, to the white leather seats. How could he? Why would he? And at my party, too. Did he want to hurt someone the way that he hurts? I don't understand why he would do this.

"I don't understand," I murmur, the first strike of the butt of my knife coming down on the driver's side of the windshield. The glass spiderwebs into a million beautiful shatters, but I don't hear it. All I hear is my heart in my ears, and the way he proudly announced me as his girlfriend.

"No!" I scream, my neck filled with strain as I scream, over and over, that I have no clue why he would do this, why he would hurt me this way. Another hard strike of the knife's handle, this time against the driver's side window, the glass crumbling with the blow, falling to the buttery leather seat. I reach in, pulling the sharp blade through the soft leather, screaming, "No, no, no!"

Sweat coats my back. There's a hush of voices. I'm no longer slashing his seats but now, tipping the blade of the knife to his car, I make a full circle around it, careful not to bump any of the surrounding cars. "Why did you do that?" I hear myself ask as the knife tears away a new layer of paint. "Why are you ruining everything?" I ask, rearing back, stabbing the knife into the tire, a fresh wave of tears hitting as air rushes out of his tire, into the night.

Making my way to the headlight, I crouch, rearing back again as I crush the butt of the knife against it. It doesn't shatter, but I only want to hit it harder, so I rear back and hit it again.

And again.

And I cream the plastic light over and over, my knife slipping in my palm as my wild sobs echo through downtown Bluebell.

"Holy shit," I hear a voice, a moment after the door dings open a few feet away. I don't recognize the voice so I don't turn. Instead, I rear back and pop the other headlight, smiling through tears as it flies off the car, tumbling through the street.

"Ivy," Juniper's voice wavers, slicing through the chaos. I rear back, slightly aware of a vibration running up my forearm, starting in my wrist.

Bam. My hand and the butt of the knife come down in the center of the hood, this time sending my knife flying through the air and onto the sidewalk somewhere. There's a splatter of blood over the hood, near the new dent in the center, and I lift my hand to see it's drenched, soaked in red.

A wide groove centers my palm, and when I look over at Trace's car, I see blood splattered everywhere.

"Ivy, sweetie," my sister's soothing voice finds me, causing my head to jerk up. She's standing in her long white sundress on the sidewalk, closing the few feet between us. She wraps her arm around my shoulders, pulling me into her as she tells me that everything is going to be okay.

"I don't—I don't want to m-m-mess up your d-dress," I stammer, and when did I start sobbing? Snot is slick beneath my nose as I bury my face against my sister's, the quiet *plunk, plunk* of blood dripping onto the ground a soundtrack to our moment.

"Shh," she says, smoothing her hand down my hair.

"Whoa," another voice sounds, but I keep my face pressed into my sister, a heartbeat throbbing in the center of my palm. I don't remember cutting my hand.

"Okay, get her in my truck," the first voice says. "The four of us need to get out of here," he adds.

"I can't—I can't walk away from this," the other voice says.

"Please," Juniper begs, her soft tone lower and more personal than I've ever heard it. "Please," she tries again, still smoothing her fingers down my hair.

The first voice speaks to the second voice. "We know there aren't cameras out here, okay? We know this, remember?" he says, pressing the other man. "So help Juniper get her into the truck, and I'll find the knife." He drops his voice. "C'mon, Dash, this is what's right, you know it."

Dash.

My mind spins.

I pull my face from Juniper's chest and turn to see Sterling Ford standing behind Trace's crumpled sports car, taking in the damage from his spot in the street. Dash Foster stands near the hood, eyes wide as he takes in the disfigured, bloody car.

"It's just a car, it's not a person," Sterling says to him, and the two of them share eye contact.

"Your guys," I whisper to my sister.

"Yes," she says, her tone still soft and detached from the moment, soothing me. "My guys. And they're going to help, okay? It's going to be okay," she promises, using the word okay at least a hundred times.

A moment later, Juniper is helping me into the back seat of a lifted pickup truck, sliding onto the bench seat with me. Using the bottom of her dress, she wraps up my injured hand, blinking at me in the mercurial moonlight.

"What happened?"

I peer out, and watch Dash and Sterling walking around the car, ducking down to look underneath. Dash even peers inside the car, swiveling his head.

They're looking for my knife. "It's on the sidewalk," I tell Juniper, ignoring her question. "It slid down past the shop on the sidewalk," I reiterate. She rolls down the truck window, whisper-hissing my secret into the night. The men go for it, and Juniper returns her focus to me.

"What happened, Ivy?"

"There's a blonde," I start, and Juni shakes her head.

"There's always a blonde."

I sniffle. "He tattooed her a few weeks ago. Maybe a month or more, I can't remember."

"Okay," Juni draws out.

I wave my good hand over the front seat, toward Ink Time. "I saw Trace holding her, kissing her, in the back of the shop. I watched from the sidewalk. I saw their tongues. She put her hands in his hair the way I do." Tears streak my cheeks as Juniper pulls me toward her body, attempting to absorb my shock and pain.

"That motherfucker," she retorts as the truck dips, Sterling sliding behind the steering wheel, Dash taking the passenger side.

With black gloves on, he holds up my knife. "We got it."

Sterling throws the truck in reverse, and the men stay quiet, and so does Juniper, holding tightly to the pressure on my hurt hand. One flash of his lips pressed to hers and blackness envelops me, and I sink into a much-needed adrenaline-crash slumber against my sister, in the arms of someone who actually loves me.

TWENTY-EIGHT

Trace

How I ended up in an intimate conversation with Rochelle the domme? I have no goddamn clue. And as much as I admit I avoided her before, now I don't want our talk to end.

"I can't believe the freedom in submission," I tell her, my gaze moving from her to her partner. He doesn't speak, and I've learned that their dominant and submissive roles span all of their lives, not just in the bedroom. It's wicked interesting.

"I know, right? Most men don't want to try it because they hear submissive and they think weak," she says, using her thumb to stroke her partner's hand, their fingers woven together.

I nod. "Yeah, that's definitely how I felt about it. But I realized there's a certain headspace to it—"

Deuce's hand comes down on my shoulder, jerking me back from the convo.

"Excuse me," I say to Rochelle, turning to face Deuce. "What's —" His eyes are wide, and his chest is heaving, out of breath. "Is everything okay?" I look him up and down. "Are you all right?"

He swallows. "Don't freak out," he starts.

I roll my eyes, panic blooming in my bones. "Oh, okay, because tearing me away by saying 'don't freak out' is a great way to start a calm conversation."

He bypasses my sarcasm, which has heat spiking up my spine. He never misses an opportunity to talk shit to me. "Someone destroyed your car."

"Huh?"

"Your car..." He glances through the crowded studio toward the sidewalk and back to me. "It's fucked up, man. Done for."

I look around the shop. "Where's Ivy?"

Deuce shakes his head. "I-I don't know. Connor was leaving and he came back in, said your car is fucked up, completely destroyed."

"She left," Connor says, approaching us from the crowd.

"Thought you were taking off," Deuce says to him. Connor shakes his head.

"Wanted to make sure Trace is okay," he says, leveling his gaze on me. "Pretty vicious attack on you, man, are you okay?"

My head spins. "Wait– Ivy left?"

He nods. "I saw Juniper and her getting into a truck out front."

Why the fuck would Ivy leave her own party? Why would she leave without saying goodbye? But... Why would she leave? It doesn't make any sense. We were going to go back to my place together, have a romantic night. The celebration of her was only just getting started. I sift a hand through my hair, the back of my neck slick with nervous sweat. My stomach clenches.

"Holy shit," Connor sputters. I look up and follow his eyes to a man moving through the crowd toward us. A man I know despite all my efforts to unknow him.

"Hey, brother."

Immediately Deuce steps between us, pressing his hand into the center of my chest, anticipating a lunge. But I don't move. I just stand there, staring into the eyes of my twin brother, the one I have purposely not seen in over a year.

I don't have to ask him how he found me. He holds up his phone, my reactivated social media account glaring on his screen, the photo of mine and Ivy's boots front and center. "You made it easy, brother," he says, wearing his usual slimy smirk.

I notice that he's copied my tattoos, his neck and hand matching mine. He's probably trying to pass himself off as me for pussy, which is par for the course for this pathetic asshole. Derek has shown me that blood doesn't make family, but loyalty makes family. And he's not loyal.

"Oh shit," Jeremy draws out, picking the worst time to appear. "So you were the one making out with the blonde," he motions this thumb between us, relief softening his features. "I was gonna say, cheating on Ivy is not cool, man," he says, eyeing me.

"Wait—" I face my twin brother. "You were making out with someone here?"

He tips his head to the side. "White tank, black skirt."

The four of us follow his orders and find the woman matching his description on the other side of the shop.

"She was a client of mine a few weeks ago," I say, irritation running through my veins. "I'm going to take a stab and say you let her believe that you're me?"

His white teeth and broad grin make me sick. I grab his wrist, holding his hand out. Connor, Jeremy, and Deuce stare at it. Releasing him, I stick my hand out, and even though he takes his back without me holding him there, they see it.

"And I'm sure it goes without saying, but I'm gonna say it, I got mine first," I say to them, earning a scoff from my twin.

"You always were cooler than me," Derek says with a smile. He can act like he's being facetious, but I know him. He's always thought less of himself. Always living in my shadow.

By fucking choice.

Derek was always a lazy, cruel troublemaker who was jealous of everything I did when he had every opportunity I had to make something of himself.

And he did.

He made his life becoming my dark shadow, the one I deny, the one who's done nothing but trail me and ruin things for me. Derek is the reason my life was turned on its head twice, and he married my first love.

Jeremy claps a hand on my shoulder. "God, though, you do really look like identical twins. I mean, sometimes twins look less alike as the elder—"

"Elder?" I cock a brow. "I'm thirty-eight and—oh fuck." My sentence dies on the vine as everything falls into place.

Ivy left.

Derek is here, and he's using my name to get laid. Or attempt to.

Interrupting my train of thought, my brother says, "I thought you'd like to know, me and Cat got separated. Legally. Getting the big D."

With my chest tight, I stand there, waiting for it to hit. Happiness. A comment about karmic retribution, something. But I feel absolutely nothing at the news that they aren't going to make it as a couple. She cheated on me with my identical twin and ruined my ability to trust but still, I feel nothing. Completely indifferent.

"Trace, I think Ivy may've—" Deuce starts, but fucking Derek opens his mouth again.

"Who's Ivy?"

I have his shirt in my fist and his face to mine in less than three seconds, I'm sure of it. "Don't fucking say her name," I hiss, spit splatting his stubbled upper lip.

"Why, scared I'll get another one?" His smile is goading, but I refuse to play into him. I lost years of my life running from what he did. I gave him way too much power. Because if you love someone, you don't cheat on them.

He's nothing, and she didn't love me.

"Because I don't want you in my life. And she is part of my life, so go the fuck away." I face Deuce. "Drive me to Ivy's. Now. Please."

Derek starts talking but Connor diffuses, stepping between us as Deuce and I take off out the front of the shop.

She's got it all wrong.

My jaw draws tight as evening nips my ears and nose. Deuce runs out onto the sidewalk after me as I take in the shape of my car.

The blood.

She did this.

I know my Firecracker did this after what she thinks she saw.

I don't give a rat's ass about the car.

I care about getting to her and explaining. Turning to Deuce, I say, "Get Derek. Get Derek or she won't believe me."

Deuce nods. "It is pretty fucking unbelievable that there are two of you."

I shake my head. "There is only one me. He's just the...

drug store knockoff." Ivy flashes through my mind as I look across the street to Goode's. "Go get him. I need to get to her."

TWENTY-NINE

"He's dead to me."

Ivy

There's a heartbeat in my palm, throbbing, sending a reminder to my brain that I'm hurt. But I don't need the reminder. Because everything hurts, and my hand is the least of it.

I thought betrayal was one-size-fits-all. But having the man you've fallen in love with cheat on you at a party he himself has thrown? At your new place of work? With all of your family and friends around?

I turn over in my bed, and face the window, staring out in the gloomy night sky. Hudson and Dolly's house lights are on, and I know it's because of what happened tonight. I heard Dolly's voice in the hall, the rough vibration of Hudson soothing her.

Trace made a fool of me, and now I have to pick up the pieces. And even though I know my family is here for me, I'm ashamed. Ashamed that I trusted too soon, got excited way too early and let myself be happy. I let myself believe my life was falling into place.

I should have known it was too easy.

Dolly had to stalk Hudson for years and beat the living shit out of her competition. A few salty remarks at a tattoo parlor? Of course that wasn't it. Of course it wasn't that easy.

My stomach burns with hunger and unease, but I can't eat. Every time I try to open my mouth, I cry. I wanted to tell Juniper exactly what happened, why I did what I did, I wanted to explain to Dash and Sterling that I'm not some brat throwing a tantrum. To tell them I destroyed Trace's car because he destroyed my heart, and when you think of it in those terms, he got off pretty easy.

But every time I tried, sobs smothered my words, and I just couldn't.

Sterling carried me from his truck, Juniper behind him, guiding him to my room. He laid me down, Dash brought his medical kit and threw some loose stitches into my palm as Juniper wiped blood from my arms and face using a damp washcloth. She brought in hot tea and toast with my favorite jam, but the tea went cold and the toast is stale, the jam now too sticky.

I can't do anything but lie here, stare at the stars through the window and wonder how. How can a person be so cruel?

And just as I'm finally finding peace in sleep, there's commotion outside.

We live in the sticks, commotion is rare. Dash promised he wouldn't say anything, so I have no worry that it's the police department. He must really like my sister if he's willing to break the law and risk his job for her.

The jam must really be good.

There's a slam, then another, and a third, and then the

doorbell shudders through the whole house. Three people, judging by the car doors, are here, on the porch.

Ev and Deuce, maybe? But who's the third?

A moment later, my bedroom door is opening, dim light from the hall pouring over the end of my bed. The light is gone just as fast, and the door clicks closed.

My heart twitches in my throat, my good hand sore from clutching the blanket so hard. My chin trembles with a sob I'm holding back. Because I know who's here.

I can smell him, pine and cedar, a scent that just hours ago would have me melting.

"Ivy," he croaks, and a moment later, my bed dips. His hand finds my calf, and tears flank my cheeks as he smooths it up my leg, over my thigh, sinking his fingertips into my hip. His touch still sends waves of heat sweeping through my insides, pebbling my nipples and tossing bumps along my flesh. My eyes roll closed at his proximity, wishing so much that I could go back in time and save my heart by avoiding this man.

He turned out to be everything the tabloids said he was, everything Google warned me about, and yet here I am, crying in bed like a complete cliché.

"Ivy," he tries again, causing me to twist in bed, jerking and thrashing until the covers are off and I'm sitting up, glaring at his beautiful face in the partial moonlight.

"Shut up, Trace, shut up. Stop saying my name. Stop ruining my name with your stupid voice!" I shout, my temples pounding, my chest racked with a constant ache, one that I don't think has anything to do with stress, adrenaline crashes or dehydration. I fear that pain is heartache.

He nods slowly, as if agreeing with the way I'm lashing out, and that only makes me angrier. Sterling took my boots off, or else I'd muster the last of my energy to kick Trace in his perfect face.

"I'm going to ask you for a big favor right now, okay? I understand what you're feeling but please, one favor, okay?"

"Why? Why should I give you anything?" I hate that I can't stop my bottom lip from giving me away. "I gave you everything and you stuck your tongue down some client's throat. I'm done giving you things, Trace, now get the fuck out of my room and out of my life!"

Rearing back, with my fist balled, I strike, aiming for his nose. But he's quick, and he catches my fist in his palm, keeping my arm suspended in air as his eyes hold mine.

"Please listen, Ivy. That's the favor, okay? I need you to listen."

He lowers my fist to the bed and starts talking, even though the last thing I want to hear is his excuses.

But I'd be lying if I said I didn't want this moment, only because I know it's our last. And a few more minutes with Trace, no matter what he did, does something for the little girl inside me who still loves his art and still aspires for his talent.

"That day in Goode's, that first time we went there together," he starts, his hand now on my thigh. He rubs small, consoling circles, and I let him. "You asked me if I had family, do you remember that?"

"I swear to fuck, Trace, there better be a point, because if you tell me some bullshit trauma about your dad not loving you and that's the reason why you had your tongue down someone else's throat, your car won't be the worst thing I fuck up tonight," I breathe, nostrils flaring as his soothing circles continue, despite my harsh threats and murderous tone.

"Remember I told you my folks are gone?" he says, and annoyingly I find myself nodding. "And you asked if I had siblings, and I said no."

His hand stops moving on my thigh. "I lied to you, technically. I have a sibling. I have one brother."

I don't know where he's going with this. "Why did you lie about that?"

Pulling at the back of his neck, he sighs. "Because he's dead to me. No part of me recognizes him as a sibling, or even a family member. And it's been that way for the better part of ten years."

I don't say anything. His expression is heavy, weighted with stress and pain. I see that now, that even though I'm in pain, so is he.

Do not feel bad for him, Ivy. He cheated on you. What's next? He's gonna hit you and you're gonna justify that, too?

"When I first started tattooing, I apprenticed for this artist. She was absolutely great. She taught me so much and because of that, I was just... in awe of her. And I fell in love."

I want to say that his story sounds familiar, but the fact that I fell for him before I knew him can stay my stupid secret now.

"Was she—" I start, and he nods in confirmation.

"Cat, she was the one. The one who cheated on me. I fell in love, my first love, actually. I loved her something fierce. I thought we'd be together forever. I bought a ring. I saw a whole life of tattoos, travel, and eventually, a family."

"If you say hurt people hurt people, I swear to God, Trace—"

At that, he glances back at the bedroom door. "No, I wasn't going to say that. I was going to say Derek Wade hurts people, but mostly just me."

"*Derek?*"

"Get the fuck in here!" Trace shouts at the closed door.

"Who are—" I'm stopped short when the door to my room flies open, Deuce eating up the frame. Into the hall, he reaches out of sight, and a moment later, he's shoving someone inside my bedroom.

I get to my knees in the center of my bed, holding my

bandaged hand to my face as my mouth gapes. My eyes bounce between Trace and—"Oh my God," I breathe, completely tripped out. "Is he?"

"This is Derek. He's my brother," Trace says, still focused only on me. "My identical twin brother."

I don't know what to say. I don't know what to do. Blinking, I look between the two of them, Deuce still lingering in the doorway.

"You know that photo I posted of our boots? The one where I was trying to let my followers know that I'm alive and well and starting over?" he asks, and of course I know. I love the photo, and I was both surprised and honored to know that he was unafraid to share this chapter of his life with his followers. He hadn't posted since he left the show, and part of me thought he never would.

"Apparently Derek, here, was waiting to find me. And he did."

My gaze slides to the knockoff Trace. Okay, I don't know if he's the knockoff because I have no clue who is older, but as I take in the identical tattoos and the attempt Derek is clearly making to nail Trace's laid-back style, I'd say he's definitely the knockoff even if he's older.

I saw Trace get the octopus inked onto his hand, live, on the show. So if Derek has that same ink, it's because he copied Trace. He wanted to look like Trace.

"He's the one who slept with Trace's girl all those years ago," Deuce adds from the doorway. "I tried to get Trace to stay, face them both and... I don't know, work it out. Figure out a way to forgive his brother because it's his damn brother. But Trace refused, then he went off for the show and... I can honestly say you were right, Trace. You were right when you said he wasn't worth it. Because he keeps finding you, only to start shit."

Derek presses his hands to his chest in mock surprise. "I didn't come to start shit, it's just... I can't help that women flock to me. I didn't know you had a girlfriend who was going to flip her lid with jealousy." He smirks, bringing a curled knuckle to his lips to absorb his stupid little laugh. "Man, you're psycho. You really fucked up his car."

In a split second, Trace grabs Derek by the shoulder, rears back, and punches him straight in the face. The sound of knuckle on nose is unnerving, but I smile as Derek stumbles backward.

"Don't call her psycho. Don't say her name. Don't look at her. Don't even breathe the fucking air around her, got that?" Trace spits at Derek, shoving him back, hard, sending him careering into the wall. My framed sketches rattle behind him, but he bounces back, taking a swing at Trace. He ducks, missing the blow, grabbing Derek by the wrist, Trace pins him against the wall.

"So, wait, why did you come to Bluebell? I know you saw his post but why?" I ask, not understanding why this man resurfaced after what sounds like years of no contact.

"Wanted to rekindle my relationship with my twin," Derek balks, his face smashed to the wall. I love watching Trace's bicep flex as he pins his brother, keeping him suspended for me.

"They're divorcing. That's what he said earlier. They're legally separated." He chuckles as something clicks in place. "She realize it was you with my assistant, and not me?" Trace looks to the back of his brother's head. "Not that it matters, but I officially lost my TV contract because of that one, Derek."

"Look, I didn't mean for that to happen. I just wanted to visit my brother onset and that assistant of yours—shit, she came for me, she really came for me." He snorts, attempting to victimize himself. "No man would say no to what she offered.

It was her unfortunate fault that she thought I was you." Derek grunts before Trace releases him. Derek stutters and steps back toward Deuce, dragging his wrist under his nose, where he's bleeding.

"Your entire life is pretending to be me," Trace says. "If that isn't fucking pathetic enough, you have to try to ruin the life you're emulating." He shakes his head, stroking his hands through his hair as he exhales. He turns to face me, and I open my arms, begging for him.

A small sigh leaves him as we embrace, Trace collecting me in his arms, lifting me into his lap as he sits on my bed. I bury my face in his neck.

"I'm sorry I doubted you," I breathe, because I did. I doubted him long before Derek resurfaced. But the shit I'd seen in the tabloids about his affair with his assistant, it wasn't even him. It was Derek.

He laughs. "You have nothing to be sorry about, Firecracker. I lied to you at Goode's because I didn't want to face what happened. I've been denying him and their marriage and that part of my life for years. But that was stupid. I was stupid. I should have told you."

"You would have, eventually," I say, lifting my face from the crook of his neck to smooth my hands down his cheeks, pressing my lips to his. Our kiss is hungry and feral, and at some point, Deuce takes Derek out and the door closes.

"I would have, yes. I mean, I was going to. But if I would have told you that day," he lifts my hand between us, gently smoothing his thumb over the white gauze. "You wouldn't have hurt your tattooing hand." He kisses the bandage, and brings my hand to his heart, holding it there. "I'm sorry my lie hurt us, Ivy. And I'm so sorry for what you must've thought tonight. Because I know that pain, and I'm so fucking sorry you went through it."

The ugly sobs hit hard. "You didn't cheat on me," I cry, tears of happiness commingling with tears of relief, my arms around him again.

"I couldn't, Ivy. I wouldn't." He peels me off of him, and takes my chin in his hand. "I love you, Firecracker."

My face tingles, and my stomach free falls, my ribs tight, a knot in my throat. "Say it again," I breathe.

"I love you," he repeats easily.

I smile. "I love you too."

"I had something special planned tonight." He skirts his lips against mine. "I wanted to tattoo you, since you tattooed me. A double rite of passage."

With my hands on his shoulders, I steal another kiss from his lips. "Yes," I breathe, "I want that."

He chuckles, smoothing his hands up my back, heat blooming between my legs at our closeness. "You didn't ask what I want to ink on you."

"I don't care," I say truthfully. "I just want your work on me."

He scoops me up. "Hospital for a check on that hand, Ink Time, then my place," he lists.

"My hand is fine. Dash sewed me up."

"Oh yeah, a crooked cop is someone I trust with your tattooin' hand," he scoffs, pushing out the bedroom door. A moment later he's lowering me to a barstool in my kitchen. Juniper, Dash and Sterling are standing around a pot of brewing coffee, despite the fact it's nearly nine o' clock at night.

They seem to be soothing her, but when we lock eyes, she smiles, rushing forward. "I heard, Deuce explained," she says, pulling my head into her chest. "I would have done the same thing and I'm just glad it wasn't true."

Sterling hands me a cup of coffee, but Trace snatches it, moving through my kitchen to find my protein powder. He grabs milk from the fridge and mixes the two, pouring it over the steaming cup of caffeine. "There," he says, passing it back to me with a wink.

"Your brother is waiting in my truck," Sterling tells Trace as Juniper toasts me a fresh slice of bread, bringing me a canteen of fresh water and some pain reliever pills. I love my sisters.

"What do you want us to do with him?" Sterling asks.

Dash pinches the bridge of his nose. "Please say take him to the airport or something."

Juniper's gaze flicks between the two men. "Let Trace answer."

Trace shrugs. "I don't care. I don't care what happens to him."

Dash's shoulders slope as he releases a long sigh, and Sterling shifts on his feet, a worried look sliding to my older sister. "We can take him to his car and let him go," he offers, and it's now that I realize they're bartering with Juni. That she clearly wants another fate for Derek.

She turns to me, smiling. "Don't worry about any of this. We're just trying to figure out a permanent solution to this problem."

I blink, unsure of what that means, but before I can overthink it, Trace is gathering my stuff in a bag and collecting me from the barstool. "C'mon, Firecracker, I want that hand looked at."

He turns to Juniper. "Can I borrow your van?"

She looks to Sterling then back to Trace. "That should be fine, if we need to—sure, yeah, that's fine."

Juniper passes her keys to Trace, kisses my forehead and gives me a final, tight hug.

With the windows down and Trace's hand securely on my inner thigh, I rest my head on his shoulder, soaking up the middle seat as he drives us into town to the hospital.

After forty minutes and some antiseptic, they turn us loose, and we head to Ink Time, parking next to his destroyed sports car.

I stop next to it, taking in the mess and destruction I created. Trace is opening the front door when he realizes I'm a few paces behind.

"I'm sorry I did this," I whisper, staring at the crimson smear across the white hood.

He waffles his fingers through mine. "I'm not. Because as soon as I realized what happened, I looked at my car again and it hit me."

"What did?"

He turns, pulling me into him, dropping his forehead to mine. "That you love me."

"And I'm jealous," I add playfully.

"That makes two of us."

He seals his mouth to mine, kissing me like he has something to prove, but he doesn't. Tonight was chaos, but I've never wanted him more, I've never been so sure of him than I am now.

"Now," he says, "let's go get you tattooed."

Lying across his chair, the aftermath of a large party all around us in the form of crumpled napkins and partially drunk water bottles, Trace slides into his chair and snaps on his gloves.

"You ready?" he asks.

I nod. "I'm ready."

He prepped the station on his own tonight, to keep me in the element of surprise, and when the machine starts, I find myself eager to know what he's up to. But I don't glance down. I keep my eyes on him.

He's so beautiful to watch while he works.

The way his brows pull together as he outlines, how he's able to chat casually while slipping the needle from the pen, switching them out. How every few minutes he pauses, leaning in to dust his lips against mine, reminding me without words that he loves me.

He chose my hip bone, right where I tattooed him weeks back.

"You really don't think Derek can change? Or, you don't care if he does?" I ask as he shades the mystery design, a needy heat moving through my groin. I love being tattooed, I love the slow burn of it, and I love being here with him.

He shakes his head. "You don't sleep with, then marry, your brother's girl. But in a way, I'm glad he did. I see now that it was the clearest most obvious way for him to tell me that I don't matter, my wellness does not matter, and that there is no respect between us." He shrugs, adjusting the pen before the needling starts up again. "What they did to me sent me in a tailspin, I won't deny it. But I wouldn't be here, with you, if it wasn't for him and what he did."

"You were fated to be with me, not her," I whisper, believing it despite the fact that, with a crumpled bloody car outside, it sounds a bit crazy. But maybe I am. And if I am, I don't care, because he loves me anyway.

"It's true. And so, no, I don't care if he changes." His eyes meet and hold mine. "He's dead to me."

The pen shuts off and Trace puts it on the tray, grabbing a paper towel to wipe the design.

"Here," he says, extending his hand to help me off the chair. Walking me to the floor-to-ceiling mirror, I lift my t-shirt up, and keep my leggings shoved down to my pubic bone as I step closer, narrowing my eyes at the reflection of my new tattoo.

Bringing my bandaged hand to my mouth, I gasp, shaking my head as tears of happiness spring to my eyes. "Oh my god, it's so good," I laugh, tipping my head to the side to get a better look of the crumpled and bloody little sports car on my hip bone.

"I'm sorry you hurt your hand, but it was fucking hot to know that you had that much passion for me." He spins me around and takes my face in his hands, not a move I'd ever have thought Trace would do months ago. "When I'm being an asshole, or, I don't know, if I relapse on booze, or if I don't say the right thing, I want you to look at that tattoo and remember how much you love me, and how far you'll go for me. I need you, Ivy. I need you to love me that way forever," he breathes, a rattle in his chest as emotion springs to his throat.

I nod. "I love it. And I promise to always be passionate where you're concerned." He crashes his mouth to mine, his tongue greedy against mine, eating me up as our moans tangle. "You'll never doubt how much I care, Trace, I promise you."

I open my mouth but he stops me. "And you will never doubt my loyalty to you, Ivy. I promise. Even if it means being jealous and overprotective and a prick to every man in Bluebell if they look at you a second too long, you will never doubt my love."

"Jesus," I breathe, making light of the beautiful promises he just laid out. "I was already gonna fuck you because of the tattoo, you didn't need a Hallmark speech."

He growls and I giggle, rocking to my toes to sink my lips against his. "Thank you," I whisper, "every girl needs a Hallmark speech once in her life. Even baddies."

"I have another surprise," Trace says, the rasp of his words making my arms and legs feel heavy. "It's at my house."

"Take me," I whisper, "take me, surprise me and fuck me."

TRACE'S LITTLE PLACE LOOKS DIFFERENT THAN I remember, and like he's a mind reader, as soon as we're inside with the door locked behind us, he says, "That's the longest you'll ever go without being here."

I nod. "Last week was... weird."

"Yeah?" he says sarcastically. "I didn't feel a thing."

I slap his bicep as he laughs, retrieving a brown box from the floor near the dining table. "I don't like the idea of you bringing a bag with you when you come over, so I bought toys for us to have here," he says, dunking his large arm into the open shipping box. He pulls out a strap-on, dropping it onto the couch where I sit down. Next he retrieves a dildo, holding it out. I take it from him, completely turned on that he bought all of these things for us.

"Last item," he says with a wink that makes my pussy weep. From the box he produces a purple gag ball with two black straps and a buckle. "For when you get tired of my mouth." He grins.

My stomach flutters.

"There's one other thing, but it's in my room." He drops the box and extends his hand to me.

I fold my arms over my chest, teasing him. "Let me guess, the surprise is in your pants."

He tips his head back, his Adam's apple sliding as he roars with laughter beneath his stubbed, inked skin. "Good one, and the answer is yes, I do have a surprise for you there but there's also an actual surprise," he says, wiggling his fingers. I place my hand in his and he pulls me to my feet and we walk down the hall together, my heart pounding.

I thought I'd never be back here, and now I feel more at home than ever.

He flicks on the light and drags me to his closet, where he shows one side completely empty. "You have half of the dresser, too," he says proudly. I let go of his hand and stand in the clear space, next to where his black t-shirts and long-sleeved flannels hang.

"You made space for me to keep things here," I stammer, completely overwhelmed by the permanency of the gesture.

He nods. "Now, please, get naked and let me fuck you because that hand," he says, nodding to my bandaged palm, "is making me hard."

Laughing, Trace steps in and starts undressing me, only making me laugh harder. I'm going a little hysterical, I think, but I choose to embrace it as I nudge off my slippers, stepping out of my leggings and panties.

"My hurt hand makes you hard?" I ask, still a bit breathless from everything.

He nods as he tears his clothes off, leaving us both completely nude in the dimly lit closet. "Knowing how big you feel," he says, smoothing his octopus-covered hand through his long hair. I reach out and wrap my hand around his erection, making him groan. "That's how it makes me feel."

Then I'm over his shoulder, his hand smacking my bare ass as he takes me to the bed. He tosses me onto the center and stalks over me, nudging my legs apart with his knee. Skating his lips down my neck, he carves kisses along my collarbone, discovering the space between my breasts. "You're a bad girl, Ivy, but you're my bad girl, aren't you?"

I nod, sifting my fingers through his hair then down the carved planes of his shoulders, my eyes fighting to stay open. "Yes," I breathe, "please fuck me, Trace," I plead. My legs tremble around him, warmth leaking from my pussy as my clit throbs, begging for touch.

He kisses his way down my belly, taking care to not touch my new tattoo. When his mouth finds my clit, my back arches and I smack my palms against the mattress, howling out for him.

"Oh god, Trace," I moan, "yes, yes!"

He nibbles my clit as he drives two fingers inside me, my body hungrily accepting him, coating him in arousal. In and out he plunges his fingers, curling them when he's deep, his tongue painting my clit with affection in slow, delicate licks.

"I need you inside me, please," I beg, my legs shaking, my core the same.

He crawls over me, kissing me with his lips flavored like me, and I moan in response, loving that I'm all he tastes right now.

Bearing his weight on one elbow, he reaches between us, notching his cock. Our eyes meet. "My girl," he breathes before he thrusts his hips, sending his cock to the hilt in one push. I gasp, clenching around the most perfect intrusion, willing my body to normalize to his size.

"You're crazy for me," he moans, the smooth roll of his body into mine making my toes curl. "You're wild for me, aren't you, Firecracker?"

Beneath him, I nod, studying the intensity in his eyes, taking note of the softness in his words. This sex we're having is different. We were both cheated on but Trace was hurt in ways I can't imagine. In and out, he fucks me as he stares into my eyes, his hand still between us, now stroking my clit.

My legs fall farther apart, my body wanting more of him as I claw at his back and writhe in the sheets. "Yes," I moan, the word stretched with desire as I hook my ankles around him, using my heels to drive him deeper.

"Yes, what?" he says, the flex of his shoulder between us as he fingers my clit setting off sparks of desire in my brain, making dirty talk even harder to focus on.

"Y-yes, I'm crazy for you, Trace," I whisper, trying hard not to lose control as he slams into me again, this time stealing away his hand. Caging me against the mattress, his hands tangle in my hair as he finds my mouth with his.

His kiss is soft, our mouths dancing together in tandem, his tongue discovering my mouth, then mine his. Inside me, he throbs, holding himself still. Each twist of my tongue along his has his cock pulsing inside me, the warmth of his balls on my ass driving me wild.

"And you—" I breathe, ready to spiral out of control but waiting as long as I can, so I can spiral with him.

"I'm fucking crazy for you too, baby," he says, sealing the promise with a kiss, flooding my mouth with moans. "I'd do anything for you, Ivy," he says, his tone rocky, his eyes set on mine. Holding my head to the pillow with his large hands, he slows his pace, fucking me in a teasing, destructive speed that has me completely unraveled in just a few minutes.

"I wanna come deep inside you, and pretend, okay? You wanna pretend with me?"

I nod, knowing I'll go to whatever fantasy he's at, just to be with him.

Another thrust and my legs grow weak, falling from his back to the mattress. My thighs tremble and between my legs, a deep ache throbs.

"Pretend you aren't on any pill," he whispers, riding me slowly now, so slow that the bed no longer squeaks and the headboard doesn't hit the wall. "Pretend when I make you come, and I come, too, that your hungry little pussy is taking in every drop I have to give, turning you into a mama, my little mama with my baby in her belly."

My eyes flutter closed at the insinuation. Trace fantasizing about our future is absolutely the hottest thing ever, because I want that too. I want a baby with Trace—no, I want a full life with Trace.

Pictures with Santa and staying up late to write the tooth fairy a letter, sporting events on Saturday mornings and birthday parties with too much pizza. Tears over homework and excitement over first dates. I want to be a parent with him, to experience all the little beautiful moments I had as a child with the man I love, helping our child.

But we're not ready. And as romantic as making a baby together is, I can appreciate that it's better for everyone if we're ready.

Still, it's just a fantasy, so I lose myself in it with my man.

"Yes," I breathe, "please, leave me full, breed my pussy," I mewl. "I need your cum!"

He drops his mouth to my breast, sucking a puckered nipple inside. "That feels so good," I breathe, completely lost in the dream of my belly being round, an adorable blonde toddler asleep in the next room over. It's hot, and god does it get me going. I wonder if he's fantasizing about something similar, because his mouth slides to my other breast, sucking me in, as his hips rove faster.

"My hot, wild, perfect little Firecracker," he groans, making his way back to my mouth. He reaches for my hand, and brings it between us, eyeing the bandages as his cock swells inside me, making me burn.

"Trace, I'm gonna come," I warn, the sight of him kissing my bandaged palm sending me into a heated, orgasmic tailspin. "I'm—I'm gonna come," I grit out, bearing down on his dick as my orgasm crashes into me, hard and fast.

"Come on my cock," he commands before crushing his lips

to mine. Our tongues twist as I come, clenching around him in violent waves, my tailbone vibrating.

He groans each time I clench, milking him for more length, more movement, for cum, for all of it. And a moment later, he's cursing in my ear, telling me he's coming, too.

There's an eruption of heat between my legs, deep inside my pussy. "Ivy," he groans, opening his eyes to find mine. He pulses, a wave of heat spreading through me, and I clench, hungry for that heat, aching to devour his cum. Trace's face goes slack, the creases falling away as he collapses on top of me, moaning.

A moment later, he pulls out and jumps to his feet, collecting a damp and a dry towel from the bathroom. Swiping through my folds, he begins cleaning me, all while staying naked.

"Wow," I say, chasing my breath. "I think you just made *loooove* to me." His eyes lift to mine and he shakes his head, chuckling.

"Well, shit, Firecracker, don't call me out like that."

I sit up as he wipes at my sensitive pussy, swollen and aching from his use. "If you're gonna make me admit how crazy I am for you, then I'm gonna make you admit you made love to me."

He tosses the towel onto the floor and grabs my face by the chin, his trademark style. "I made love to you because I love you, now I'm gonna feed you."

Bringing our faces together, he kisses me then helps me out of bed, redressing me in one of his t-shirts and a pair of his sweatpants. "You're either naked or you're in my clothes after we fuck, we clear?"

I move past him into the hallway, scooping my hair up to get it off my neck and back.

"Let me," he says, rolling an elastic from his wrist, tying my hair up in a knot as I tease him.

"I have cute pajamas, you know. And now that I have space here, I can bring them, so I can technically wear my own clothes to bed, Trace..." I say, and even though it's true, and I do have adorable pajamas with skulls and roses all over them, I love pissing him off. He finishes off a perfect bun, and squeezes my shoulders.

"My clothes or no clothes," he growls, stomping after me toward the kitchen.

I yawn as I hop onto the counter, peering around the space that has way more stuff in it. A chopping block with knives, a cutting board propped on its side, a case of canned sparkling water on the floor, and an empty vase. "Fine," I say, "I guess I agree."

He winks, filling the vase full of water.

"You have way more stuff than last time I was here," I comment, watching him pull dyed black roses from kraft paper on his table. "Those are beautiful, Trace."

He slides the vase toward me. "Arrange them. They're yours. I was going to take them to Ink Time for the party but I thought you'd want something to look at when you wake up here tomorrow."

Running my thumb along the silken petal, I sigh at their beauty, and the fact that he ordered these especially for me. "Thank you for the party, by the way. Despite how it ended, it was so thoughtful of you and I want you to know, I really appreciate it," I tell him as he pulls a frying pan from the cabinet.

"Grilled cheese?" he asks, and I nod. Gathering the ingredients, he says, "You're welcome. I liked doing it. And ordering all the things I needed made me realize that I could easily fill my house and make it a much more enjoyable place for us to live." He nods to the frying pan. "Like being able to make grilled cheese after hot sex."

Grilled cheese after hot sex in the arms of the man I've adored for ages? He was right. Tattoos and fairy tales—life is perfect.

THIRTY

Not for the rest of our lives.

Trace

"I don't like feeling jealous and out of control, do you?" Ivy asks, her hand pressing my face against the wall.

"No," I say, the singular word jumbling as it passes by the gag in my mouth.

"No, no, you don't," she says. "And there was a lot of laughter after your last session today. A lot of... friendliness not needed to retain the client."

Fuck, I love this. I love how worked up Ivy gets when we have a new female client that requests me. You'd never know it, not even if you knew her, because she does such a great job of being professional. But when new clients flirt with me, it drives her fucking wild.

Then we come home and she fucks me wild.

I've been hard for the last four hours, anticipating my Firecracker being upset.

"You'll learn," she breathes against my ear, the warning sliding down my core, leaving me edgy and achy. "Keep your hands on the wall." She slaps my bare ass and I jump, but my hands don't move. I know better. Last time I disobeyed my Firecracker, my balls took a whack that still makes me cough when I think about it.

Her hands smooth over the globes of my ass before she gently parts me, rocking to her toes, pressing her bare chest to my naked back.

Her tits smashed against me as she drags the head of the toy through the split of my ass is driving me mad, so I groan, but the gag ball stops me.

"Oh, you want relief?" she whispers, her words trickling down my spine as her velvet lips graze my earlobe. "I'll give you relief, and when you come all over the fucking wall for me, remember who made you feel this way. Remember me when you're flirting with some babe in the shop," she hisses, surging forward, making me gasp from the intrusion.

One hand keeps me spread, the other loops my waist as she grabs my throbbing cock. I can't help but moan against the gag, the feel of her slick palm jacking me and her cock in my ass making me crazy.

I needed to come hours ago, when she showed me her tits in the office at Ink Time. It's why I flirted with that client, to rile her up. I've been dreaming about being her plaything all damn day. And now that I am? I want it to last.

But she makes it so hard.

Releasing my cock for a second, she twists my nipple, making me jerk. She takes the opportunity to slide deeper inside me as I flail, using where we're joined to push me into the wall. My hands stay up, but my eyes flutter closed as the pressure in my groin skyrockets.

When her hand comes back to my cock, she strokes me while pumping into me from behind. "If you want to play games with me, Trace Wade, you can. But there's a price to pay for upsetting me." She fucks me harder then, my stomach coiling as my balls pull tight. Looking down, I drool and moan against the gag at the sight of her fair hand pumping my hardened pink dick, the tip slick with precum, angry veins tracing the shaft.

"You wanted to fuck her?" she breathes, and though this is part of the punishment role-play, I still try to say no, I try to let her know that even in role-play she's the only one I want. But she won't let me. "Now I'm fucking you," she says, laughing as she releases her grip on my cock, denying me the slight relief.

Digging her nails into my hips, she holds me, and says, "Here comes your punishment. Look down and watch, or else," she commands before picking up her pace, rolling her hips so that the toy prods and fills me at the exact right angle. She always knows the right angles.

"No—" I slur against the gag, desperate for her to stroke me as I come. She loves ruining me, and as hot as it is, it also drives me fucking crazy. "No—" I beg, a completely hopeless slut for her hand.

"Watch," she moans, and that's it. Hearing her get off to fucking me and ruining me is all it takes to push me into oblivion.

"Iv—" I try to shout her name against the gag as the first rope shoots from the angry slit in my cock, painting the wall in front of me. She thrusts into me again as I come again, white ribbons of cum decorating the wall, floor and my feet as she fucks me dry.

"There," she breathes, her voice shaking as she catches her

breath after her own orgasm. How hot is it that she comes when she fucks me? Fuck hot, thats how hot. "Now, if you want to touch yourself, you can, but face me first."

I'm her eager whore, and I don't pretend I'm not.

Spinning, drool sliding down my chin and neck, I face her and reach down, gripping my still hard cock. I groan at the slick feel of my cum coating my shaft as I pump madly, trying desperately to intensify the orgasm I just had. But like waking up in the middle of a dream you can never return to, despite how hard I jerk, the moment has passed.

Ivy, the dildo shiny between her legs, reaches up, unbuckling the gag behind my head. Stepping out of the harness, she takes the toys to the sink and begins washing them, tossing me a damp towel to clean up the mess I made.

"God, I love fucking you." She smiles, pumping soap onto the dildo. "And you really deserved that ruined orgasm tonight, too."

My chest tightens as I wipe my cum from the wall, something I can honestly say I never thought I'd be doing. Then again, with Ivy, that's how life is. She's given me things I never imagined having, yet I'm happier and luckier than ever before.

"That was so hot." I dispose of the towel before joining her in the kitchen, wrapping my arms around her from behind. "You know I was just being extra nice to that woman to get you to destroy me tonight, right?"

She twists in my arms, smirking. "Of course. And I love you for it."

I kiss her temple and take in a noseful of her hair. I love the way she smells, and I hate how her scent only lives on my bed sheets.

"I wish I could smell you all the time," I tell her, watching her lean hands coated in suds stroke the toy clean before rinsing.

"Wanna wear my skin too?" she teases.

But then it hits me, so I knock the cock from her hands and spin her around. "Move in with me."

Her mouth opens but closes as she searches my eyes. "What?"

"Move in with me. I mean, we're headed to forever, right? This is a step to that." I bend down and kiss the shocked look off of her face, then nuzzle my lips against her neck. "C'mon, Firecracker, don't make me beg."

"But you look so hot begging," she simpers, so I drop to my knees with my dick out and steeple my hands together, bottom lip in a swell.

"Please, baby, please come live with me so I can talk to you, see you and touch you all the time."

"And smell me," she adds, sassy despite the shine in her eyes.

"And smell you."

She rolls her eyes, wearing the most beautiful grin. "Yes, I'll move in," she finally agrees.

I have her over my shoulder in a second, patting her naked ass as I parade around the house, whooping and hollering, all the while she screams and giggles and begs to be put down.

She doesn't really want me to put her down, and I won't. Not for the rest of our lives.

EPILOGUE

I want to own a business with my wife.

Ivy

"I hope it's not cancer," I whisper, fiddling with the edges of my ripped shorts as Trace flicks on his blinker. His hand comes to my thigh, tenderly giving it a squeeze.

"It's not cancer, it's... I don't even think it's bad news," he says, but I notice that he's chewing the inside of his lip like he's not so sure himself.

"Everly is pregnant. Oh God, what if something is wrong with the baby?" I breathe, panic coursing through me in waves. Deuce and Everly are family to me, and if anything happened to either of them—

"Stop spinning out, Firecracker, okay? Don't borrow trouble. Let's just see what's going on," he soothes, using his thumb to stroke down my leg.

He puts his new car in park—the sports car was replaced

with an SUV, a normal priced SUV that makes more sense in Bluebell than a fast car ever did. He unbuckles his seat belt and turns to face me. "So they asked us both to come, and it sounded serious, I'll give you that. But... if something were really wrong, I don't think they'd tell us at the shop, you know?"

"I guess," I say, still nervous as I peer through the windshield at Ink Time.

"I mean, if you were gonna give someone shitty news, you'd, like, I don't know, ask them to your place and make scones and coffee and shit," he offers, trying to soothe my worries. And in a way, it works. I arch an eyebrow.

"Are scones what you'd serve if you told someone you were dying?"

"C'mon," he scoffs, giving my leg a pat. "Let's go put your mind at ease."

We get out and Trace leads us into the shop, holding the door open while his other hand stays linked with mine. Inside, Deuce and Everly stand behind reception, she's in his arms, and he's kissing her head.

"Oh god, he's dying," I whisper, my eyes threatening to water.

He squeezes my hand. "Hey," he greets, and they snap to focus, Ev smiling as Deuce does the same.

"Is everything okay?" I blurt out, my eyes darting between the two of them. "Please tell me you're both okay."

Ev's eyes widen as she processes. "Oh, honey, no, everything's fine," she says, taking me from Trace to pull me into a hug.

"I thought—I don't know, I was worried," I admit as she pulls us apart, smiling at me.

"Everything is actually really great. But... we wanted to talk to you two alone about something... pretty serious," she says, making eyes to her husband. They agree on something without words, and I love how couples communicate that way. Trace and I do the same, and it feels so good to be part of that secret language. Right now, though, their secrecy has me nervous.

My mind careens back to Trace and I closing up last week. We were on each other's nerves all day and by the time the front door was locked, I couldn't wait to get his dick in my mouth in the back office.

Have they caught on to us using the office as our "we can't make it home" place?

I roll my lips together as we sit in Connor's station, Deuce and Trace taking the rolling stools, Ev and I sitting in the extra chairs. Between us is the tattooing chair where clients sit, and silence. So much silence that Trace begins tapping his foot.

Finally, Deuce speaks.

"Ev and I think it's time to sell Ink Time. With a toddler and another one on the way, managing this location is just... too much. And quite frankly, I don't really need the income. I don't need any part of it." He twists, his black-and-white flannel shirt bunching on his large torso as he does. Facing Trace he says, "But it would be roots for the both of you, and we wanted to give you two the opportunity first."

My heart leaps, as happiness tingles through my cheeks. Holy shit. Me and Trace, owners of Ink Time? Juniper loves owning her own business, and Dolly is thrilled being her own boss. And as for Trace and I? We work so well together, even when we're annoying the ever-living daylights out of one another.

"No," Trace says, getting to his feet, "and can you excuse us for a second?" he says, yanking me to my feet by my hand.

"No?" You're just gonna answer for us? I don't have a voice? Fuck off, Trace, I want this place. And honestly, I want this place with you—"

He shuts me up with his mouth pressed to mine, shoving

my back against the closed office door. Grinding his erection against me, he pulls back. "Your mouth gets me so hard," he groans, nipping at my bottom lip.

I smack his chest, pushing him back. "And your assumption that we don't want Ink Time makes me mad," I say, shoving him again as he moves to kiss me.

Finally, he steps back, pulling his hand down his new beard. Trace with a beard, by the way, is *four orgasms a night* levels of hot. Trust me.

"Ivy, I want to own Ink Time. I want to own it with you, too." He studies me. "Badly."

"Okay," I draw out, confused as ever.

"But I want to own a business with my wife."

"Yeah but, by the time that happens, someone else may want to buy or will already have bought it and—"

His mouth curls into a smirk as he reaches behind me, twisting the knob, giving the office door a push open. "Turn around, Firecracker," he rasps.

Turning, I find the shop suddenly full. Hudson, Dolly, Honey, Bear, Juniper, Dash, Sterling, Deuce, Everly, their daughter—everyone stands with black silk roses in their hands. Trace moves out of the office, in front of me.

"The first time I filled this space with your loved ones, I fucked up. We need a redo." He drops to one knee, making my legs wobbly and tears spring to my eyes. "Ivy, you are the one true love of my life. Marry me, own this place with me. I promise to always love you, and always fall to my knees for you and give you everything you've ever wanted." He digs a blue box from his pocket and pops it open, revealing a marquise cut diamond, onyx in color, a string of clear diamonds glittering around it.

I look up at my sisters, who are both tearily nodding.

I look back down at Trace. "Yes," I breathe, "yes."

Everyone cheers for us, but the noise falls away as Trace rises, pulling me into his arms. We hug so tightly before he pulls back, slipping the perfectly sized ring onto my ring finger.

"I've never seen a black diamond before," I breathe, my tears making it hard to study the ring the way I'd like. "I love it, it's so perfect, thank you."

He grabs my chin. "Are you mine? Forever?"

I nod, the weight of his ring on my finger making me delirious. "I'm yours."

He shakes his head, as a bottle of sparkling cider pops open in the background. "I can't believe I'm this lucky." He crushes his lips to mine, repeating the command I gave him when I was sucking the dildo and torturing him. "Say it again."

I take his face in my hands. "I'm yours, truly."

The End.

IF YOU LIKED THIS STORY...

Next to reading our books, reviews are the next best gift! If you have time, I'd love to hear your opinion.

Thank you again for reading!

Sign up for my newsletter to keep up-to-date with my projects, deals on books, sneak peeks, and much more.

ABOUT THE AUTHOR

Daisy Jane is an indie author writing contemporary romance with kink. In her stories you'll find small towns, ordinary people and extraordinary sex lives.

Daisy enjoys reading, finding new ways to eat peanut butter, black coffee, funk music and cool cover bands, Yosemite, 90s movies, true crime, and so much more.

She lives in California with her husband of sixteen years, their two daughters and three cats.

ALSO BY DAISY JANE

Series:

Twisted Sisters

All My Love / age gap female stalker / MF / Book 1

Yours Truly / age gap enemies to lovers / MF / Book 2

Crave & Cure (3 Books)

Stuck With Tuck / male porn star / MF / Book 1

Cohen's Control / subtle femdom / MF / Book 2

Bound By Brielle / pet play workplace / MMF / Book 3

Wrench Kings (3 Books)

The Wild One / a reverse age gap romance / MF / Book 1

The Brazen One / a grumpy/sunshine romance / MF / Book 2

The Only One / a femdom romance / MF / Book 3

Men of Paradise (3 Books)

Where Violets Bloom / a stalker romance / MF / Book 1

Stray / a femdom romance / MF / Book 2

With Force / a CNC romance / MF / Book 3

Oakcreek

I'll Do Anything / a bully femdom romance / MF / Book 1

After the Storm / an alpha MM romance / MM / Book 2

Standalones:

Undeniable / dual POV / MF / age gap / mom's ex

Raleigh Two / a taboo MFM romance / MFM

The Man I Know / a married couple romance / MF

The Other Brother / dual POV / MF

The Corner House / single POV / MFMM, MFM, MFM with an HEA

Hot Girl Summer / a taboo step sibling romance / MF

Release / a taboo MMF, MM, MF romance

Novellas:

Cherry Pie / very taboo why choose / MFMM

Sweet Clementine / why choose / MFMM

Peaches & Cream / step mom/sons why choose / MFMM

Candy Cane / why choose / MFMMM